Marrying Miss Martha

Anna Jacobs is the author of over eighty novels and is a natural storyteller. She grew up in Lancashire and moved to Australia in the early seventies. She comes back to England every summer to visit her family. Married with two grown-up daughters and a grandson, she lives with her husband in Western Australia.

Also by Anna Jacobs

Anna JACOBS

Marrying *Miss* Martha

🔟 CANELO

First published in the United Kingdom in 2004 by Severn House

This edition published in the United Kingdom in 2024 by

Canelo
Unit 9, 5th Floor
Cargo Works, 1–2 Hatfields
London SE1 9PG
United Kingdom

Copyright © Anna Jacobs 2004

The moral right of Anna Jacobs to be identified as the creator of this work has been asserted in accordance with the Copyright, Designs and Patents Act, 1988.

All rights reserved. No part of this publication may be reproduced or transmitted in any form or by any means, electronic or mechanical, including photocopy, recording, or any information storage and retrieval system, without permission in writing from the publisher.

A CIP catalogue record for this book is available from the British Library.

Print ISBN 978 1 80436 722 3
Ebook ISBN 978 1 91142 096 5

This book is a work of fiction. Names, characters, businesses, organizations, places and events are either the product of the author's imagination or are used fictitiously. Any resemblance to actual persons, living or dead, events or locales is entirely coincidental.

Cover design by Diane Meacham

Look for more great books at www.canelo.co

Printed and bound in Great Britain by Clays Ltd, Elcograf S.p.A.

Part One

August 1828

Chapter 1

Martha sat bolt upright on a wooden chair in the lawyer's office listening to Mr Droffington read her father's will, though what he said only confirmed what each of the three persons present already knew.

'…and to my beloved daughters, Martha and Penelope Merridene of Rosemount Lodge, Woodbourne, I leave the residue of my estate, to be divided equally between them. I am aware that this is not as much as I would have wished, since my naval pension will die with me, so I commend my daughters to the protection of their cousin, Edward Merridene, of Poolerby Hall, Leicestershire, to whom I also bequeath the gold signet ring that has belonged to the head of the family for nearly two hundred years.'

Edward nodded his head in satisfaction and turned to smile reassuringly at his two cousins. 'You may rely upon me *absolutely*.'

Martha decided that Edward's resemblance to a rabbit was increasing rather than decreasing with the years. As if she would let *him* manage her life!

Mr Droffington lowered the paper from which he had been reading. 'There should be no difficulty in settling affairs within a few weeks, my dear ladies. Not a complicated estate, since there is no property involved.'

Edward nodded. 'Might I ask—as head of the family—how much you estimate will actually be realised for my poor cousins?'

How dare he call us 'poor cousins', Martha thought, anger momentarily overcoming her grief. She opened her mouth to protest but closed it again as Penelope gave her a quick nudge.

'Well—er—not quite two hundred pounds, I'm afraid. And the furniture, of course.'

'As little as that, eh?'

'Unfortunately, yes. Captain Merridene was not an extravagant gentleman, but his private means were small. He only rented the house and the naval pension was not exactly generous.'

Edward shook his head and looked at his cousins pityingly.

Martha scowled at him. 'We had the best of fathers and I wouldn't have changed a single thing about him!' Which was not quite true. Her father had never been good with money and his unthinking generosity had sometimes made for difficulties, given their restricted budget.

An uneasy silence followed her words then Mr Droffington cleared his throat and continued, 'The lease on the Lodge will expire in December, but as it would be beyond the ladies' means to renew it, this is very timely. Of course, they each have a small annuity from their mother's marriage settlement, so they will not be entirely penniless.'

Martha listened indignantly to the two men discussing the situation as if she and Penelope were not there—or were too stupid to understand money.

Edward shook his head sadly. 'I cannot consider a hundred pounds a year each anything more than pin money. However, you may rely upon me, my dear cousins, to deal with all the business details and supply the masculine guidance which you have sadly lost with my uncle's passing.' He slid the signet ring on to his finger and held his hand up to admire this symbol of his new position in the family, then stood up to signify that it was time to leave.

Martha found the sight of her father's ring on Edward's plump white hand painful in the extreme and was unable to keep silent a second longer. 'That will not be necessary!' Her voice came out more loudly than she had intended and both gentlemen gaped at her.

'I beg your pardon?' Edward said, looking puzzled.

'I said: that will not be necessary,' she repeated, standing up and facing the two of them. 'My sister and I are quite capable of settling any business arising from Father's will ourselves.'

'You had much better leave such things to those who understand them, Cousin.' Edward drew himself up to his full five foot five inches and stared resentfully across the table. There was something very unladylike about such a strong-looking woman. Penelope was slightly taller than he was, but Martha must be all of five foot nine! She was handsome enough—or she would be if she did something with herself—for she had regular features and hair of an attractive chestnut hue. But he didn't approve of the aggressive jut to her chin and he preferred Penelope's slenderness and softer prettiness to Martha's generous curves and look of strength.

The chin was even more pronounced as she continued, 'You forget that it was I who handled all our business matters after Mother died because Father could never understand accounts, so I can probably tell you to the farthing how we're left.'

'My uncle might have allowed you to organise the *housekeeping money*, Cousin Martha, but that is quite different, believe me, from managing one's income! And I must insist...'

Penelope swayed and clutched her sister's arm. 'Oh dear! I'm afraid I feel rather faint! I...'

In the bustle of getting Penelope out to Edward's carriage, further discussion was postponed, but Martha knew her sister had not felt faint—neither of them was prone to that sort of thing—and had done this on purpose to prevent a quarrel. Well, perhaps it would be as well to discuss matters privately, but she had no intention of biting her tongue if Edward continued to speak to them in such a patronising manner and she would definitely not be giving her affairs into his hands.

—

Once back at Rosemount Lodge the two ladies served tea in the front parlour and as nothing further was said about financial matters, Edward was able to give himself up to enjoyment of the feather-light scones. 'By Jove! My own cook could not have done better!'

'Do have another!' Penelope said quickly. To her relief, her sister only watched grimly as Edward consumed a second scone and followed it with a generous slice of plum cake.

Afterwards Penelope invited Edward to take a turn round the garden with her and listened meekly to his views on how *he* would have set out the vegetable patch. With true heroism she refrained from interrupting or pointing out the glaring faults in his schemes, which took no account of the prevailing winds or the amount of shade in each area.

Well aware of what her sister was doing and grateful for the respite from Edward's inanities, Martha went to help their maid, Sally, prepare an evening meal which would not disgrace them in their cousin's eyes. When she heard Penelope bring Edward back into the house, she went upstairs to change for dinner, donning her one black evening gown.

Her sister joined her a short time later, similarly clad but with her hair still loose about her shoulders. 'Could you help me put up my hair?'

'Of course, love.' Martha pinned her sister's soft brown waves into a high chignon twisting the shorter hair at each side of the face into curls. Penelope was calm again, with that distant look on her face. Martha wished, as she had so many times, that her sister's fiancé had not died so suddenly. The look of bright interest and anticipation which used to light up her sister's face had rarely returned, though it was well over two years since that dreadful day when Mr Medson had arrived to tell them that his son had died of a putrid sore throat—just one month before Penelope and he were to have been married.

Banishing such depressing memories firmly, Martha stood back. 'There. You look charming, Pen. You always were the pretty one of us two. I wish we could afford a new evening dress for you, though. Even the vicar's wife is wearing wider sleeves than ours now.'

Penelope stood up and gave Martha a hug. 'Thank you. No one can put up my hair as well as you. And I don't care about fashion any more than you do, as long as I'm decently clad.'

Martha sat down in front of the mirror to attend to her own coiffure, clicking her tongue in exasperation at the unruly mass lying on her shoulders. 'Strands will escape, however firmly I pin it back,' she grumbled.

'If you didn't try to push your hair into such a severe style, it might behave itself better. I wish you would let me—'

'I can't be bothered to fuss. There. That's the best I can do. At least it's neater now.'

'Why will you never let me help you look your best?'

'What's the point? At twenty-eight I'm well beyond trying to attract a husband and a neat hairstyle is easier to manage. Don't look at me like that, Pen. You won't change my mind.'

Penelope sighed, but refrained from arguing. At the door she stopped again to say, 'Do try to bite your tongue tonight, dear. Edward can't actually *force* his wishes upon us, after all, and he'll soon be gone.'

'I'll try, I really will, but I can't promise anything. He's such a fool. And I'm not—' Martha's voice wobbled for a minute, '—not quite myself at the moment.' She took a deep breath and led the way downstairs.

–

'I have been considering your position,' Edward announced abruptly after spooning up the last of his second helping of stewed apples and cream.

Martha looked up, her own spoon poised half-way to her mouth, ready to take issue with the idea that their position was any concern of his, but he didn't give her time to protest.

'Although you are not precisely young any more, it would still not be seemly for you to keep house without the support of a gentleman's presence. I am not, in any case, a believer in female independence.' He waved a nearly empty wine glass at them. 'But you are not to worry! No, indeed! I spoke to my dearest Rosemary before I left the Hall and we are as one in this, as in everything else. We shall be happy to offer you a home.' He sat back and smiled benignly at them.

He spoke as though they would be reduced to starvation or the workhouse otherwise, Martha thought, when they had a perfectly adequate income if they lived modestly and moved to a smaller house or took rooms. But even if they didn't have enough money, she would rather hoe turnips than live with their cousin! Far rather!

Edward continued to explain the situation. 'Rosemary and I are, as you know, blessed with three children.'

Poor little things! thought Martha. *They already favour their parents.*

'I am happy to inform you that we expect another addition to our family in three weeks' time. In these circumstances, my dear wife will positively welcome the support of her two cousins, for she does tend to become a trifle out of spirits when she is—ahem—' he lowered his voice, 'great with child.'

As he seemed to expect some comment, Martha managed a 'Mmm'.

'And with *three* ladies in the house, I'm sure we shall be able to dispense with the services of the housekeeper. That and the savings on hiring a governess—for we all know how well-read you are, my dear Martha—will more than compensate us financially. So you need have *no* fear of being a burden.'

Both sisters gaped at him, astounded by this meanness.

'And you will have your annuities,' he continued, 'which will provide you with enough pin-money to buy the material to make yourselves the simple gowns which will be in keeping with your new station in life. So you see, it all works out very neatly.' He leaned back in his chair, drained the last of the wine and beamed at them.

Martha could hold back no longer. 'Thank you, Edward, but I'm afraid we must decline your generous offer!' She had the pleasure of watching his smile fade as her words sank in.

'*Decline!* Decline my offer! But—but—you cannot! Whatever will Rosemary say? She is quite counting on your help, as am I. Our eldest son had been growing somewhat naughty lately—such a spirited lad, dear little Ned!—and he needs a firmer hand than poor Rosemary—the most sensitive of females!—can provide.'

'Well, I'm sorry but we do decline, Edward!' In response to a well-aimed kick from her sister, Martha tried to modify her tone and find more conciliatory words, but could only repeat, 'We are, however—as dear Penelope would agree—grateful.' The word nearly choked her. *Grateful!* For a mean-spirited offer like that! Well, she had no intention of becoming the unpaid slave of her Cousin Edward and his wife, thank you very much.

Penelope stood up. 'This has been such a wearing day and my head is aching abominably. I do think we ought to postpone further discussion until tomorrow, my dear cousin.'

Martha pushed her chair back abruptly. Pen was right. They were both tired and sad; not in the mood to manage a polite conversation with their fool of a cousin. She took their candlesticks from the mantelpiece, allowed Edward to light them with the taper that stood ready near the fire, and then went upstairs with her sister.

'We'll talk in the morning,' Penelope told her soothingly as they went to their own rooms. 'Early.'

Martha nodded, so weary now she could hardly set one foot in front of the other. Tears filled her eyes as she passed the door of what had been her father's bedroom and she whisked into her own room before her sister could see them.

-

In the bedroom at the end of the landing Penelope went to stand by the window, drawing the curtains back and staring out across the moonlit gardens. Her father's death had made her think very deeply about their personal situation. Since John's death she had felt only half-alive, deprived of the future she'd looked forward to. Now, she knew she must pull herself together and become stronger, more like she used to be. She did not intend to be a burden on Martha.

She gave a wry smile at her reflection in the mirror. Stronger was one word for her old self, rebellious was another. Father had called her that several times, because he hadn't wanted her to marry John and she'd defied him. He'd said the fellow was not only short of money but had dangerous radical tendencies, just because John cared about the poor. Well, what else should a curate care about but those who needed his help most?

The rebellious part of her seemed to be surging up again now, pulsing with life, and it was disconcerting.

She might not speak as bluntly as dearest Martha, she might sometimes try to avoid trouble rather than confront it head on, but she was equally determined that they should make a life for themselves, and oh, most definitely not one dependent on their cousin.

On that thought, she drew the curtains firmly and got into bed. But it was a long time before she slept, and she could hear Martha's bed creaking next door as her sister tossed and turned too.

–

Seven o'clock the following morning saw the sisters sitting with a tea-tray in the parlour, knowing they were safe from interruptions because their cousin had never been an early riser.

'Edward's a fool!' stated Martha, stirring her cup of tea so vigorously it slopped into the saucer. '*You* can go and live with him if you want to, Pen! I'd rather go out as a governess. Far rather!'

'That's just what he was offering you,' Penelope pointed out with a chuckle.

'Unpaid! And as if he were doing us a favour, too!'

'Yes, but what *are* we going to do, Martha? We shan't be able to afford to live here any more. He's quite right about that.'

'We can manage on our annuities if we're frugal and go into rooms, but personally I'd prefer to find some way to earn a living. Otherwise what should we do with our time?'

'We ought to have made plans before now.' She frowned and fell silent for a moment, then asked, 'What *can* we do, though? You wouldn't really go out as a governess, would you, Martha?'

'I would if I had to! Only I'd prefer us to stay together. Wouldn't you?'

'Oh, yes!'

'And besides, governesses lead awful lives. Look at Jenny Barston. The poor thing can't call her soul her own, and if it weren't for us, she'd have no friends at all, because the Warings rarely include her in their social life unless they need to make up the numbers. Anyway, I know exactly what we can do. I've had it in mind for a year or two now, only you were grieving for John and it didn't seem necessary to discuss it yet.' Her voice wobbled as she continued, 'I didn't expect Father to die so soon.'

Penelope squeezed her hand in sympathy. 'What can we do?'

'Open a school.'

'A school! But there's one in the village already!'

'I know that! We shall have to go somewhere else, somewhere that doesn't already have a school for young ladies.'

'Leave Woodbourne?'

'How can we stay? There isn't enough money and that's that!' Martha stood up and went to gaze out of the window, her arms rigid at her sides, her hands clenched in tight fists. 'Even Edward couldn't offer us a solution that would allow us to stay here, Pen.' She swallowed the lump in her throat as she turned round. 'Anyway, I refuse to live on his charity! I just won't do it! I can't abide him or that silly moon-faced wife of his. I should be at outs with them in hours—no, minutes!'

'Then it seems we must try your school idea.'

Martha glanced sideways. 'I didn't think you'd agree so easily.'

'As you say, we have no choice.'

'Good. That's settled, then.'

She didn't say so, but there was another reason she would be glad to leave quiet little Woodbourne. All the unattached males there were either elderly or mere boys. Penelope was very pretty and surely, if she got the opportunity to meet some eligible gentlemen she'd find herself a husband?

Martha had no such hopes for herself. She'd read novels about people falling in love, but it had never happened to her. She was, she supposed, too practical and as for moderating her own opinions to suit those of a husband, she could never do it. So she'd resigned herself to spinsterhood.

But if Penelope were married and had children, then Martha's life would be richer, too.

–

Immediately after breakfast Edward again broached the question of his cousins' future and refused to be diverted from the subject. He spoke soothingly and every third or fourth sentence assured them that their presence would be no financial burden upon himself and his dearest Rosemary.

'Edward, you know perfectly well that you and I could never live in harmony,' Martha snapped when his tedious peroration came to an end. 'I don't know why you're even considering the idea. Anyway, Penelope and I have other plans for the future. We've decided to open a school and that'll suit us much better.'

He goggled at them, then positively shouted, '*Open a school?* I forbid it, absolutely and utterly forbid it!'

Martha began to enjoy herself. 'You can't prevent us, Edward! We're of full legal age and we have our own money, so it's got nothing to do with you!'

'Nothing to *do* with me! My own cousins talk about setting up as schoolmistresses—schoolmistresses of all the shabby genteel things!—and you say it's got nothing to do with me! Have you thought what people will say? Merridenes reduced to running a school. It's shocking—unthinkable. I won't have it!'

Penelope joined in. 'Rubbish, Edward! Teaching is a perfectly respectable occupation for a lady in reduced circumstances.'

He opened and shut his mouth a few times. 'You must be mad to refuse the offer of a good home at Poolerby Hall—every comfort—the bedroom walls repapered only last year—new curtains, too—ruinously expensive and fading already. I never heard of anything so ridiculous in all my life! Anyway, the risk is too great! You could lose what little money you do have. Schools cost money to set up—if one does things properly, that is.'

'We're not fools!' replied Martha. 'We shall choose a suitable town most carefully. We have no intention of failing in this venture.'

He stared at them in horrified dismay as the only possible meaning sank in, opening and shutting his mouth several times before he managed to speak. 'You don't—you can't mean you intend to leave Woodbourne and go to some strange place where you know nobody and are utterly without masculine protection!'

'You can't have been listening, for I told you so quite plainly.'

Penelope stepped in. 'We shan't rush into anything, Edward, I promise you.'

He stood up and marched across to the door, belly and jowls quivering with the violence of his steps. 'I shall wash my hands of you! And so will Rosemary! I'm not having people saying that I encouraged you in this ridiculous venture! Or that I didn't offer you a home. I shall pack my bag at once.'

He waited, clearly expecting them to beg him to stay. When they didn't, he withdrew behind a wall of icy dignity, summoned his carriage from the inn and took his leave in the curtest possible manner.

'He'll be back,' said Martha cynically as they stood at the gate and watched the dust settle in the lane.

Penelope laughed. 'If only to see how we're managing.'

Martha threaded her arm in her sister's and turned towards the house. 'Now, love, we must start doing some careful calculations. We have to go into this in a very businesslike manner. Remember, if we fail, we shall be dependent upon Cousin Edward's charity!'

They both shuddered at that thought.

–

Finding a place in which to open a school was more difficult than they had expected and the problem had not been resolved by the time winter approached and with it, the date they had to move out of their old home. By then, even Martha was beginning to worry that they might have made a mistake.

They studied advertisements in newspapers and dipped into their slender capital to go and inspect a few schools that were advertised for sale. But these were in districts that were distinctly shabby or else in remote villages. All of them had a sad air, as if the buildings themselves were tired of being schools.

This was not at all what Martha had in mind. Better-class persons wouldn't send their daughters to be educated in such places, she was sure, and she intended to run a successful school, not a scratch-quill establishment.

Chapter 2

Over a hundred miles to the north in a small Lancashire town called Tapton, Ben Seaton opened a letter and cursed fluently as he read its contents. Within the hour he had hired a carriage from the livery stables and was driving across the Pennines to Yorkshire.

He arrived in Bradford at dusk, weary and still angry. Not waiting for the groom sitting beside the coachman to jump down and open the carriage door, he let himself out with a curt, 'I'll expect you back here at ten o'clock tomorrow morning.' Picking up his valise, he strode up the steps and hammered impatiently at the door of the commodious three-storey residence.

When a maid answered his knock, he thrust his hat into her hands and walked inside. 'Where is your mistress?'

The sound of raised voices coming from the room to the right told him before the maid could do more than open her mouth, so he set down his valise and moved in that direction.

Mrs Seaton was the first to notice him. 'Ben! Oh, thank goodness you've come!'

He trod across to take his step-mother's hand and clasp it for a moment then turned to his half-sister, his expression hardening as he took in the elaborate clothes which didn't suit a girl of her age. 'Playing off your tricks again, Georgie?'

She scowled at him. 'It wasn't so bad. Other girls go out driving with their beaux and—'

'Not girls of sixteen and not in a carriage on their own with a man!' her mother snapped. 'And that particular beau is not only ten years older than you but more intent on winning himself a fortune than observing the proprieties. I told you so when you first met him.'

How had she managed to meet him in the first place? Ben wondered. Belinda had always given his half-sister too much freedom.

'Harold *loves* me!' Georgie cast a resentful look towards her mother. 'Besides, I got home safely, didn't I? What harm was there in it?'

Her mother was not to be persuaded. 'If Mr and Mrs Gralling hadn't seen you at the inn—looking uncomfortable, she said—and brought you back in their carriage, I shudder to think what might have happened once *that man* had got you out into the countryside on your own.'

Georgie pouted and flounced across to the window. 'Well, nothing did happen and if Harold had tried anything—he's not nearly as gentlemanly as I thought—I would have stabbed him with my hat pin. I think it very mean of you, Mother, to write to Ben about it when nothing bad happened.'

Mrs Seaton began to fan herself in agitation. 'Ben *is* your guardian.'

'Goodness only knows why! I don't know what Father was thinking of, leaving a will like that. Why, I can't even marry till I'm twenty-five without Ben's permission or I'll not gain access to my fortune. And he may be fifteen years older than me,' she added with monumental scorn, 'but what does *he* know about love or—or anything? All he understands is running that dirty old mill. No wonder

Miss Gayle broke off their engagement! He'll no doubt die a rich old bachelor, but *I'm* not going to follow his example and… and…'

Under her half-brother's stern gaze the flow of words gradually trailed off and she flounced one shoulder, turning away from him.

Mrs Seaton looked at Ben and spread her hands helplessly. 'I can do no more. Georgiana is becoming so wilful and,' she blushed, looking suddenly younger than her forty-one years, 'since I am shortly to re-marry, I shall have even less time to devote to her from now on.'

Ben wasn't surprised that Belinda had found herself another husband. She was that sort of woman, the clinging type. Why hadn't she mentioned her engagement in her letter? He guessed suddenly that the main reason she'd summoned him wasn't Georgie's escapade—though that was bad enough—but because Belinda had found an excuse to hand her daughter into his care. That was probably the best thing for the poor girl, if not for him, for his step-mother never had spent much time with her daughter, preferring to gossip or go shopping with her friends.

He realised she was looking at him expectantly so said quietly, 'My congratulations on your coming marriage, Belinda. Do I know the gentleman?'

'I think not. Ambrose is from near York—one of the Perrings—and I shall be moving there as soon as we're married, only—' She looked at her daughter and bit her lip before adding plaintively, 'Georgiana doesn't get on with him.'

'The man's a fool!' his sister said without even turning round. 'A *rich* fool, I'll grant you, landed gentry, no less. She's done even better for herself this time moneywise, but he's four years younger than Mama, so she doesn't want a daughter as old as me making *her* look older.'

Ben was sure Georgie was right, but that still didn't excuse her recent behaviour or this open rudeness to her mother. He frowned at her and turned back to the older woman. 'I dare say you'll wish some privacy to settle in with your new husband, then, Belinda?'

She nodded, a pleading look in her eyes.

'And in any case, I believe the time has come for me to take charge of Georgie. Shall I take her back to Tapton with me tomorrow?'

'Oh, Ben, that would be so kind of you.' She beamed at him.

But it was the girl by the window he was watching and he didn't miss the way she made a furtive swipe at her eyes with one hand. 'I'll be happy to have your company, Georgie,' he said in a softer tone. 'Really I will. I've missed having family nearby.'

She swung round, looking very young suddenly. 'Well, *I* won't be happy to go back to Tapton, not without Father. And since I'm tired now, I'm going to bed.' She whisked out of the room, slamming the door hard behind her.

He looked at his step-mother. 'Perhaps you'd ring for a maid to pack her things tonight? I've asked the carriage to come at ten tomorrow morning.'

She nodded.

'Is there any chance of something to eat… ?'

'Mercy, I'm forgetting my manners.' She rang the bell and began to give orders, her expression now smug.

Ben stared into the fire, leaving his step-mother to maintain the conversation by telling him all about her dearest Ambrose. He knew only too well what he was taking on, because he had been called upon before to sort out Georgie's scrapes. He had already decided that this time he would need help. A governess, perhaps— although he knew his sister considered herself too old for a governess at sixteen.

Belinda had foolishly dismissed the last woman a few months previously and made no attempt to find another. Well, that particular governess had never managed to control Georgie. It would take a very special sort of woman to manage such a wilful girl, and how he was to find such a person he didn't know.

He sighed. His peace in his own home was undoubtedly at an end and duty made a hard bedfellow. He was already fully engaged, trying to sort out a cotton spinning mill that his father had allowed to run down into near bankruptcy. Perhaps he should start thinking seriously of marriage himself so that he could provide a proper home life for his sister? *If* he could find a woman he could trust this time.

Oh, hell, why should he lumber himself with a wife when Georgie would undoubtedly marry and leave him within a few years? He had decided when Amanda jilted him for someone richer that he would never marry and he wasn't about to change his mind.

There must be someone available to look after her each day, though.

—

At nine o'clock on the second morning after his return to Tapton with Georgie, Ben walked across from the mill to his house, which was situated at one corner of the big yard, separated from it by a low wall. After washing his hands and changing his jacket, he went into the breakfast parlour. His sister's place was untouched so he rang for Hepzibah. 'Is Georgie not up yet?'

She shook her head. 'I sent Nan upstairs a few minutes ago with the hot water and Miss Georgie told her to go away.'

Hepzibah, who had been housekeeper to the Seatons since his mother's time, and who had not been grand enough for Belinda to take with her to Bradford, thank goodness, screwed up her lips in a way she had when she disapproved of something and didn't feel it her place to say so openly.

Ben held back a smile only with difficulty. He usually had breakfast sent across the yard to his office at the mill on a tray, but after being accused yesterday of leaving his sister alone all day, he'd decided to make the effort to eat breakfast at home from now on. It was only a short walk, after all.

He sighed. Georgie had turned up her nose at coming to live here because it was the original mill house. She had grown up in a grander place outside town because Belinda had refused point-blank to live so close to *that dreadful noisy mill* so his father had built her a new house. Ben had moved back here when he'd grown too old to live with them and Hepzibah had come with him. After his father's death he had needed capital, so had sold the new house to some county gentry who considered themselves too grand to associate socially with a mill owner, but not too grand to snap up a bargain.

'It was near eleven when she got up yesterday,' the housekeeper told him with a sniff. 'She says she doesn't like early mornings.'

Ben didn't try to hide his own disapproval. 'I'll go and see if she's awake.'

He took the stairs two at a time, impatient to get on with his day, and rapped on his sister's door. When there was no answer, he knocked more loudly.

A voice yelled from inside. 'I told you to go away.'

'It's me, Ben.'

'Well, you can go away too. Why does everyone want to wake me up? I can't possibly get up this early.'

He opened the door and scowled to find Georgie still lying in bed. 'We all get up early here, as you well know. And you did too when Father was alive.'

'Well, I don't any more. Mama says real ladies don't rise at the crack of dawn like servants.'

'It's inconvenient for Cook to have to provide two breakfasts and for Nan to keep setting and clearing the table, so you'll get up in time to join me for breakfast at nine o'clock from now on.'

'I shan't and you can't make me.' She slid down and pulled the covers over her head.

He walked over and dragged the covers off again, ignoring the screech of outrage and pulling her out of the bed when she remained huddled where she was. 'I'll expect you downstairs in twenty minutes.'

'It takes me far longer than that to dress.'

'Then we'll have to get you some simpler clothes.' He cast an angry glance at the garments scattered all over the floor. Fussy, frilly things, none of them pleased him and they certainly didn't flatter his sister who was as short as her mother. 'Who do you think is going to pick these up?'

'The maid, of course.'

'Nan has enough to do without you adding to it. She'll clean your bedroom, but you'll need to keep it tidy yourself. If it's not tidy, I won't allow her to clean it.'

Georgie burst into tears. 'Mama said I was old enough now to have my *own* maid, a lady's maid. She was going to get me one, too, until she met Ambrose.'

'Why? Can't you dress yourself? Twenty minutes,' he repeated. 'And if you're not in the dining room by then, I'll come and carry you down, whether you're dressed or not.'

'You wouldn't dare!'

'Oh, but I would.'

Their eyes met and hers fell first. Her noisy sobbing followed him down the stairs. He popped his head round the kitchen door to ask Cook to send breakfast through in twenty minutes, then told Hepzibah that Nan wasn't required to pick up after Miss Georgie and was only to clean her bedroom if it was tidy. 'Just tell me if there are any problems.' He saw the housekeeper smile and grinned back at her. 'She's been rather spoiled.'

'And neglected.'

That surprised him. 'Why do you say that?'

'From what she's let fall, that mother of hers hasn't spent much time with her. That's a very lonely and unhappy girl, Mr Ben.'

He was surprised by this, but valued Hepzibah's opinion, so vowed to be more patient with Georgie and perhaps win her confidence.

Twenty-two minutes later, just as he was about to go upstairs again, his patience already fading fast, Georgie came down with her hair hanging unbrushed down her back. She flung herself into the chair next to his, drank a cup of tea and spurned the food offered with every appearance of loathing.

'There'll be nothing else to eat until one o'clock,' he warned, but she didn't respond so he ate a hearty breakfast, made one or two remarks to which she replied in monosyllables, then dismissed her from the table. He left the house via the kitchen, telling Cook, 'Miss Georgie refused to eat breakfast, so don't give her anything to eat until I come back from the mill at one o'clock.'

'There'll be ructions before we're through, Mr Ben,' she replied.

'Then there will have to be ructions.'

The midday meal was again marked by a lack of conversation, but at least Georgie ate well.

'Did you go out at all this morning?' Ben asked.

'No. There's nowhere to go in Tapton.'

'What did you do?'

'Nothing.'

It was, he decided, like living with an angry wasp. And it was hard to win over someone who refused to hold a proper conversation and did nothing but sulk.

On Saturday morning Ben invited his sister to go for a walk with him that afternoon once the mill had closed.

'No, thank you.'

'You used to enjoy walking with Father.'

She blinked her eyes furiously and tried to hide the tears.

Ben's voice softened. 'You need some exercise. If you don't come willingly, then you'll come unwillingly.'

'I don't want to walk anywhere with *you*.' The look she gave him would have curdled milk.

When he got back to take her for a walk, having left several jobs at the mill until later, he had to go up to her bedroom and personally select some stout shoes for her to wear, since she turned up in soft kid slippers more suited for an evening engagement and an elaborate hat that would have blown away in the lightest of breezes.

'Those shoes hurt my feet.'

'Then we'll walk slowly.' What excuse would she offer next? he wondered.

She got tired very quickly even though he'd chosen a gentle stroll, and she was as grumpy as ever, with hardly a word to say for herself.

When they got back she retreated to her bedroom and he went to sit in the parlour, at his wits' end about what to do with her. He couldn't go on like this.

And Hepzibah was right. Georgie was a very unhappy girl.

After much thought, he decided to consult his friends, Jonas and Libby Wright. Jonas owned the largest of the three mills in Tapton, and although Libby was now an invalid, she was a woman of sound sense and had four delightful daughters of her own. She might have some ideas.

If she didn't, he couldn't think what he'd do.

–

Having heard nothing from Edward for over a month, Martha and Penelope had quite forgotten his promise to help them and were debating where to look for lodgings while they continued to pursue their inquiries about schools. Then he turned up unexpectedly on a bitterly cold day in early November.

After waxing lyrical over his wife and new daughter's excellent state of health, he asked abruptly, 'Have you found anywhere to set up your school yet?'

'Not yet,' Martha admitted.

'Well, in that case I might just be able to help you. Not that I approve of what you're doing any more than I did before, mind. Let that be clearly understood from the start.'

'You mean you actually know of somewhere suitable?' asked Martha in surprise.

'I may do. Though it's not exactly a school, but rather a private arrangement with two gentlemen.' With a smugly triumphant glance at them both, he continued, 'Through a mutual friend I made the acquaintance of one of these gentlemen when he was visiting his wife's relatives in the district.' He frowned, then qualified this statement, 'Well, he's a mill owner, so one can hardly call him a *gentleman*, but his wife is gently born and he's done well for himself— one has to respect that, at least—and no one could fault his manners.'

Penelope made an encouraging noise.

Martha kept her lips firmly pressed together.

'This Mr Wright comes from somewhere in Lancashire—now what did he say it was called?' Edward began drumming his fingertips on the table, muttering syllables beneath his breath and shaking his head. Then suddenly his expression cleared. 'Tapton, that's it! Such a vulgar-sounding name. No wonder I had trouble recalling it.'

He nodded approval of himself and continued, 'Anyway, Mr Wright's wife is an invalid and his children are all girls. He doesn't wish to send them away to school, so he and his wife have decided to find a lady who will act as governess-companion to them. A house will be provided nearby for the governess, and the children are to go to her every day because his own house is next to the mill and isn't large enough—imagine living so close to one of those dreadful places! Mr Wright's offer would possibly suit you for the time being and it is, at least, respectable.'

'It's worth considering,' Martha admitted. Maybe they'd be able to turn it into a proper school once they'd settled down.

'After I'd questioned him about the details I mentioned you two, though I made it very plain that I wasn't happy about your taking up employment and—'

'What is he offering to pay?' Martha inquired.

'I will engage to make suitable arrangements for your remuneration.'

'I'm doing nothing unless I know that from the start.'

He breathed deeply and let out a sniff. 'Wright is prepared to be generous, amazingly generous, actually—I should never pay a governess that much—and his friend Mr Seaton is to pay you an additional emolument as long as you will tutor his younger sister during the day as well.'

'How—much?' she repeated.

'If you didn't interrupt me so often, Martha, I'd be able to get on with my tale.' He saw her opening her mouth again with that stubborn expression on her face and added hastily, 'Mr Wright will pay sixty guineas a year for the two of you, plus providing the coal. Mr Seaton will provide the house and pay a further thirty guineas per annum. Oh, and Mr Wright will supply all the materials needed for teaching his girls—paper, books and so on—because he doesn't want any skimping on that side of things.'

Knowing that the more she questioned him, the more stubbornly Edward would withhold information, Martha picked up Penelope's embroidery to distract herself and began stabbing the needle viciously into the material. 'Pray continue.'

'Well then, where was I? Ah, yes… We decided in the end that I should take the two of you to Tapton because he wishes to meet you and introduce you to his wife before he will commit himself, which is only right and proper. And of course, for our part, *we* cannot decide anything either until we see the town and the house being offered, as I told him.'

Martha opened her mouth to protest his assumption of having a part in the decision making, but Penelope forestalled her. 'How very clever of you, Edward, to seize the opportunity so promptly! We're extremely grateful for your help, are we not, Martha?'

'Yes. Extremely.' Stab went the needle, giving the flower a garish yellow stem with big, uneven stitches. 'We must definitely arrange to go and see this Tapton place.'

'My dear Martha, you cannot have been listening. I have already arranged it. That's why I'm here today. Mr Wright is impatient to get matters settled, so if you could be ready by tomorrow morning and could offer me my old room for tonight, I'll take you there in my own carriage. Two ladies travelling all the way to Lancashire without a gentleman's escort is not to be thought of.'

He leaned back in his chair and beamed at them, abominably self-satisfied, and they could do nothing but thank him and accept his kind offer, because this way they would not even have to pay coach fares.

–

In Tapton Jonas Wright settled down in front of the blazing fire and looked at his younger friend, whom he hadn't seen for several days. 'Are things going any better at home, Ben?'

'No. I had to threaten to drag Georgie to church last Sunday and well, you saw what she was wearing...' He sighed and ran his hands through his short, dark hair. 'I need to do something about her clothes, but what do I know about how a young woman should dress?'

'Libby was wishing she could help you more, but she hadn't been at all well lately. The slightest movement hurts her.'

'I'd not inflict my sister on your wife, Jonas. Libby has enough to bear already. Quite frankly, Georgie's been spoiled rotten since my father died, but neglected too, and although I blame Belinda for that, I must blame myself as well. I should have paid more attention to what my dear step-mother was doing; not let her move so far away— though she does have cousins in Bradford and it seemed reasonable for her to go and live near them. Anyway, she's no longer my responsibility.' And thank goodness for that. Georgie was more than enough for a busy man to deal with.

'Did the wedding go well?'

'Very smoothly. His side paid, of course, because Belinda had some very extravagant ideas and I declined to spend my money on them. Besides, my father left her a very comfortable sum and I saw no reason why she shouldn't use that to pay for her wedding.' He grinned. 'It took a couple of quarrels to persuade her she couldn't twist me round her little finger as she did him, but in the end she accepted that I wasn't going to waste my money on one day's fuss.' His smile faded. 'Anyway, I couldn't have afforded such a large outlay just now, as you know.'

'I do and I think you're right to get new machinery for your mill. It'll soon pay for itself. Tell me more about the wedding, though, because Libby will want to know all the details. What did the bride wear?'

Ben frowned. 'Something frilly and blue with the widest sleeves I ever saw and a hat so large I kept expecting it to slide off her head. The whole thing was a much bigger affair than I'd expected and to tell the truth, I felt out of place among county society.' He pulled a wry face and they both smiled, for even in Tapton there were sharp lines drawn between families in trade and the county gentry, who lived on nearby estates.

'Georgie was so sulky at the wedding I felt downright ashamed of her and so I told her. She would hardly open her mouth to her new step-father and scowled the whole time, so it's not just me she's angry with, it seems to be the whole world. Oh, and you can tell Libby my sister was wearing something frilly, too, pink and white.' He sighed and lapsed into contemplation of his various problems.

'Are the new machines completed?'

'Nearly. Then we have to get them here safely. There's been rioting over in Netherdene and I've heard that some of the operatives in Tapton are upset, too. I've tried to make my own employees understand that these are new spinning machines not power looms.'

'I've spread the word among my workers, too.'

'But that still leaves Noll Brindley's workers, who seem determined to see the machines as threatening their jobs.'

'I've heard Brindley's behind all that, stirring them up.'

'Who else could it be? He's been behind a few bits of trouble since I took over and we both know why: he wants my mill. Well, even if I wanted to sell, I'd not offer it to him. But I don't want to sell. I want to make it thrive again as it did in the old days.' Before his father had met

Belinda and lost interest in his business. 'I can never thank you enough for your help this past year or two, Jonas.'

His friend waved one hand dismissively. 'It was my pleasure. After all, we didn't want Owd Noll getting his hands on another Tapton mill, did we? The way he treats his workers is a disgrace.'

Ben nodded agreement. They had both seen the gaunt, starveling children who worked at Brindley's. After a moment or two he dismissed that unpleasant picture and smiled at his friend. 'Well, that's enough about me and my problems. What did you want to see me about?'

'I may have found someone to teach the children and keep an eye on your Georgie.'

'That'd be a huge relief!'

'I met this fellow in Leicestershire, Edward Merridene, he's called. A fussy fool in some ways, but a shrewd enough businessman. It seems he has two female cousins whose father has just died and left them short of money. They're looking to set up a school. And the terms you and I agreed upon seemed acceptable to him.'

He grinned. 'Merridene was at great pains to tell me he'd offered them a home but they'd refused—which I thought spoke in their favour—but if they're anything like him, they won't do. Anyway, he's bringing them up to meet us and they'll be arriving the day after tomorrow.'

'They'll probably take one look at Georgie's sullen expression and run for their lives,' Ben said glumly.

'Nay, lad, never despair. You'll find some way to manage her. My Libby says she needs your love.'

Maybe she did and maybe he would find a way, Ben thought glumly, but in the meantime it was heavy going. Even Hepzibah was having trouble with Georgie, and there had been several scenes and tantrums.

What the hell did he know about bringing up girls of sixteen? Especially girls as contrary and wilful as his half-sister. He prayed these schoolteachers would be up to scratch.

–

When Ben got back to the mill, he found a man waiting to see him, a man ill-dressed for such a cold day and who looked vaguely familiar. He nearly refused to see him, then chided himself. Had he not vowed when he took over the mill to treat decently and kindly all the people with whom he dealt? 'What can I do for you?'

'I'm looking for a job, Mr Seaton.'

'We're not taking on any more hands at present, I'm afraid.'

'I heard you're getting new machinery. I'm good with machines.'

Ben frowned. He did need an Assistant Engineer, but this man looked more like a labourer than a skilled worker. 'Where did you train? Do you have references?'

'I don't have references and I trained by working on machines whenever I could. I'm good with them.'

'Where did you work last?'

'Brindley's. He dismissed me yesterday.'

Ben knew he should send the other away, but there was something about the man's expression, dogged and yet desperate, that touched him. 'Why did he do that?'

'Because I wouldn't take the guards off the machinery and make it unsafe for the little 'uns who clean it. I've been working as his engineer.'

'What's your name?'

There was the slightest hesitation, then, 'Daniel Porter.'

Of course! That hair colour. 'You're James Porter's son.'

'Aye.'

'My father dismissed yours.'

'I'm not like him. Are you like *your* father?' When no immediate answer was forthcoming, Porter sighed and turned towards the door.

'Wait!'

He turned round.

'I'll take you to see Ross Turner, my engineer. If you can convince him you know how to work with machines, I'll give you a trial. But at the first sign of trouble, you're out.'

'I'm *not* a troublemaker and I'll be grateful for a chance to prove it, Mr Seaton. I have a mother and sister dependent on me.'

When they went to see Ross, Ben stood back, watching as his engineer checked out Porter's claim to understand machinery. Soon the two men were leaning over some engine parts talking eagerly, hands waving, completely forgetting their employer. He had to move forward and take Ross's arm before his engineer could be distracted from the piece of equipment he was stripping. 'Well? Does he get the job or not?'

'What? Oh yes, of course he does.'

Ben saw Porter close his eyes for a moment and relief play starkly over his thin face. 'You can have a month's trial, then.'

'I shall need a house, too, Mr Seaton. We've to be out of Brindley's house by the end of the week. He only gave us that time because he thinks I'll go begging for my job back and when he hears I've been taken on here, he'll have us thrown out. I know he will.'

It was very likely. Everyone knew that Noll Brindley did nothing out of kindness and cared only about money. 'Ross will arrange that for you.'

As Ben walked slowly back to his office, he wondered if he'd done the right thing. Well, if Porter caused any trouble he'd be out on his ear. But if he did know about machines, he'd be a godsend.

–

The journey north severely tried the patience of all three travellers and made Edward turn peevish, but soon after noon on the second day they saw the small town of Tapton lying below them in a narrow Pennine valley. As the coach jolted down the deeply rutted road they were able to take a good look at their possible future home.

'Wright told me Tapton was little more than a village at the turn of the century and has grown rapidly, thanks to the mills offering employment to so many people,' Edward said. 'I'd guess those stone dwellings near the church are the older part and those larger buildings must be the mills, but look at all those cottages, rows and rows of them. I never saw such a thing.'

The newer buildings spread out along the sides of the valley like smutty fingers grasping at the grey-green skirts of the hills. There were many terraces of workers' dwellings, built right up the slopes of the valley sides in places, some on land supported at intervals by steep retaining walls. The red bricks of the narrow houses were already streaked with soot and their roofs were of grey slate. The three large square buildings were several storeys high and were each dominated by a tall chimney pouring black smoke into the sky.

'The mills are much bigger than I'd expected,' Penelope said after a long scrutiny.

'I didn't expect them to be built *inside* the town!' exclaimed Edward in tones of deep distaste. 'And look at that smoke. I can only be thankful I don't have to subject *my* family to such outpourings of filth! I cannot like this, my dear cousins. You must tell Mr Wright that you've changed your minds.'

The sisters ignored him, continuing to stare through the carriage window, avidly taking in every detail of what might be their new home.

He raised his voice to gain their attention. 'As soon as the horses can be changed we'll set off for home again. I daresay we can cover quite a few miles before dusk. How glad Rosemary will be to see me again.'

'Oh, we may as well look round, now that we're here and we can't leave without seeing Mr Wright,' Martha said.

Penelope rubbed her temple and added, 'Anyway, I really couldn't face any more travel today, Edward. I'm feeling quite nauseous and my head is aching.'

Her cousin edged away from her with a worried glance.

Martha looked at her compassionately, but knew her sister hated to be fussed over when she was feeling unwell, so turned back to gaze out of the window as the main street widened out into a rather pleasant square. The carriage crossed it to turn into the yard of a commodious inn, above whose door swung a crudely-painted sign depicting a sickly-looking dragon writhing on the ground beneath a plump knight holding a gore-tipped lance. The knight definitely reminded her of Edward and she couldn't help smiling.

An ostler came running out to hold the horses and the landlord of the inn surged forth to greet them in person, flanked by his wife. He offered just the sort of fussy attention that Edward enjoyed and Martha watched in amusement as her cousin mellowed rapidly beneath an expert touch.

'Mr Wright has booked rooms for you and the ladies, sir—the best the inn can provide—and fires have been burning in them since early morning. No need to fear damp sheets in *our* establishment. And he wishes to be informed the minute you arrive.'

It was obvious from the landlord's tone that Mr Wright was a personage of considerable importance in the town.

'Very civil of him,' Edward murmured, mellowing still further when the three visitors were shown up to comfortable bedrooms with blazing fires and a good hot meal promised within the half-hour. Their baggage was brought up with panting promptness by the boot boy, and a young maid followed soon after with copper ewers of piping hot water.

Penelope begged them to excuse her for a while and retired to her bed, looking wan and shuddering at the thought of food, but Edward and Martha did full justice to the excellent meal that was served in a cosy private parlour.

Afterwards Edward decreed that they should both take a rest before venturing out for a stroll round the square. Martha wasn't surprised that he needed to rest after consuming so much food and didn't bother to argue with him. She tiptoed in to see her sister, but found Penelope fast asleep, the frown already smoothed from her face.

On returning to her own room she hesitated, then told herself there could be nothing wrong with going out for some fresh air. She needn't go far, but was bursting with curiosity about the town.

Outside she paused for a moment, deciding that even the air tasted strange here—sharp and invigorating, but with a hint of soot and other odours she couldn't identify. The people looked different too, striding along briskly as if they hadn't a moment to spare, which was very different from the slower pace of the villagers in Woodbourne. These folk also called out cheerfully when they met an acquaintance, their voices louder than she was used to in public.

The breeze was invigorating after the stuffiness of the carriage and she decided to go and inspect the church on the other side of the square. It was surely one of the ugliest she had ever seen, for it was topped by a stubby spire out of all proportion to the rest of the building and was surrounded by sagging gravestones. So engrossed was she in studying the peculiarities of its architecture and in controlling the wild flapping of her cloak and bonnet strings that she didn't pay attention to where she was going and collided with someone.

The encounter knocked the man's hat sideways over one ear and made him drop the hand he had been using to hold it on, upon which the wind whipped the hat right off and sent it bowling across the square. As he steadied Martha, he let out an angry exclamation and once he was sure she wasn't going to fall, he stepped back to watch the progress of his hat. Her reticule had been knocked from her hand, scattering its contents in the mud, but he didn't seem to notice that. A Woodbourne gentleman would have ignored the hat and picked her things up, regardless of whose fault it was.

This man yelled, 'You, boy, get that hat!' to an urchin loitering on the corner.

'Yessir!' The lad set off at a run.

Not until he had seen the hat retrieved did the gentleman turn his attention back to Martha, who was picking up the last of her things.

'Why didn't you look where you were going?' he demanded. 'My hat'll be covered in mud now.'

'I could ask you the same thing, sir!' Her anger grew at being addressed so rudely. 'And if you have such difficulty with your hat, I would suggest you either carry it in your hand or purchase a better-fitting one.'

He looked as if he were about to snap back at her, but the boy came up with the offending article at that moment and by the time the man had dropped a penny into the child's grubby paw, Martha had stuffed her things back into her reticule anyhow and was walking away.

'Hoy!' bellowed a voice behind her, but she ignored it. Who did he think he was, shouting at her like that?

Footsteps pounded after her and she quickened her pace, made nervous by the pursuit. When he grabbed her arm she cried out in shock as she was pulled forcibly to a halt. Heart pounding, she swung round to face her pursuer and for a moment they stood staring at one another, so close they were separated by only a few inches.

She was tall and used to being on a level with, or taller than, other people. But he was taller by several inches, with broad shoulders and a general air of strength and vigour. His hair was dark and wavy, and the wind had sent it into tangles. His eyes were stormy, as if he was angry about something—not their encounter, surely? That wouldn't generate so much anger. The breath caught in her throat and for a moment she couldn't speak, only stare back at him.

He let go of her arm and stepped back. 'Didn't you hear me calling?'

'I'm not in the habit of answering to shouts of "Hoy!" from complete strangers.'

'What *are* you in the habit of doing, then? Throwing your purse away?' He brandished it in her face.

'Oh.' Flushing with annoyance at being caught in the wrong, she took it from him and tried to frame an apology.

But he interrupted her to say, 'I'd advise you to watch where you're walking in future. I give you good day, ma'am.' Touching his hat brim as the merest afterthought he marched away towards the rear of the church and vanished round its corner.

Once he was out of sight Martha realised with a start that she'd been standing staring after him like a bumpkin at a fair. But then she'd never seen anyone quite like him! Although well dressed, he didn't seem to be a gentleman and his voice had a certain northern tone to it, a slowness of enunciation and a way of rolling the vowels, as if every letter of each word must be given its full value.

And what was she doing standing here thinking about a complete stranger?

She went briskly on her way but on getting back to the inn she stopped, unwilling to return to Edward and the overheated stuffiness of the parlour. Perhaps she would just take a quick turn to the other end of the square.

There she discovered a linen draper's shop displaying an excellent range of goods. Beside it was a grocery store, the many panes of its big bow windows twinkling in the light of the setting sun and its shelves also well-stocked. The shoemaker's shop nearby displayed an elegant lady's and a sturdy gentleman's shoe in the window, so clearly catered for citizens of the better sort, and the apothecary's had a row of matching storage jars of various sizes each set in the centre of one of the many panes of glass in the window. The sign said *Chemist and Druggist* which meant, she hoped, that the owner compounded his own medicines and remedies, something which was always more convenient.

It would be pleasant to live in a larger community, she realised, not only for the convenience of having shops like these within easy walking distance but also because she and Penelope might make a few new acquaintances.

If Mr and Mrs Wright and this Mr Seaton approved of them. *If* they succeeded in their little enterprise. So many uncertainties!

There were two streets leading off the far side of the square, each lined with comfortable dwellings set in small gardens, the sort of places usually referred to as villas. She ventured a little way along the first one, but found that it narrowed after about fifty yards and from then on was lined with much smaller terraced dwellings without gardens.

Turning round, she began to make her way back to the inn, but for some reason she couldn't get the face of the man she'd bumped into out of her mind. He wasn't handsome, exactly—or was he? No, it was the aura of strength and energy that emanated from him and the light of intelligence in his eyes that made him attractive, or would have done had he controlled his anger.

Of course such a person wasn't suitable for her sister, and he might well be married, but surely there must be some eligible gentlemen in a town this size? She did hope so. She really wanted Penelope to find someone again, a kind man but with more money than John Medson, who had only been a curate with a small stipend to live on and no immediate prospects of advancement. Penelope had always insisted that she didn't care about money but it was much better to be *comfortable*.

And if Martha could run a school in the same town, why, they would both be happy, because they would see one another quite often. She pushed aside the thought of marriage and a family of her own but couldn't hold back a sigh. She had never attracted the attentions of any eligible gentleman and doubted that this would have changed.

Still, all in all, Tapton seemed very promising.

–

Ben Seaton walked on, conscious that he had taken out his worries on the stranger, regretting his display of bad temper. Who was she? He had never seen her before and knew all the ladies in the town, by sight at least. Suddenly it occurred to him that she might be one of the new governesses and he muttered, 'Oh, hell!'

But he soon forgot her because there was definitely trouble brewing in Tapton and he wouldn't know until the following day whether he'd managed to avoid it. Machine breaking had been rife in the north in the past few years, because handloom weavers resented the machines which were taking away their independence. As if you could hold back progress! And even spinning machines were not immune from the hatred some operatives bore to machinery of all sorts, for these machines had forced men to work outside their own homes and worse, provided more jobs for women and children than for grown men, so that wives were growing too independent, some said.

He grinned on that thought. Some wives had always had minds and ideas of their own, his mother for one. It was with her behind him that his father had become a successful mill owner, for she'd done the accounts and discussed business matters with him. When she died so suddenly, his father had gone to pieces and the mill had never flourished in quite the same way again.

His smile faded. He had so much at stake with these new machines, into which he'd invested every spare penny he possessed, that he was having trouble sleeping at night, worrying about getting them here safely. Brindley would like to see him go under, but he didn't intend to do so. However, he also didn't want to ask any further help from Jonas. He had more than served his apprenticeship as a mill owner now and must stand or fall by his own efforts.

He was determined not to fall, determined to make Seaton's grow and expand, not for the money alone, but for the satisfaction of a job well done and of providing work for so many people whose whole lives depended on his efforts. And he would do it in a way that didn't leave his operatives in grinding poverty. It sickened him how little Brindley paid his workers and how badly he treated and housed them. It would sicken any decent man.

But it would also upset Ben if those same unhappy workers wrecked his new machinery.

Chapter 3

Martha arrived back at the inn at the same time as a gentleman turned off the square into its yard. He held the door open for her and she preceded him inside, murmuring her thanks. He seemed to be studying her rather closely, but perhaps that was the northern way. Smiling at the landlady, she went straight up to her room, the clatter of her sensible leather half-boots not quite hiding the effusive welcome that was being accorded to the gentleman or the words, 'Mr Wright'.

She couldn't resist stopping to peep over the banisters at the man who might become her employer, but by that time he had left the hall. Then she caught sight in a mirror of her windswept appearance and exclaimed in dismay. No wonder he had stared at her. The wind had whipped strands of her unruly hair from its pins, her bonnet was askew and her cloak badly crumpled from the journey, while her cheeks were blooming as rosily as a milkmaid's.

He could hardly have failed to guess who she was. What must he think of a governess who looked such a hoyden?

Before she could get into her room to repair the damage, Edward appeared at the end of the corridor.

'Ah, there you are at last!' He stopped short and frowned. 'My dear Martha, whatever have you been doing to get yourself in such a state?'

'Taking a walk. It's very windy.'

'*Walking unescorted in a strange town?* Have you run mad?'

'I needed some exercise.' He was still frowning, so she forced herself to add, 'I've only walked round the square, I promise you. It was all quite proper and I was never out of the sight of the inn.' Except that Edward would not have considered her encounter with the dark stranger at all proper.

He ignored this attempt at conciliation. 'But just look at you! What *will* people think? I hope you can tidy yourself up quickly, for we're expecting a visitor at any moment. I received a note from Mr Wright immediately he heard of our arrival, saying he would call on us directly, which shows him not to be lacking manners, at least.'

'I think he's just arrived at the inn. In fact, I heard the landlady greet him by name.'

Edward clicked his tongue in annoyance and gave her a push. 'Then for goodness sake, go and tidy yourself quickly!'

She whisked into her bedroom, casting off her cloak and bonnet, then sitting down in front of the mirror to attend to her hair. There was a tap on the door and Penelope came in.

'Our dear cousin sent me to check that you make yourself decent and ladylike. He's been in a great fussation for the past half hour, ever since he found out you weren't in your room.'

'I'm sorry to have left you to face him on your own. Did he wake you up?'

Penelope chuckled. 'He got the landlady to do that, as he has too much delicacy of mind to knock on the door of an unmarried lady's bedchamber. When he found out you weren't in the inn, he became almost hysterical. Does he really believe we never walk out alone? One would think there were quicksands underfoot and brigands round every corner to hear him talk. What a fool he is! Now, let me pin up your back hair again, love! You've missed a bit.' She coiled the heavy locks into a more flattering arrangement.

Martha frowned at her image in the mirror. 'It's too loose. You know I like it tighter than that.'

'There isn't time to do it again.'

'I suppose it'll have to do, then. You look a lot better now, Pen.'

'Oh, yes. The nap soon settled me. And the landlady brought me up some tea and cake when she came to wake me, so I'm feeling quite myself again, I promise you.'

'What do you think of Tapton?'

'I haven't seen as much of it as you, but as long as we're together, I don't really mind where we live.'

'It's an ugly town. Edward was right about that.'

'Oh, stop worrying, Martha. Let's go and face this Mr Wright.'

–

'Ah, here are the ladies!' Edward said unnecessarily as they entered the private parlour. 'May I present my cousins, Miss Merridene and Miss Penelope Merridene? Cousins, this is Mr Wright.'

Martha was for a moment embarrassed to think how dishevelled she must have appeared when they met in the entrance and was relieved when he didn't refer to their encounter. She was immediately struck by his wide smile and sturdy appearance. He was her own height, probably forty or so, with greying hair and a strong, square face. His northern accent was even more marked than that of the man she'd met in the square, and he was eyeing her and her sister far more closely than was polite.

'So you two ladies want to start up a school, eh?'

'Yes.' Martha automatically acted as spokeswoman, something she had started doing in the past year or two.

'In spite of my offer of a good home at Poolerby Hall,' put in Edward.

There was a moment's silence and Martha wondered if she had caught just the hint of a smile on their visitor's face.

He addressed them, not Edward. 'Let's get it straight from the start: it's not me who'll decide whether we employ you or not, but my wife, so I've come to invite you ladies to visit her this afternoon—if you're not too tired, that is. She can't go out these days because she has trouble walking. Rheumatism.' He paused for a moment, looking sad.

Penelope murmured, 'It can be a terrible affliction.'

He nodded. 'Aye. Don't try to shake hands with her. It hurts too much. You can meet my little lasses while you're there. They're in sore need of schooling, I'm afraid. We did have a governess but that didn't answer at all, because she was a starchy female and never stopped nagging them. I don't want my daughters turning into quiet little mice, so she and I were soon at odds. Nor will I send them away to school. I don't hold with children living apart from their families, especially girls. Besides, I should miss mine too much. They're grand little souls.'

Martha leaned forward, her eyes bright with interest, and Mr Wright mentally revised his opinion of her looks. Not such a plain Jane, after all, with that intelligent expression lighting up her whole face. He had been doubtful about even considering that silly fellow's cousins, but he'd been desperate for help. And he was beginning to feel more optimistic already because he liked the looks of the younger sister, too.

'There's also Georgie,' he added reluctantly, knowing he and Ben must be open about that problem.

'Georgie?'

'Aye. Georgiana is her proper name, but everyone calls her Georgie. She's Ben Seaton's half-sister, sixteen and trying to act like twenty. Eh, she's a real minx, spoiled rotten by her mother, and that's one of the reasons why Ben's prepared to pay generously. She'll need some firm handling.'

'I cannot like the thought of my cousins taking on a troublesome chit of that age,' protested Edward. 'If her brother cannot control her, why should he think they will be able to?'

'He *can* control her, but he wants more than that. He wants to see her happy and acting like a lass of almost seventeen should.'

Martha cut in quickly before Edward could say something else tactless, 'We'd need to meet her as well, then. I couldn't agree to supervise her unless I thought she and I could come to terms with one another.'

'I'll take you round to their house if you get on all right with my wife. We live quite close to one another in Tapton, close to the mills as well, which is why we don't bother much with carriages.' He glanced at Edward with a barely concealed smile. 'I know we seem to be hurrying things, Mr Merridene, but if your cousins and the children aren't suited to one another, then why waste more of everyone's time?'

Edward breathed deeply and looked as if he was about to say something.

Penelope interrupted quickly with, 'Why indeed?'

Jonas leaned back in his chair and stared at the two women. 'Just tell me before we set off what makes you think you can run a school, Miss Merridene, Miss Penelope? You've no experience of teaching, after all.'

'True I have no experience of actually running a school, but I have run my father's house since I was fifteen, which included taking care of the money and accounts, and it was I who helped educate my sister. You'll find us well-read, we speak passable French, play the piano and can do fine needlework. My sister is skilled in drawing and the use of water-colours, and I intend to teach the older girls practical skills like managing the household accounts.'

When he didn't immediately respond, she asked, 'What more do you ask of a schoolmistress? Or do you wish your daughters to study Latin and Greek? If so, I'll admit we can't help you.'

Mr Wright was in no way abashed by her spirited defence. 'Of course I don't want them to study Latin and Greek. What use are such things to a woman—or to a man, either, come to that? This is the nineteenth century, not the first!'

He slapped his thigh and let out a crack of laughter. 'Well, at least you can speak up for yourself, which is more than I can say for most of the governesses I've interviewed in the past few months. And to answer your question, what I want from a schoolmistress, apart from teaching the three Rs, is that she allow my daughters to develop a bit of character and sense without spoiling them—and that she play with them and take them for walks so that they grow up strong and healthy. That's something their mother can't do. Practical skills are good, but I don't want mine stuffing full of useless accomplishments such as playing the harp and painting on china!'

'I assume you wouldn't mind them learning to sketch, though,' Penelope asked.

'Not at all. My wife used to be a good artist before her hands grew so twisted.' He stood up. 'Well then, if you two ladies will fetch your outdoor things, I'll escort you round to my house. After that, if my wife thinks you're suitable, I'll take you to see Ben.'

He turned to give Edward a firm look. 'We'll leave this part to the ladies, eh Mr Merridene, and not drag you out into the cold again? I'm only acting as guide and shall not be there while your cousins talk to my wife.'

Edward opened his mouth to protest, looked at Mr Wright and closed it again. 'Oh, very well!'

—

In a comfortable house near the third mill in Tapton, Oliver Brindley, known to his workers and enemies as Owd Noll, walked across the yard to take his afternoon tea in solitary state in front of his own hearth. The small table was perfectly set, but he found fault with it anyway and sent the maid back to the kitchen in tears because he reckoned servants had an easy life and he wasn't letting his get slack in their ways.

When she'd gone, he poured his own tea, as he had done since his wife had died several years previously, and helped himself to a generous slice of cream cake. As he ate it in great chomping bites, he studied the letter that had arrived that afternoon and was now propped against the teapot. He knew the handwriting. It was from his only son, who had been educated to be a gentleman and who now despised him—though Peter didn't despise his father's money. Oh, no! In fact, he only wrote when he wanted more of it.

Well, Peter hadn't done what his father asked and found himself a well-bred young lady to marry, so Noll was damned if he'd hand over any more money. On a sudden impulse he sent the letter spinning into the fire without opening it, cutting another slice of cake and cramming some into his mouth as he watched the paper shrivel and flare into nothing.

When he went back to the mill which lay behind his house, Gerry Cox was waiting for him.

'You'd better come into the office, lad.' Noll shut the door, then went to sit behind the big mahogany desk while Gerry perched on one corner of it. 'Well? Did you threaten to throw them out?'

'They'd already gone. Seaton's set Porter on as Assistant Engineer and they've moved into one of his new houses in Reservoir Lane.'

Noll swelled with indignation. 'I told Seaton I wanted Daniel Porter out of this town. Seaton's doing this to spite me and is getting altogether too big for his boots since his father died. If Wright hadn't stepped in to help him, I'd have had his mill off him by now.'

He fumed silently for a minute or two, tapping his fingers on the desk. 'We'll leave things as they are with Porter for a bit because we've that other matter to deal with first. But I won't forget this. Seaton will regret taking that cheeky young devil on—and Porter will regret disobeying my order to leave town.' He gave Gerry a sly grin. 'Just as his dad did, eh?'

Gerry summoned up a grin in return, though he couldn't see what Noll was making such a fuss about. As long as Seaton was out of their mill, what did it matter where he went? He changed the subject. 'How's your Peter going on in London? Found himself a fancy wife yet?'

Noll's smile vanished. 'No, he hasn't. As far as I can tell, all he's done is throw good money away. I had a letter from him this morning.'

'Oh? What did it say?'

'How should I know? I didn't open the damn thing, just threw it into the fire. He only writes when he wants more money. He's far too fine to associate with a common fellow like me the rest of the time. Well, I'm not giving him any more till I see some return on my investment. I need a grandson I can train up to run this mill when I die, and I mean to have one.'

'Your Peter always looks as fine as a fighting cock.'

'Looks are one thing, turning up his nose at his father's another and I'm not having it.'

'You'll soon bring him to heel.'

'Mebbe. He's too like his mother, though. She could be damned stubborn when she'd set her mind on something.'

Gerry didn't comment. Noll could get very touchy about his son, though what else could you expect when you sent a lad off to a fancy school? The place seemed to have taught him only to despise the hand that fed him.

They sat on together for a while longer, discussing various details about the mill. He and Noll had been lads together, then his friend had risen in the world, as Gerry knew he never could have done, though he'd not done too badly for himself, ending up as Chief Overlooker, responsible only to Noll, the Master.

But for all the differences between them now, his master still treated him as a friend—or as close to a friend as a man like that ever got, for everyone in Tapton was well aware that Owd Noll preferred money to anything and anyone else in the world, his son and heir included.

–

It took only a few minutes for the ladies to walk to Mr Wright's home. His wife was waiting for them in the front parlour but she didn't attempt to rise and greet them. Martha was shocked at how unwell Libby Wright looked, for pain had etched deep lines on her gentle face. Her hands were twisted with rheumatism and she was lying on a day bed with a blanket across her lower body.

Mr Wright went across to her. 'How are you, my dear?'

'A little better, thank you.'

His expression said he knew this to be a lie, and the mixture of love and sadness in his eyes as he looked at his wife made a lump come into Martha's throat. How would it feel to have a man love you like that?

Having introduced their two guests, he turned and left the room.

A blazing fire was burning in the grate and the parlour was so cosy after the chilly dusk outside that Martha said without thinking, 'How welcoming this room feels. Oh, I'm sorry, Mrs Wright. That's not a polite way to greet a new acquaintance.'

'I'm not interested in what's polite today, but in meeting two ladies who may or may not be looking after my girls, something I can no longer do properly myself.' She gestured to two chairs opposite her. 'Please sit down. We've interviewed several governesses and I must say you don't look like the others.'

'I hope that's in our favour,' Penelope said at once.

Libby smiled. 'Oh, yes. That's a very good point as far as I'm concerned. I don't want my girls stifling or regimenting, as I was. My parents and governess were far too strict. But I do want to know why two ladies like you have decided to become teachers? I gather you've been left without much money, but my husband tells me your cousin has offered you a home, so you aren't obliged to go out and work for a living.'

Martha hesitated but didn't feel it would be loyal to denigrate their cousin to a stranger. 'Let's just say that we prefer our independence and don't get on well enough with Edward to live at Poolerby Hall. Besides, what would we do with ourselves all day if we had no occupation?'

Libby looked at Penelope. 'You're very quiet. Do you agree with your sister?'

'I wasn't sure at first, but now I'm beginning to think a complete change may be good for us both in many ways. My sister's worked so hard since our mother died thirteen years ago. I don't think she ever had a chance to enjoy her girlhood.'

Martha looked at Penelope in surprise. That thought had never even occurred to her. She had helped Sally look after their mother when she grew ill, then taken up the household reins without hesitation when her mother died, out of love for her father and sister. It embarrassed her to talk of herself, so she quickly changed the subject and they went on to discuss what and how they intended to teach.

Then Penelope noticed Mrs Wright shifting uneasily on the sofa. 'We're tiring you, I think. Would you like us to leave now?'

'No. I get uncomfortable if I lie in one position for too long, that's all. If you could help me sit up straighter? Thank you. Now, if you have no more questions, let's bring the girls in.' She rang her handbell twice and there was the sound of footsteps and scuffling in the hall outside, then four girls filed in. They went to stand near their mother, the two eldest behind the sofa and the others at one end. Each of them took great care not to bump into the sofa, even the smallest child.

It was such a lovely family group that Martha felt her old desire to have children, long repressed, surface suddenly and bite into her like acid.

'Let me introduce Beth, Helen, Jenny and Alice.'

The four chorused a greeting, staring at the two strangers with the clear-eyed, open gaze of happy children. The oldest girl must have been twelve or so and the youngest around five. For a moment or two Martha felt intimidated then pulled herself together. 'Perhaps you girls could tell us what you were learning with your last governess?'

It was Helen who answered. 'We learned the Kings and Queens of England. It was a *very* long list.' She sighed.

'Countries and their capitals,' Beth offered without enthusiasm.

'I always hated learning lists,' Penelope smiled at the youngest child. 'Do you like reading stories?'

'She can't read yet,' Helen said scornfully. 'She's just a baby, still learning her letters.'

'I like listening to stories, though,' Alice volunteered. 'When Mother's well, she reads to us sometimes.'

'We'll all have to help you learn to read, won't we?' said Penelope. 'Then you can read to your mother, for a change. Books are such good companions. I don't know what I'd do if I couldn't read. And I know lots of stories.'

'I like drawing best,' Helen volunteered.

'So did I when I was your age,' Martha said. 'But my sister is much better at it than I ever was.'

Mrs Wright had been watching them carefully, but she now intervened. 'I think you can go and get your tea now, girls.' When they had gone she turned to her visitors. 'I'm prepared to give you a try.'

The words were out before Martha could stop them. 'Whatever made you decide that so quickly?'

'The way you talked to my daughters. I won't have anyone hectoring them or forcing them to be silent all the time—though I don't want them spoiling, either.'

Martha could see that her hostess's face was visibly paler. 'We're delighted that you approve of us, but I think we should leave you to rest now, Mrs Wright.'

'Yes. I'm sorry. I had a bad night, just when I wanted to be at my best.' She rang the bell once and her husband came in. 'Jonas dear, perhaps you could escort our visitors round to the Seatons'. I'd be happy for them to teach our daughters, but they need to meet Georgie first.' She looked at Martha. 'Georgie behaves badly, there's no denying that, but she's a very unhappy young woman who is missing her father greatly. Her mother has just remarried and has never been very attentive to her needs. Perhaps you'll be able to find a way to help her. I do hope so.'

Mr Wright led them into a study and waved them to big leather armchairs. 'There's another thing I want to ask of you before we set off. I need some better educated workers and so does Ben Seaton. We'll pay you extra to run reading and writing classes for our overlookers and any men with promise. The classes would have to be in the evenings, but the men would give you no trouble because they're eager to learn.'

It was Penelope who spoke this time. 'I used to do this with my fiancé for a while, teach ordinary people to read, I mean. I found it very rewarding and would be delighted to do it again.'

He looked at her in surprise. 'You're engaged?'

'Not now. John died.'

'I'm sorry.'

'It's all right. It was over two years ago.'

He waited a moment then stood up. 'Well, then, it seems we're in agreement, so let's go and see Ben.'

Outside the sun had already set but next to the house was a big square building, its windows brightly lit, revealing large machines and people toiling around them. 'I spin cotton,' Mr Wright said, noticing them staring, 'or rather my machines do. And I live next to my mill in case I'm needed. If you come to Tapton, I'll show you round the place one day.'

Without waiting for an answer he led them across the square, which was lit by lanterns hanging outside the shops and inn.

'That's Seaton's,' he waved a hand towards another brightly-lit building looming behind the houses on the opposite side of the square.

Martha noticed that it wasn't as big as Mr Wright's mill, but it still seemed large to her and was just as brightly lit.

'And at the other end of the town is Brindley's. You can just see the lights from his place over there.' He pointed to their right.

By the light of a nearby lantern Martha could see how tight his expression had become at the mention of the name Brindley and was intrigued. Clearly he didn't get on with the third mill-owner. She didn't pursue that point now, just enjoyed the brisk walk past the inn towards Mr Seaton's house, which also lay next to his mill. Their breath clouded the chill air and their footsteps sounded clearly on the square stone setts that paved the streets in this central part of the town.

'Does Mr Seaton spin cotton too?' Penelope inquired.

'Aye. Towns usually specialise in either spinning or weaving. In Tapton it's spinning, though there's a small dye works too. We use steam engines to drive our machinery nowadays, but we used to use water power. Ben's bringing some new machinery into his mill soon, so it'll be more efficient. His father let things run down, I'm afraid, and Ben's had a hard time of it since he inherited. But he's pulling things into shape at the mill now.'

He hesitated, then added, 'If he seems a bit short-tempered, well, he's got a few problems at the moment, so please bear with him.'

He stopped in front of a square, stone-built house. It stood neat and solid in front of the mill and something about it appealed to Martha.

The door opened before Mr Wright could raise the knocker and a plump elderly maid stood there beaming at him. 'I saw you walking down the street, Mr Jonas. Come inside quickly, ladies. It's bitter cold out.'

He gestured to the two sisters to precede him, then said in his easy manner, 'This is Hepzibah Carr, who's been with the Seatons since she was a lass and who rules this house with a rod of iron.'

'Get on with you, Mr Jonas,' she chided with a fond smile, then turned to study the visitors quite openly before saying, 'I'll just send Nan across the yard for Mr Ben. Miss

Georgie is waiting for you in the front room.' She threw open a door, calling, 'Here they are, love.'

From the rear of the room a girl moved forward into the brighter circle of lamplight. She was pretty, but her appearance was spoiled by a sulky expression and her clothes were far too grown-up for a girl of sixteen, in Martha's opinion, and far too fussy.

'Good evening, Georgie,' Mr Wright said. 'I've brought Miss Merridene and her sister Miss Penelope to meet you.'

'Good evening. Won't you please sit down?' Her voice was wooden and when the sisters had sat down on the sofa, she chose a chair set further back while Mr Wright went to stand in front of the fire, one hand on the mantelpiece. 'Ah, here he is.'

There was the sound of footsteps and as she'd suspected Martha recognised the gentleman who had picked up her purse. He stopped just inside the doorway, looking somewhat abashed as he recognised her too, then turned to Mr Wright, smiling a greeting. She decided that when he wasn't scowling he was, as Sally would say, a fine figure of a man, if not strictly handsome.

Mr Wright made the introductions, saying frankly, 'Libby sent the ladies round to meet you because she's happy for them to teach our girls.' A clock chimed on the mantelpiece and he looked at it with a frown. 'Can I leave you to escort them back to the inn, Ben? One of the older machines has been giving us some trouble and I want to check it before the men leave for the day.'

'Yes, of course.'

'And someone will need to show the ladies round the house in the morning.'

'Hepzibah's agreed to do that. I'm going to be busy tomorrow, as you know, or I'd do it myself.'

'Aye, well, it'll probably be better for a woman to do it, anyway. I hope things go well for you, lad.' He clapped Mr Seaton's shoulder and turned to say, 'Goodbye, ladies. I'll see you tomorrow before you leave.'

When Jonas had gone, showing himself out, Ben took the big armchair opposite his two visitors and sat in it with his hands resting on the arms. He looked tired but alert.

His sister was leaning back so far in her chair that her face was mostly in shadow.

'I'll come straight to the point,' he said. 'Georgie here doesn't feel she needs any more governessing, but I don't want her idling the days away—or getting into any more mischief.'

Martha was dying to ask what sort of mischief he was referring to, but refrained. 'How old are you, Miss Seaton?'

'Almost seventeen.'

'Not for three more months,' her brother corrected sharply, earning himself an angry look.

'Then you're definitely too old for normal lessons,' Martha said. 'What you need to know now is how to run a household, do the accounts, deal with servants, plan meals—that sort of thing.'

The girl shrugged. 'I shall be able to afford servants to do all that. My father left me plenty of money, so *I* shan't have to lift a finger.'

Ben growled in anger and opened his mouth. Martha was afraid he was going to correct his sister again and make her even sulkier, so shook her head at him. She was pleased to see him take her meaning and snap his mouth shut again.

'You'd be very bored if you sat around doing nothing all day,' Penelope said lightly. 'And you'd get very fat, too, if you didn't take some exercise. Women do, you know.'

Martha saw Ben's hastily suppressed amusement as Georgie looked down at herself in horror and she too had to hide a smile before turning away from that point. 'If you don't understand the work your servants do, how will you check that they're doing their jobs properly?'

Georgie frowned but said nothing more.

There was silence then Ben said, 'Well, if Libby approves of you, then it's all right with me if you take the job, ladies.'

'Don't *you* want to ask us anything, Mr Seaton?' Penelope ventured.

'I shouldn't know what to ask a governess, but I trust Libby Wright's judgement implicitly. Did Jonas speak to you about the other thing, helping our men?'

'Yes. I've already done similar work,' Penelope said. 'My fiancé was a clergyman and we were helping some of his poorer parishioners to better themselves.' This time she added before he could ask, 'Sadly, John died two years ago, so I wasn't able to continue the work. I've missed it.'

Ben nodded and when no one said anything else, asked impatiently, 'Well, shall you take the job?'

Martha said what they'd agreed beforehand. 'We'd like to think about it overnight and give you our decision after we've seen the house you're offering.'

'Aye, well, that makes sense. I'd do the same myself. Hepzibah will come and collect you from the George and Dragon tomorrow. It's only a short walk to the house. Nine o'clock do you? The town should be quiet enough by then.'

'Nine o'clock will suit us perfectly, Mr Seaton.' She wondered what he meant by 'the town should be quiet by then' but didn't ask.

'Good. I'll escort you back to the inn.' He stood up and the ladies followed suit. His sister didn't stir. *'Georgie! Where are your manners?'*

The girl came slowly to her feet, muttering a farewell.

Martha gave her a brief nod, then turned back to Mr Seaton. 'We can find our own way back to the inn. It's not far.'

'I'd prefer to go with you.'

He barely said a word as they walked briskly back and at the inn he tipped his hat before striding off into the darkness.

'He's very abrupt,' Penelope said, pausing to watch him go.

'He's downright rude most of the time,' Martha said, chin jutting dangerously. 'And I mean to treat him in exactly the same way from now on and speak my mind when I'm with him.'

'Was it my imagination or did he look surprised to see you?'

'We'd already met, but not in such a way as to exchange names. I didn't have time to tell you but I bumped into him when I went for a stroll and we—um—disagreed about something.'

'Oh.' Penelope didn't comment further because she had never seen her sister get flustered for so little reason and was intrigued by this reaction. 'Georgie is going to be difficult to deal with, don't you think? We shall probably earn every penny of what he's offering.'

'Yes. In fact—I'm not at all sure about this venture now, what with the classes for men from the mill as well. What do *you* think about that? Really.'

Penelope looked at her in surprise. 'You know I've always believed in universal literacy. I'd love to help the workers from the mill. And I think the Wright children are sweet. I'm sure I'll enjoy teaching them and playing with them. Did you see how careful they were not to bump their mother's sofa? Her illness must be very hard for them all.'

'Especially her.' But Martha was still thinking about Ben Seaton, not at all sure she wanted to work for him. She found him very—she fumbled mentally for a word and could only come up with *unsettling*. 'Well, we can't stand here all evening. Let's go inside and beard the lion in his den.'

'Lion? Edward? He's more a rabbit, wouldn't you say?' They both chuckled.

Their cousin darted out of the sitting-room as soon as he heard their voices in the stairwell. 'There you are at last. What kept you so long? It's almost time for dinner.'

'We'd better go and change, then.'

'No, no! Come and tell me what happened first. I'm sure there's no need to change, given the circumstances.' He led the way back into the sitting room. 'I think it was extremely rude of Mr Wright not to invite me to accompany you. After all, I *am* the head of the family. But I didn't make a fuss, not when your livelihood might depend upon the fellow's goodwill.' He looked expectantly from one to the other. 'Well?'

'The Wright children seem delightful,' Martha said, 'but their poor mother is very twisted with rheumatism. She must be in great pain.'

'Yes, yes! But I do hope you convinced her that you would be able to keep them in order. No one is going to hire a governess who can't control her charges. I meant to have warned you of that point before you met her, but you left so quickly.'

Penelope stepped in hastily as she saw her sister begin to bristle with indignation. 'We—um—satisfied Mrs Wright that we could offer her the sort of service she required and she sent us to meet Mr Seaton and his sister.'

Martha joined in. 'They would definitely like to employ us but we said we wished to inspect the house they're offering tomorrow morning before making our decision.'

'Very sensible. I shall come with you for that. As the landlord of several properties I can give you the benefit of my experience.'

'Mr Seaton's housekeeper will be collecting us at nine o'clock,' Martha warned him. 'Won't that be a little early for you?'

Edward gave an aggrieved sigh. 'I grudge you no exertion in this venture, though I still cannot like it. But—a mere housekeeper? Mr Seaton isn't conducting you over the residence himself?'

'No. He'll be busy at the mill.'

'And if the house is all right—?' He looked at them expectantly.

'We shall probably accept the positions,' Martha said.

'Hmm. I still cannot like it. Now that we've seen what a rough, dirty place Tapton is, you must surely realise that as gentlefolk, you owe it to your family to set yourselves up in a more salubrious area and—'

Fortunately the landlady knocked just then to see if they were ready for their dinner and Edward was distracted by the need to check exactly what she was offering them for their meal.

Chapter 4

The following morning Hepzibah arrived promptly at nine o'clock, just as Edward was complaining about the lack of consideration of people who expected a gentleman to do business at this ungodly hour.

The housekeeper took them along one of the side streets leading off the other side of the square. Half-way along it she stopped and gestured to a house. 'This is it. Fern Villa.'

The two sisters studied the outside, exchanging pleased glances at what they saw. Like the neighbouring residences, it was a neat three-storey building, double-fronted and with a very small front garden—but at least it had a garden, which many in the town didn't. Hepzibah also pointed out that all the houses in the street had the luxury of piped water from the Tapton Municipal Water Company, which had been formed only three years previously at Mr Wright's instigation.

'I wouldn't advise you to trust a water company,' Edward declared at once. 'I don't use any water not drawn from my own well.'

'Mr Wright mistrusts the wells in the town,' Hepzibah remarked. 'Says they're poisoned by the seepage from the cess pits and won't let his childer drink owt that hasn't come from his own water company, yes and been boiled, too. Cook does the same for Ben and Georgie, just to be safe.'

'Shall we go inside?' Penelope asked quickly, seeing that their cousin was looking thunderous at the house-keeper's familiarity in using her employers' first names. She was quite sure Hepzibah wouldn't put up with him hectoring her without responding sharply, because Sally wouldn't have either and the two women seemed rather similar in nature.

Luckily the house distracted Edward. Fern Villa had two parlours, one on either side of a narrow hallway, with a large dining-room at the rear on the left and a much smaller room on the right. The kitchen was behind that and had a modern kitchener, all shiny with blacklead, with a closed fire in the centre giving out gentle heat, a hot water tank on one side and a double oven on the other.

'I came and lit the fire earlier this morning,' Hepzibah said. 'Thought it'd take the chill off the house a bit, make it seem more welcoming.'

'That was kind of you.' Martha held her hands out to the warmth.

'There's a scullery, pantry and coal house through here,' Hepzibah went on, opening another door that led to a small corridor.

'Sally will love this kitchen,' Penelope murmured after they'd examined everything and come back to stand looking out of the window. The rear garden was larger than she'd expected, with a gate at the far end, newly painted in a bright green colour. She saw Hepzibah looking at her questioningly and explained who Sally was, then added, 'The house has a nice feel to it.'

'It was where old Mr Seaton lived with his first wife until he built the mill house, and they were very happy here. I worked for them for many years, until we all had to move. My poor mistress died when Ben was only nine, just as the master was starting to do well. He never cared as much about the mill after that and although he missed her greatly, he married again only a year later.' Hepzibah's lips tightened. 'Miss Georgie is the result. Spoiled, she's been, but she has a good heart if she'll only stop trying to show off.'

Martha looked at her with interest. This was the second person to defend Georgiana Seaton from possible criticism. She didn't comment, however, just turned back to the window. 'The garden has been let run wild.'

'Ben never did care about gardens, only about that dratted machinery of his. There used to be some very pretty ferns in the front garden. He's kept the house well maintained, though, and 'twas he put the new stove in for the last tenant. You won't find any damp, either.' She looked from one to the other. 'Are you going to take the job?'

'Yes.' They both spoke at once then laughed.

'I'm glad to hear that. I'll leave you to look round at your leisure, then, ladies. We've a busy morning on at home and I don't want to be away too long. You may as well keep the front door key.'

Martha was surprised at her leaving, but Hepzibah had seemed on edge the whole time, not because of them but because of something that had her glancing regularly out of the window and listening—though what for, Martha couldn't tell.

Edward had allowed the ladies to inspect the kitchen without him, having little interest in such domestic minutiae. They found him pacing out the front parlour, shaking his head over how small it was, only five yards square.

'Once you have your piano in here, it'll look over-crowded. And the hall is too narrow, not a gentleman's hallway at all.'

'We like the house,' Penelope declared. 'We'll have to decide what furniture we'll keep and what we'll sell, if we're to fit in.'

'But...' he broke off to stare at them. 'You've decided, haven't you? And without even consulting me. Well, I haven't taken to Tapton and I won't *allow* you to do this!'

'Edward, you can't stop us.' Martha was growing weary of repeating this.

'But you haven't even considered the practicalities. Look how cramped you'll be if you try to run a school in this house. Why, the front parlour is barely adequate for ladies of your station as it is. No, no. It won't do.' He let out a gusty sigh. 'If you won't make your home with us, I shall be obliged to rent a house for you somewhere more genteel. Buxton, perhaps? I'll give you an allowance *and* pay Sally's wages. Now what do you say?'

They looked at one another and smiled, not needing to put their thoughts into words.

'Thank you. It's very generous of you. But we'd prefer to come here and earn our own way in the world,' Penelope said.

He looked from one determined face to the other and drew himself up. 'I can see I'm wasting my time talking to you. You always were stubborn when you had your mind set on something. I'll return to the inn and leave you to finish going over this house, but please be ready to leave in two hours. I've done my best, but some people simply won't be helped.'

He swung on his heel and left without another word.

They both breathed sighs of relief as the front door slammed behind him.

Martha couldn't help asking, 'You're sure, Pen?'

'Yes, I am. We'd better not waste our time talking, though, if we're to leave in two hours. Why don't you pace out the downstairs rooms and I'll do the upstairs ones? I brought a little notebook, just in case, and we can surely spare an hour before we return to the inn to pack.'

When someone knocked on the front door a few minutes later, Martha opened it to find Ben Seaton standing there.

He didn't waste time on civilities. 'Hepzibah said you liked the house.'

'Yes. It feels to have a happy atmosphere.' He looked round and his expression became sad, so she guessed he was thinking about his mother. When he walked through to the kitchen she followed, trying not to intrude on his memories.

'I used to come here to eat hot scones,' he said in a softer tone of voice than usual. 'My mother and Hepzibah would be working together. They always seemed to be laughing and there was a fire burning brightly, copper pans shining on the shelves and...' He broke off and the guarded expression came back on his face as he went on in a more formal tone, 'I'm glad you intend to accept the position because Georgie needs something to occupy her time. How soon can you come here?'

Martha had been dreading Christmas in Woodbourne without their father and would far rather they spent it here in Tapton, even if they knew no one. 'Give us a week to pack after we get home, then we'll find a carrier and...'

'No need. Jonas and I can send a couple of our mill drays for your stuff if you'll write down directions before you go.' He turned towards the door. 'I must leave now. They're delivering some new machinery to my mill. We started during the night in case there was trouble and I'd better get back to keep an eye on things, though we're mostly home and dry now.'

'Why should there be trouble?'

'Some folk don't like progress and blame it on the machines, so they try to destroy them. I just wanted to see you before you left.' He looked at her, wondering why it had seemed so important that she and her sister take the position, important enough for him to leave the mill at a crucial time. Though there had been no sign yet of the trouble-makers he'd expected, thank heavens.

He'd come because he liked the Merridene ladies, he decided. Yes, that was it. Martha was straightforward and sensible, as unlike his step-mother as a woman could be. As for Penelope, she had a warm smile and a chin as stubborn as her sister's. Surely they'd be able to control his sister, and under their influence Georgie would learn to behave more reasonably?

He realised he'd been standing lost in thought, which was hardly polite. 'I really must get back.' He stepped aside to let her go first and as she passed him, he smelled lavender and soap. Her face was shining as if she'd just washed it, her cheeks were as rosy as apples and her eyes— well, they were surprisingly beautiful, of a hazel colour and full of smiling warmth, as if she liked the world she lived in.

He breathed in deeply, annoyed at himself for wasting time on such fanciful thoughts. 'Leave a note for me at the inn with directions to your house and we'll send the drays to arrive one week from today, if that suits you.'

'Thank you. It'll be a great help.'

As Martha took the hand he held out, she stilled because that strange feeling of awareness was running through her again. It was unnerving. She had never felt anything like it and didn't understand why it kept happening. It must be because he was so very large and masculine. Yes, that was it. Even her father hadn't been as big as this man. It wasn't that Ben Seaton was intimidating, not at all, but you just couldn't help noticing him—and reacting.

Closing the front door firmly behind him, she went back to taking notes, pacing out the rooms as carefully as she could.

When she had finished she went upstairs to join Penelope, feeling happier than she had since her father's death. 'We'd better get back to the inn and pack our things now or Edward will complain all the way back to Woodbourne.'

'I woke early and couldn't sleep, so mine are packed already. Why don't you go back and see to yours? I'll join you in another half-hour. I haven't paced out the attics yet.'

'Are you sure you'll be all right on your own?'

'Of course I shall. It's not very far to walk.'

'Here's the front door key, then. Be sure to lock up carefully.'

As Martha walked back to the inn she thought the square seemed rather empty considering how busy it had been the day before, but perhaps people of the better sort did their shopping later on. She heard a few shouts in the distance, but thought nothing of that, her mind focused on their coming move and what needed to be done.

–

The man known mainly as Croaky Jack went into the office at Brindley's first thing that same morning, looking angry. 'Seaton's tricked us.'

Noll scowled at him and gestured to Gerry to stand back. 'What do you mean?'

'He brought them machines in during the night. They're uncrating them now. If we hadn't been housed outside town in that old barn of yours, we might have noticed that something was happening. We were taking too much care to keep out of sight and should have kept a watch on the western road all night instead of sending out watchers at dawn. The men didn't see any drays arriving this morning because they were already in town.'

Noll's face went deep red with anger and he thumped the desk several times with a clenched fist, muttering, 'Damn him!' in a low voice.

'And with Porter to help set the machines up, they'll soon be spinning extra thread,' Gerry put in. 'You should have kept that fellow here, Noll. He's really good with machines, which Ridley will never be.' He heaved a sigh. 'Eh, we'll not stop Seaton now.'

Jack cleared his throat and said in his peculiar, husky voice, 'He can't have them installed yet, surely? And now he's got them inside the mill, he'll mebbe not be keeping watch as well as he should be.'

'You mean...' a grin slowly creased Noll's face, deepening the wrinkles.

Jack grinned back. 'I could tell my men to gather a crowd and then attack the mill head on. The lads can egg folk to knock down the gates and try to damage the new machines.'

'They're to be ready to pull out if anyone calls out the militia,' Noll put in sharply. 'I don't want the magistrate tracing this back to me.' He chewed his forefinger for a moment, then added, 'It's a bit risky.'

'Not with your operatives rioting. Trust me. I'm good at getting crowds het up.'

Noll stared at him, then nodded slowly. 'I can give you some fuel to get 'em started.' He turned to his overlooker. 'Gerry, lad, spread the word that I'm going to cut wages again. I'm not, but that'll shake the operatives up good and proper.'

'It'll send 'em into a mad frenzy an' they'll down tools, then we'll not make our quota of yarn this week.'

'Can't be helped.'

Stifling a sigh, Gerry hurried out to do his master's bidding, still not convinced it was the right thing to do. He knew who always got the blame when they fell below the set quota. Why could Noll not be satisfied with what he'd got? Gerry would be satisfied with a quarter of what his employer had, by hell he would!

Jack nodded farewell and slipped outside in that way he had of doing things before you'd realised it.

When he was alone, Noll began to pace to and fro. He'd tried to hide his anger but he was furious and if Croaky Jack thought he was getting paid the full amount for this job, he could think again. They might still be able to do some damage to Seaton but it wouldn't ruin the fellow.

Well, he wasn't finished yet. No man had ever got the better of him without him finding a way to get his own back.

–

Ben arrived back at the mill to find the gates standing open and men bustling to and fro round Ross Turner, who was uncrating the new machines. 'Close the gates!' he ordered. 'Anyone could walk in.'

'They're not likely to cause us any trouble now, are they?' Jem Saverby asked. As head of the mill stables at Wright's, he'd supervised the loan of his master's drays so that Ben Seaton could bring the machinery into town in one fell swoop. He'd wanted to be there in person to watch over his horses and the well-kept drays for which he was famous.

'You can't be too careful. Where's Porter?'

'Your engineer sent him out to get another crowbar from the ironmonger's. Them crates are so well put together we've broke a couple of hammer shafts trying to lever out the nails without damaging the wood.'

'Never mind that now. Let's get all the gates shut and locked.' Ben went across to help him with the heavy wooden gates, which were nearly twice as high as a man, but they'd only managed to get one closed when a group of men with blackened faces rushed round the corner and tried to shove their way into the mill yard, yelling threats and obscenities.

A desperate scuffle began, with every man on the premises rushing to try to help repel the invaders and even some of the women workers joining in, because the machines meant their livelihoods too, as Mr Seaton had explained only the morning before.

The would-be invaders were driven back slowly.

Why? Ben wondered as he stood panting behind the now closed gates, listening to the shouts and yells still coming from the street outside. What could Brindley hope to gain now? For he was quite sure who was behind this.

When her sister had left, Penelope went up to check the attics, deciding that the biggest of these would make an excellent bedroom for Sally. As she strolled round the whole house again, she wondered what it would be like to live here. Very different from the much larger Rosemount Cottage, but interesting, she was sure. In fact, excitement was rising in her like leaven in a loaf.

She hadn't realised until her father's death changed their lives so greatly how stuck in a rut she'd been, because there had always been plenty of household tasks to fill her days. Perhaps she had deliberately sought refuge in that rut after John's death? She'd missed him so much. And her father had always been protective of her—too protective for her own good, she knew—while Martha and Sally had been treating her like fragile china for the past two years, now she came to think of it.

And she wasn't fragile, not a bit of it. In fact, she felt to be brimming with energy and life, just as she used to be.

John wouldn't have approved of her letting people over-protect her. He'd admired her partly for her practical nature and energetic, independent ways. Her father hadn't approved of the match at all, because John had only his stipend as a curate, but Penelope hadn't cared about that. She was sure her fiancé would get his own church one day and then he'd earn more, and anyway, she had her hundred pounds a year from her mother. That made enough difference for them to feel it all right to marry. They'd been so happy, full of plans for helping their poorer parishioners.

Sighing, she banished the sad memories. She must look forward not back from now on. And she intended to do something about Martha as well as herself. Although people considered her sister the capable one, Penelope knew that Martha had the same fears and vulnerability as any other woman, only she hid them underneath that brisk exterior. She'd had the same dreams too when they were girls—to be a wife and mother—and had given them up without complaint to look after her father and sister.

Was it too late now for Martha to find happiness in that way? Who could tell? All Penelope knew was that there was more chance of *something* happening here than there ever had been in Woodbourne—for them both. She admitted to herself that she would still like to marry and have children.

She stretched, raising her arms and twirling round. She could almost feel herself breaking free of the protective shell. Once, when she was sixteen, she had crept out to dance barefoot on the lawn in the moonlight, wearing nothing but her nightdress—a shocking thing to do. Now that same joy in life was bubbling up inside her and she wanted to weep for her father, cry out with the pain of the new life surging through her, laugh at Edward and his foolish ways, exult in their coming move—all at once.

As she ran lightly down the stairs she heard a noise in the distance that she couldn't quite place, a faint roaring sound almost like the distant rumble of thunder. Perhaps it was one of the new steam engines? There it went again. What did she know about mills and machinery? Nothing. But she could learn, couldn't she?

Only when she opened the front door did Penelope realise that people were running along the street, glancing backwards over their shoulders as if terrified of whatever they were fleeing from.

'Is something wrong?' she called, but no one answered.

She hesitated, but as the number of people passing had lessened and she could see nothing pursuing them, she decided it must have been a false alarm and locked the front door, turning towards the square and moving briskly. The inn was only two or three minutes' walk away. Nothing could happen to her in that short distance, surely.

But when she was only a few steps along the street she heard voices yelling behind her and turned to see a group of rough-looking men run round the corner pursuing two others. Even as she looked, they bowled over an old woman who was hobbling along painfully and pounced on one of their victims, kicking him and punching him so that he screamed in pain.

Terrified, Penelope turned to run, but someone grasped her arm and pulled her into a narrow passage between two houses. As she squeaked in shock, he said, 'It's all right. I'm just getting you out of their way, miss. I doubt you could outrun them, so we'd better get you out of sight quickly.'

Although he was carrying a big iron bar under his arm, he had a transparently honest face, the sort you trusted instinctively, so when he pulled her along the narrow passage she trusted her instincts and went with him.

'We'd better get you back inside your house quickly. If they see you with me, they'll come after us both.' He turned right into the narrow muddy lane that lay between the rear gardens of the villas and the back yards of a row of terraced mill workers' dwelling. As he came to the bright green gate, he tried to open it and when it proved to be locked, cursed under his breath and glanced back the way they had come.

Penelope could hear voices yelling queries at one another.

'*Have you seen Porter?*'

'*Where did the sod go?*'

'I'll have to break it open, though it'll show them we're here,' her companion said. 'It's me they want and I've no mind to let them kick me to death, let alone what they might do to you.'

His words were so shocking she gaped for a moment, then pulled herself together and asked, 'Can't we climb over it?'

He glanced at her in surprise. 'I can, but what about you?'

'I used to climb trees as a girl.' She hitched up her skirt, blushing as she exposed her lower limbs, then telling herself that didn't matter if it was a question of saving a man's life—and perhaps her own. 'Give me a push up.' With his help she put one foot in the latch hole and with a further shove from the stranger—she carefully refrained from thinking which part of her anatomy he had had to shove—she managed to climb over the top of the gate.

'Stand back! I need to throw this over.'

With a thud the iron bar landed on the bare earth near the wall.

Her rescuer clambered over the gate to join her and picked up the bar. Seizing her hand, he pulled her towards the house. 'Hurry up. We have to get you inside, out of their way.'

'I have a front door key, but not a back,' she panted.

'Let's try it.'

But the key didn't fit this lock and the voices were getting closer.

He felt along the top of the door frame, but found no spare key in this favoured hiding place.

She glanced round them, then saw a single, empty plant pot beside the kitchen step and lifted it. 'This might be it.'

He took the rusty key from her and to her relief it turned in the lock.

'Look along the backs!'

He pushed her inside and when he hesitated, she pulled him with her. Closing the door, they locked it again and stood staring at one another, panting. For a few moments time seemed suspended then more voices outside broke the spell. With a start she realised her skirts were still kilted up and pulled them down, blushing hotly.

He put the bar carefully on the floor. 'Don't move,' he breathed in her ear. 'They can't see us if we stay here in this passage, but if we go into the kitchen or the scullery, they'll be able to spy us through the windows. I bet they come and look, because everyone knows this house belongs to Mr Seaton.'

They stood close together behind the door. His body felt warm against hers, but the wall was cold against her left hand and she suddenly realised that her leg was hurting. She could feel something trickling down it—blood, she supposed. She must have grazed herself getting over the gate. Well, she could do nothing about that in front of the stranger. The graze was quite high up her leg. How much flesh had she been showing when she climbed over the wall, for heaven's sake? She felt her face burning again, but hoped he couldn't see her embarrassment in the shadowed passageway.

Another outburst of yelling from the laneway made her flinch and let out a faint whimper. She wasn't a coward, but the voices outside sounded full of raw anger, and the way the men had kicked their victim showed how violent they could be.

He put his arm round her shoulders, whispering, 'Hold still, lass. They can't see us and I doubt they'll try to break in.'

His arm was warm and comforting and she leaned against him, thankful she wasn't alone.

The rioters broke down the back gate and came right up to the house, rattling the door and peering through the windows, but after a minute or two they went away again, arguing all the way down the garden path about where Porter could have disappeared to. After a few minutes the voices faded into the distance and she let out a long, shuddering sigh of relief.

Her companion took his arm away from her shoulders and stepped away. 'Sorry, miss. Wasn't thinking. I didn't mean to take liberties, but you seemed upset.'

She studied him covertly. He wasn't much taller than she was but he looked lean and strong, as if he'd been honed by hardship. She'd let herself get soft, she knew, far too soft. 'I'm grateful. I don't know what I'd have done without your help. Does this sort of thing happen often in Tapton?'

'Only lately, since Owd Noll's decided he wants to own Seaton's Mill.'

'Owd Noll?'

'Brindley. The man I used to work for. Nasty old devil he is. Owns the third mill in town, the smallest one. Jonas Wright has the biggest, Ben Seaton the next biggest, and then there's Brindley's. Terrible place it is. His machinery's downright dangerous an' he pays the least of any master.'

'Why were they chasing you?'

'Because I'm Assistant Engineer at Seaton's now, but I used to work at Brindley's. I reckon Owd Noll wants to stop me helping Mr Seaton set up his new machinery. I reckon he thought he'd easily buy Seaton's after the old master died, but Mr Ben wouldn't sell. He's a good master, he is, like Mr Wright.'

She could hear the admiration in his voice and felt pleased that she and Martha had not misjudged the nature of their employers. 'Well, I'm all right now, so if you think it's safe, we'll move into the kitchen. There's a fire in there and I don't know about you, but I'm feeling chilled through.'

'Aye, we should be all right now.'

She led the way. A glance through the window showed her the tops of heads bobbing past in the back lane. Voices continued to howl and shriek faintly in the distance. At one point there were sounds of breaking glass and once a woman's scream, high-pitched, cutting off abruptly.

'Is it a riot?' Penelope whispered.

'Aye. I saw some of Brindley's folk running round. They're usually at work at this time of the morning, but today they've downed tools. Don't know what he's done to upset them now.' There was a grim tone to his voice.

She held her hands out to the fire and he did the same. 'What made you help me today?'

He shrugged. 'I could see you were a lady, but I knew that bunch would have taken no account of that. Brindley's brought in some trouble-makers from Manchester, you see, men as'd murder anyone for a few shillings.' He looked into the distance, his face tight with unhappy memories. 'As well as destroying Seaton's new machinery if he can, Brindley wants me out of town. Or better still, dead.'

She could only stare at him in shock for a moment, then whisper, 'Why? Isn't it enough to dismiss you?'

'Not with him. I defied him, you see, refused to make his machinery even more dangerous to the children who work on it, not if I starved for it.' He gave her a mocking bow. 'My name's Daniel Porter, by the way, miss, and I'm a fool. I want to be an engineer, you see. I'm self-taught, still have a lot to learn, but I *do* understand machines.'

She held out her hand, feeling a link to him forged in their joint escape from danger. 'I'm Penelope Merridene and I don't think you're a fool. My sister and I are moving to Tapton soon to teach Mr Wright's children and Mr Seaton's sister. We're also going to teach some of their workers to read and write better, so maybe we'll see you in our classes.'

'Just give me the chance!' he said fervently. 'I'd heard they were bringing in a governess, but not that they were to let the men have lessons too.' Another frown, then, 'If you're going to live here, you'd better not let on that you know me if we pass in the street. Brindley's hatred seems to spill over on to anyone who's a friend of those he considers his enemies.'

She stared at him in shock. 'I hadn't realised the situation here was so—volatile.'

'I don't know what that word means, but I'd liken the situation here to a keg of gunpowder. If someone sets the fuse carefully and then lights it, the keg will blow up. Boom!' He made an expressive gesture with his hands. 'Normally no one would think twice about Seaton putting in new spinning machinery—not unless someone stirred up trouble deliberately.'

'And that someone is Mr Brindley?'

'I reckon so.'

This town wasn't, she realised now, quite as peaceful as it had seemed. But that made no difference to her decision to come here. The riots wouldn't last long, surely, and she wanted very much to live a useful life again. 'If I meet you in the street, Mr Porter, I shall definitely speak to you. My father brought us up not to give in to bullies.'

He looked at her with a wry smile. 'Then *I* shall have to avoid *you*. I don't want you getting hurt, miss, and any road, it's not your fight.'

She looked into his clear blue eyes and something warmed still further inside her. 'Don't avoid me,' she said softly. 'We all have a duty to unite against evil.'

'Eh, you don't know Owd Noll.'

But she smiled and shook her head. Nothing would make her ignore this man, not after the way he'd saved her today. Besides, she liked him, she really did.

Outside there were still occasional shouts and running footsteps, but they didn't seem nearly as loud as before. 'Shall we go and peep through the front parlour windows?' she asked.

'Aye, why not? I've never been inside one of these big houses afore. My mother and sister will want to know all about it. You're called Miss Merridene, aren't you?'

'My sister is Miss Merridene because she's the eldest. I'm Miss Penelope.'

'Is that how the nobs do it?' He was grinning.

She smiled back. 'People do have some silly rules, don't they?' She saw him staring round as they walked through the empty house and once heard him mutter to himself. 'Eh, to think of living like this!'

In the front parlour the noise was greater and men were still pounding up and down the street. Penelope and

Daniel peeped out from the side of the window, trying not to show themselves.

'We s'll have to wait a bit afore we go outside again,' he said, frowning once more.

Penelope looked at him and forgot what she had been going to say. He was thin, too thin, and his hair had been hacked off unevenly. But in a woman that hair would have been much admired, for it was the colour of new honey, neither blond nor red, and certainly not ginger, but a rich amber colour, curling slightly around his narrow features. His forehead was high and his eyes were bright and intelligent. She had seen that look before in working men and John had taught her that intelligence could be found in any class and was always to be respected.

She realised suddenly that time was passing. 'I'm going to be late. My sister will be worried and my cousin furious.'

'And you?' he asked softly.

'I'm enjoying myself in a strange sort of way.'

There was warm admiration in his eyes as he nodded. 'Well, you certainly haven't fainted on me, as I thought a lady might.'

She guessed that if they were to be friends, and somehow she was sure they would be, she'd have to make the overtures. Society imposed rules about who you should and should not associate with, but John had taught her to ignore these. Besides, if she got to know Mr Porter, she might be able to help him achieve his ambition to become an engineer. That would be a very rewarding thing to do.

It was two more hours before Daniel thought it safe to venture out, because the rioters seemed to be rushing to and fro without rhyme or reason. Even then he insisted on going outside first to check that the danger really was past and they could get to the inn safely. When he came back, he nodded. 'It's all right. I'll just go and get Mr Seaton's crowbar then I'll take you to the inn.'

When they arrived, she stood at the door watching him walk away, that bright amber hair standing out like sunshine on a winter's day. It made him too easily recognisable, though. Then she shook her head and grew angry at herself. Why was she worrying about that now? She'd better go and tell her sister she was safe. And after that she'd bathe her leg. But she wasn't going to tell Martha about her small injury or exactly how she got it. She didn't want a scold about rash behaviour.

She had enjoyed talking to Mr Porter and was determined to know him better, but she wasn't going to mention that, either.

–

In the event the Merridenes didn't leave Tapton that day. Mr Wright sent a message to the inn as soon as things had quietened down in the town centre, advising that the roads nearby might be unsafe because of the riots and suggesting they stay on for another night. Edward complained unceasingly but took this advice.

On the journey back both ladies were quiet and thoughtful, and although Edward tried again to persuade them to give up this foolish idea of going to live in a town where the poor rioted and put their betters' lives in danger, he found them unshakable in their determination to move to Tapton. Eventually he subsided into a sullen silence and left them to their thoughts.

Chapter 5

It was one thing to plan a move, another actually to make it. Both sisters were deeply upset at having to leave Rosemount Lodge, with all its memories. They had already cleared out their father's possessions during the months of searching for a place to live and work, but now they had to decide which furniture to take and which to sell or give away, then empty their own cupboards and drawers and pack their china in straw.

Penelope wept several times but tried to hide that from her sister.

Martha toiled fiercely, giving herself as little time as possible to think and tumbling into bed each night exhausted, to lie tearless and wish she could weep out her pain as she knew her sister did. There were some nights when it took a long time to succumb to her tiredness.

She knew Sally was watching them both anxiously, hiding her concern for them under gentle scolding and regular cups of tea. It was a comfort.

Late in the afternoon of the day before they were due to leave, the promised drays turned up in Woodbourne and one of the drivers, a man with grey hair and a kindly face, came to present his master's compliments to the ladies and check that they would be ready early the next morning. 'I'm Jem Saverby, miss, head of the stables at Wright's. My master sent me with the men to make sure everything was done proper. And I were glad to see a bit of the world, too. Never been out of Lancashire afore.'

'Leicestershire is a lot prettier in the summer than it is now.'

'Aye, well, isn't everywhere? You wait till you see our moors on a summer's day. There's nowt to beat it, in my opinion. Now, I'd be grateful if you'd show me what there is to load tomorrow.' He followed them round the house, not saying much, but occasionally making shapes in the air, as if fitting pieces of furniture together. In the end he nodded. 'Aye, they'll fit all right if we load 'em carefully, but it'll take us a few days to drive back to Tapton, so Mr Wright's booked rooms for you at the Dragon again.'

'That's very kind of him.'

'If you don't mind, we'll start loading tomorrow as soon as it's light. It's too late to start now.' With a cheery wave he made his way back to the village inn, where he and his companions were to stay.

That evening the three women sat together in the kitchen sharing a final meal.

'I'm exhausted and shall be glad to leave tomorrow,' Martha admitted, yawning over the stew made from their own potatoes, carrots and onions with a bit of ham.

'Well, at least Mr Edward has done his duty by you, sending his carriage for you to travel in again,' Sally said. 'It's a very comfortable one.'

Penelope chuckled. 'Oh, he always sees to his own comfort. His economies usually affect others, not himself.'

The following morning they watched their possessions carried out to the drays one by one, and roped into place. The men worked quickly, with the skill of long practice. The sisters took a last walk round the echoing house and by the middle of the day were able to climb into Edward's carriage.

'Thank goodness that's over!' said Penelope as the horses moved forward.

Martha didn't reply; couldn't trust herself to speak steadily and was relieved when no one tried to make conversation for the first few minutes. She could only hope she didn't look as sad and weary as her sister.

They couldn't make good time on the muddy roads and so were unable to reach the inn where they'd stayed last time. But as nightfall approached they found another inn which offered them a similar level of comfort.

Once installed there, Sally didn't try to hide her enjoyment of the rare treat of being waited on and that cheered up both sisters.

–

The next day they set off at first light, driving through a bare winter landscape under lowering skies which were becoming increasingly overcast. Just after ten o'clock the first flakes of snow began to fall and soon were settling on the ground.

They were all worried about whether they would manage to reach Tapton before the roads became impassable. Edward's carriage was solidly-built and the team of horses from the last inn was strong and willing, but still, you never knew what would happen when travelling in winter.

An hour later they rounded a corner and the coachman yelled out in shock and reined in his horses sharply to avoid a shabby vehicle which had lost a wheel and run into the ditch. The carriage rocked wildly, tumbling the ladies against one another like skittles, but it drew to a halt with no harm done other than bonnets knocked askew, a bruise or two and pulses beating faster.

The groom jumped down and ran to the horses' heads, gentling them until they stopped edging about and tossing their heads.

The other carriage had lost a wheel and lay tilted on one side, half in the ditch. A young man was leaning against a tree nearby, his eyes closed. His clothes were in disorder and there was a large bruise on his forehead. He was holding his right arm as if in pain and looked ready to collapse at any moment.

Martha flung open the carriage door and hurried across to him. 'I fear you're hurt, sir. Can we do anything to help you?'

He opened his eyes and turned towards her, but didn't seem able to speak coherently, only groan then mumble, 'Think I've—broken my arm'.

She looked round for help but the coachman of the wrecked carriage, a surly-looking fellow, was still trying to disentangle his horses, one of which looked wild with fear. Even as she watched, he yelled to their groom to come and help him before the creature damaged itself.

Martha beckoned to her sister. 'I think we'd better get this gentleman into our carriage.'

The two of them supported the injured man as carefully as they could, but he moaned in pain when he stumbled getting into their carriage.

As Martha brushed the snowflakes from her bonnet and shoulders, she was relieved to see him sink down on the seat and lean back against the corner because she'd been afraid he would faint. He was still supporting his right arm with his left and his face was now as white as the snow whirling down outside.

'We'll have to get him to a doctor to set the bone,' said Sally in a low voice. She leaned out of the carriage to call to the driver of the other vehicle, 'Hey you! Where's the nearest village?'

But the man just shrugged and when she called to their own coachman, Tom said, 'I don't know this road well enough, Mrs Polby, I'm afraid.'

When the horses were freed, he came to check that his passengers were all right. 'Shall I help the gentleman out and get him into his own carriage, Miss Merridene? I think it's propped up steady now. We can send help back to him.'

The other man had followed Tom across. 'There'll be no use him staying here, miss. It'll be tomorrow at the earliest afore I get away because I'll have to wait for a new wheel to be fitted.' He looked at his passenger. 'You'd best hire another vehicle, sir, and get yourself home where people can look after you.'

The gentleman roused himself to glare at him. 'Then give me my money back.'

'I ha'nt got it. It's my master you should see about that.'

'Damn you, how am I to continue without money?'

'I think we'd better take you to a doctor before we decide anything else, sir,' Martha said soothingly and looked at Tom. 'We'll have to stop in the next village.'

'Mr Merridene wouldn't like this,' he grumbled. 'It's not safe taking up strangers, let alone this gentleman's not our responsibility.'

'We can't leave him here with a broken arm!' Martha snapped, thinking that even Edward's servants had adopted his mean-spirited attitude towards the world. 'Kindly get his luggage and stow it with ours.'

Tom jerked his head towards the groom, who did this with ill grace before swinging up into his place again.

'Sorry to be so much trouble,' muttered the stranger, groaning involuntarily as the carriage jerked into movement.

'We couldn't pass by and leave you in distress.'

Martha studied him surreptitiously. He was quite young, with a thin face, full lips and fine, mousy hair. This had obviously been crimped with hot irons to give it a fashionable curl but was looking rather limp now. He was wearing side whiskers and had left a tuft of hair growing on his chin, not large enough to be called a beard. This must be the latest London fashion, though she couldn't like it. His neck cloth was now somewhat battered, but had obviously been very high, and though his cravat had slipped sideways a little, it was still tied in an over-large bow.

She was sure her father would have called him a coxcomb and become very stiff when dealing with him. Indeed, she felt the same way herself, hadn't taken to him at all. But still, she couldn't feel it right to leave him.

He leaned back in the corner, wincing as the carriage bumped along, but although the movement tried him considerably, he insisted on talking.

'Allow me to introduce myself—Peter Brindley—' He stopped talking to grunt in pain as the carriage bumped into and out of a series of particularly large potholes.

Martha made the introductions for the ladies.

It was a moment or two before the man could reply, then he started speaking but couldn't finish his sentence, 'Pleased to meet you. Grateful...' For the next few minutes, while they continued to watch him anxiously, he remained slumped in the corner with his eyes closed.

Suddenly he roused himself again, blinking across at Martha. 'May I inquire where you're heading, Miss Merridene?'

'We're making for a town called Tapton. Perhaps you know it?'

'Tapton!' He let out a bitter laugh. 'The last place to which anyone as kind as yourselves should be going!'

'Brindley!' Penelope exclaimed suddenly. 'One of the mill-owners in Tapton is called Brindley. Are you related?'

'He's my father. Ah, I see you know of him. He's a hard man.'

'Yes. So I gather.' Penelope's tone was curt. She didn't like to hear him speak so disloyally of his father to strangers.

She remembered the riot in Tapton and the fact that this man's father was the one who had brought in trouble-makers. She compared Peter Brindley to Daniel Porter and found him greatly lacking. Daniel might not be a gentleman, but he had an open countenance and blunt, honest speech. This man had tried to overlay his northern accent with a more refined one and succeeded only in sounding affected.

'I think you would do better to lie back quietly and conserve your energy, Mr Brindley,' she said quietly.

A sigh was her only answer.

When she glanced out of the window she saw that the snow had now all but covered the grimy-looking winter grass in the fields, though it was not yet too deep to prevent travel, nor did it seem to her to be falling as thickly. But perhaps that was wishful thinking.

Mr Brindley kept quiet for a few moments, then asked abruptly, 'Did you say you were going to Tapton?'

'Yes.'

'I wonder… Could I beg you to take me with you? The thing is—I've run out of money. Spent my last few guineas on hiring that carriage and unless there's somewhere I can pawn my watch in the next village, I won't have enough even to pay for a night's lodgings, let alone a doctor.' He saw that they were looking at him in disapproval and flushed, then bowed his head for a moment, before saying in a low voice, 'I've been foolish, I admit. London can be very tempting to a young man from the country. I shall know better next time, believe me.'

As they still made no answer, he added desperately, 'There's no need to worry about the money. My father will reimburse you for anything you spend.'

Penelope exchanged speaking glances with her sister. 'Well, we can't abandon you in that condition, Mr Brindley, especially in this weather, so yes, we'll take you with us to Tapton.'

'Thank you. Most grateful.'

At the next village they were fortunate enough to find the local doctor just returning from a call. While he attended to Mr Brindley's arm in his surgery, Martha and Penelope were given a most welcome cup of tea by his wife and Sally was entertained in the kitchen.

The doctor came bustling in to join them after a while. 'Well, he bore it bravely enough, but what that young man needs now is to rest. As he insists on continuing the journey, I've given him a dose of laudanum. He should be drowsy enough not to feel the worst of the pain. Relative of yours, is he?'

Martha answered. 'He's a complete stranger. We came upon him just after the accident and were able to be of assistance, but as it seems that we have the same destination, we've agreed to take him on to Tapton with us. He's—er—anxious to rejoin his family.'

'Well, on his own head be it, then. That'll be half a guinea, if you please. He says you'll pay.'

After a startled glance at her sister, Martha reached into her reticule and gave the doctor the money. Within ten minutes they were on their way again.

After their next change of horses the weather grew steadily worse. Heavy clouds hung low in a leaden sky and snow began to fall more thickly again, building up on the roads so that the carriage wheels made a faint crunching sound as they compressed it and the horses' hooves sounded muffled. They stopped only to change horses and use the inns' conveniences, not even waiting for a proper meal at noon, but taking with them what food the landlady could provide and eating it in the carriage as they drove.

By early afternoon the light was so poor it looked like dusk outside and the cold had penetrated even their thick rugs, for the hot bricks at their feet soon lost their warmth. Mr Brindley's presence put a constraint upon any conversation so they could do nothing but sit and endure this last stage of the journey and pray that the snow wouldn't stop them so close to their destination.

By the time they began their descent into Tapton, it had stopped snowing and the icy wind had eased a little. Sally peered through the carriage windows disapprovingly. 'It looks a dirty sort of place to me. Do them chimneys always puff out black smoke like that?'

'Not all day, I think, but at regular intervals,' said Martha.

'Where's our house, Miss Martha?'

'On the other side of the town square. You can't see it from here.'

'We shall have trouble with our washing,' Sally predicted, eyeing the smoking chimney attached to the largest mill.

'Are we here?' a faint voice asked.

Martha turned to him. 'Yes, we are. Do you feel well enough to direct us to your home?'

Mr Brindley struggled into a sitting position and muttered directions. It was obvious that he was more than a little feverish now and she would be glad to pass on the responsibility for his welfare. She only hoped there would be someone at home to look after him. Had he a mother? He'd only talked about his father and that without any sign of affection. She pulled the checkstring and passed on the directions to Edward's coachman.

Again the house was next to a mill, but it was smaller than Mr Wright's or Mr Seaton's and the door looked in need of a coat of paint. They left Mr Brindley in the care of his father's housekeeper, refusing her civil invitation to step in for a cup of tea. His father was at the mill behind the house at that hour of the day and it didn't sound as if anyone would be sending for him.

'And good riddance to that fine gentleman!' declared Sally as they pulled away from the house. 'I don't like to hear a young man speaking ill of his father.'

'Yet it was his father who caused the riot last time we were here,' Penelope said.

Martha stared at her in surprise. 'Are you sure of that?'

'Mr Porter said so and I believed him, but there was no proof of course. Who else would want to damage Mr Seaton's new machinery, though, except a rival?'

Further discussion was prevented by the carriage pulling up in front of the inn. The sky was darkening rapidly now as the early winter evening set in and it seemed even colder than before.

They climbed out with sighs of relief and hurried into the warmth.

'We'll take you to see the house tomorrow,' Martha told Sally as they ate a hot meal. She tried and failed to stop herself from yawning and was glad to seek her bed at an early hour. As she snuggled down into its softness she murmured in appreciation for whoever had passed a warming pan over the sheets and laid a hot brick lapped in flannel just where her feet could touch it.

Her last thought was relief that the move was over and they could now start to make a home for themselves again.

–

Noll had been informed of his son's arrival, but didn't think it worth going home from the mill until his usual time, short as the distance was. He didn't find Peter in the parlour, so tugged on the bell for his cook-housekeeper, tapping his foot impatiently as he waited for her to puff her way to the front of the house. 'Where is he?'

'In bed, sir. We sent for the doctor like you told us and he said Mr Peter should stay there till he'd recovered from the journey and his injuries.'

'What's wrong with him?'

'Broken arm, sir. Hit his head, too, the doctor thinks.' She explained about the carriage accident and how lucky

Mr Peter had been to escape so lightly and find help. 'He says the ladies paid the doctor who set his arm.'

Noll glared at her. 'Trust him to sponge off people. Which ladies?' He snapped his fingers. 'Not those new schoolteachers?'

'I believe so, sir.'

'Dammit, they're sitting in Wright and Seaton's pockets. I'm not having them telling everyone a Brindley couldn't pay his way. I'll have to call and see them, pay them back. *Thank them!*' The latter stuck in his gullet most of all because he hated being beholden to anyone. He waved dismissal, yelling after her, 'Dinner in fifteen minutes.' Then he went upstairs to his son's room.

But he was balked of an opportunity to vent his anger on Peter, who was deeply asleep, and even Noll couldn't deny that his son looked pale and battered, so he didn't wake him as he'd intended. Instead he stood looking down at him. Good looking, resembled his mother, but what use was that? It was money that counted most, not good looks.

'I'd ha' done better to marry Gerry's sister,' he muttered as he went downstairs. 'She's given that no-good husband of hers eight children, and all I got was one—and a finicky, useless one at that.'

-

The following morning dawned with clear skies, but snow still lay in patches on the ground and frost glinted everywhere. As soon as they'd finished breakfast, the three ladies set off for the house, Sally commenting favourably on the way the shopkeepers and owners of the larger houses had already cleared the ground in front of their establishments.

There were footprints in the snow of their own path, looking as if they belonged to a woman. 'Someone's been here before us,' Martha said as she turned the heavy, old-fashioned key in the lock. She again experienced that indefinable sense of welcome and couldn't help exclaiming, 'I do love this house!'

Penelope shivered as she remembered the last time she'd been here and how afraid she'd felt of the violent men rampaging through the streets. As they went inside, she could still see Daniel Porter standing in the kitchen doorway with his alert expression, taking in what were to him the splendours of their new home. It occurred to her suddenly that if she'd married John, she wouldn't have had a house nearly as comfortable as this. And it wouldn't have mattered to her at all! It was Martha who needed a comfortable home and she suspected that her sister was a great deal more upset by the move from Woodbourne and Rosemount Cottage than she was.

They found a fire burning in the kitchen range and Sally moved forward to view this item of modern domestic comfort with undisguised pleasure, making a soft aaahhhh sound of approval in her throat.

'It's a lovely kitchen, isn't it?' Penelope teased, knowing how Sally had longed for a modern closed stove like this one.

'It will be when we're settled in,' Sally allowed. 'And it'll not take me long to get used to that new stove, I'm sure.'

Discussing where they would put the furniture, they walked round the house, choosing their bedrooms and making sure Sally would be happy in the attic. Since her room was quite spacious and had the kitchen chimney running through it, the chill was taken off even on a cold day like this, so she professed herself well suited.

When someone knocked at the door, Sally insisted it was her place to answer it, opening it to find a very tall man standing there. 'May I help you, sir?'

'You must be Sally. I'm Ben Seaton. Are your mistresses here?'

Martha, who had recognised his voice, ran lightly down the stairs, feeling a warm rush of pleasure at the sight of him. 'Mr Seaton! Do come in.'

He did so with a bob of his head for greeting. 'Did someone light the kitchen fire for you? Hepzibah guessed you'd want to come here and look round.'

'Oh, yes. Such a kind thought.'

He nodded and as the two of them stared at one another, there was another of those bewildering moments when the rest of the world seemed to recede into the distance. It wasn't until Sally cleared her throat that Martha was suddenly jerked back to reality and realised he was looking at her with an air of slight puzzlement not unlike her own.

'How can we help you, Mr Seaton?' she asked hastily to break the spell he seemed to cast upon her.

'It's the other way round. I came to check that everything was all right and see if you ladies needed any help.'

'I don't think there's much we can do until our furniture arrives. Shall we go into the kitchen to talk? It's much warmer there.' She led the way to the rear of the house, hearing Sally walk up the bare wooden stairs. No doubt Penelope would come down to join them at any moment.

Upstairs Sally went to find Penelope. 'It's Mr Seaton. I thought it best to leave them two alone.' She cocked one eyebrow at Penelope, as if uncertain whether to speak.

'You sensed something between them as well?'

'You couldn't miss it.'

Penelope smiled. 'Whether it'll come to anything is another matter.'

'He's not married?'

'No. But I don't think Martha understands what's happening to her.' She looked into the distance and said softly, 'I couldn't help noticing because I still remember what it was like when I first met John. My attraction to him was immediate—and his to me.'

Sally put her arm round her shoulders and gave her a hug. 'Miss Martha abandoned all thought of marriage long ago, and you know what she's like once she's settled something in her mind. She doesn't *see* other paths. I always did think it a shame, though, that she's not married because she'd make a wonderful mother.' Another pause, then, 'Do you really think he's attracted to her?'

'I don't know him well enough to form a definite opinion.' But Penelope couldn't resist asking, 'Did you like him?'

'Well, he looks you straight in the eye, at least.' Sally hesitated. 'But Mr Seaton isn't exactly a gentleman, is he? The way he talks is not quite—and his clothes are very— um—sensible. What would the Captain have said about him, do you think?'

'The same as he said about John. My father had some very old-fashioned and impractical ideas about what sort of gentlemen would be suitable for his daughters, I'm afraid. He didn't think John was nearly good enough for me, but I knew how I felt and no amount of reasoning would have changed that, nor would I have let it.'

She sighed, then spoke more briskly, 'Anyway, times are changing, especially in the newer towns like this, and I never did consider that being born with money or being able to trace your pedigree back several generations was more important than being honest and decent and—and hard-working. I'd have been happy with John even if he'd stayed a curate all his life and never got his own living, I know I would. It'd have been such a *useful* life.' She broke off, too full of emotion to continue.

Sally patted her shoulder, pleased that her dear girl was talking more openly about the past.

Penelope took a deep breath, stepped away from her companion and turned towards the door. 'I'd better go downstairs or it'll look strange.'

She found Mr Seaton in the hall, already taking his leave, and he barely looked at her as he greeted her, then said farewell to Martha.

And Martha, who prided herself on being the practical one of the family, stood staring into space for a few moments.

Penelope didn't interrupt her till Sally came down to join them. 'Right, then, let's go and see what the grocery store is like in this town. We can stock up on dry goods while we're waiting for that furniture to arrive. In fact, there's quite a lot we can do here. It's nice being waited on at the inn, but I shouldn't know what to do with myself all day if I always lived like that.'

-

As they sat over their evening meal, which Sally again took with them in their private parlour, Martha said thoughtfully, 'We should find a girl to help you, Sally, and a scrubbing woman for the rough work. We know how we stand with our money now and can easily afford it. We'll be too busy to help you as much as we did in Woodbourne.'

'Well, I should think so. It's more than time you two stopped doing the housework and behaved like proper ladies.'

Penelope laughed. 'I doubt we'll ever be "proper ladies" in that sense, Sally. We've never had enough money to sit around idly and I think it's too late to develop the habit now.'

'I'd be bored to tears if I had nothing to do but sit and embroider.' Martha looked round the hotel parlour regretfully. 'Oh, I wish everything would arrive and we could move in! I'm itching to set to work on our new house. I'm sure we'll be able to make it into a real home.'

Chapter 6

Since his father always made it plain that he expected his son to rise at the same time as the rest of the household, Peter Brindley got up when the mill siren went. While he waited for the maid to answer the bell and bring his hot water, he stood by his bedroom window watching the operatives hurrying towards the mill. He rubbed his aching arm as he yawned and stared out.

Below him a child echoed his yawn, looking tired before it even started work. Was it a boy or girl? He couldn't tell. All the operatives' bodies seemed stunted to him, their clothing ragged, their hair matted and hanging around their faces. It was the small children who upset him. He watched one girl, not even grown into a woman herself yet, put down the child she'd been carrying and shake it awake.

He hadn't realised how young they started work. Dear God, did his father's money come from the toil of this stream of tired creatures? Why had he never really looked at them before? He grimaced. Well, he knew why. Because his mother had protected him, talked of her fine family, made him believe they'd help him to a better life away from Tapton.

Only they hadn't, so he'd gone to London, where he'd found nothing to do except gamble, and although he'd won at first, he'd lost the money again bit by bit till there was only his father left to turn to. Humiliation speared through him. He'd never gamble again, knew now he'd been set up deliberately to lose everything, that those men hadn't really been his friends—but what *was* he to do with his life?

There was a tap on the door and he opened it to find the young housemaid. 'Is there any hot water, Jane?'

'Sorry, sir. Not yet. We've only just got the fire burning up again.'

'Then I'll shave and wash later. Thank you.'

He struggled into his clothes as best he could. Poor Jane had looked nearly as tired as the lasses outside, worn down by life—though she was plumper because she was better fed, at least. She couldn't be more than sixteen or so. Did she have nothing to hope for but hard work and exhaustion like this? Or did she have hopes and dreams, as he'd had till recently?

When he was as ready as he could manage, with the shirt and coat sleeves hanging loose on one side, there was no putting off the meeting with his father, so he walked slowly down the narrow stairs, taking care not to jolt his arm.

Noll Brindley looked up as his son came into the dining room and felt sourness rise into his mouth at the sight of the foolish clothes and slight figure. What a useless fribble he'd produced! He should have stopped his wife from spoiling Peter as a boy and not sent him to that fancy school, which had cost so much and done little except fill the lad's head with foolish ideas of being a gentleman of leisure while others earned his bread for him.

But Noll had been too busy making money and by the time his missus died and he was forced to deal with his son himself, it had been too late. So he'd allowed Peter to visit his wife's family in the south regularly, then the lad had gone on to London to stay with some of his fine friends. He'd given his son strict instructions to find himself a wife, preferably one with money, but more important a healthy woman who'd produce sons—and by hell, Noll would make sure the next generation was raised properly and knew how to work for its living.

Surely he would last long enough for that? Why, he wasn't even sixty yet and his father had lived to seventy, so why should he not reach eighty? He ate better than his father ever had and lived more comfortably, too.

'Well?' he asked. 'What have you to say for yourself, having to be brought back home like that by two ladies?'

'What is there to say, Father? The carriage had an accident and the Merridene ladies very fortunately brought me the rest of the way to Tapton in theirs. But we need to repay them because they spent half a guinea on the doctor.'

'*We?*' Noll asked with monumental sarcasm. 'There's no "we" about it. You've no money, so it's *me* as'll be doing the paying! As usual.'

'Well, yes.'

Noll mimicked the fancy accent, '*Well, yes!* You sound like an actor on the stage.' He'd been to the theatre in Manchester a few times with his wife, at her insistence, and thought it a stupid waste of time and effort. But it had pleased her greatly, so he'd done it. He hadn't gone there after she died, though. Not he! No need to pretend to enjoy it now.

'Father, you sent me away to learn to be a gentleman and can hardly complain now if I've achieved it.'

'Your mother sent you away. All I did was pay for it and if I'd my time to do again, I'd not agree to it. No, by hell! When it came down to it, those fancy relatives didn't do much for you or help you find a wife, any more than they helped your mother when her father died, except to send her out as a governess. Eh, I should have sent you into the mill at seven to work your way up like I did. I'm not sure I shouldn't do that anyway.'

Peter looked at him in such horror Noll almost laughed aloud, but didn't pursue that threat because he knew he'd never carry it out. He didn't want his workers seeing what a ninny he'd sired. All he wanted was a grandson or two. A sudden thought struck him. 'How did you get on with those two ladies?'

'Pardon?'

'The teacher ladies. Did they take to you? Would one of them be a suitable wife for you?' After all, money wasn't everything.

'I doubt it. They're both years older than I am. I can meet more people if you'll let me have enough money to maintain my status as a gentleman. My cousins are still in London and will introduce me around. And I shan't be so foolish as to gamble my money away again, I promise you. I've learned my lesson there.' He hesitated, then added, 'I had to pawn some things to get back here because you didn't reply to my letters. Didn't you get them?'

'Aye, I got them, but I knew you'd only be writing to ask for more money, so I tossed them in the fire. No use throwing good brass after bad. From now on you'll be *maintaining your status as a gentleman* here in Tapton because I'm not letting you out of my sight again. The amount of money you wasted in London makes me want to puke. I shall have a look round this neighbourhood and see if there are any suitable young ladies for you. We're bound to find one if we're not too fussy.'

Peter closed his eyes as despair flooded through him. His father's voice always grated on the ears and the thought of the old man choosing a wife for him made him feel sick. What sort of woman would 'Owd Noll' consider suitable? An ugly one with money, that's what. Probably older than him, too.

A door slammed shut and he opened his eyes to find himself alone. With another sigh he rang the handbell standing by his father's place. He might as well eat something. Then how would he spend his time? From what the old man had said, he'd be expected to rise at this ungodly hour every morning. He couldn't spend all day walking the streets, had no friends or acquaintances in Tapton.

Or would his father really put him to work in the mill? He looked down. Well, he wouldn't be able to do much until his arm mended. He didn't know whether to be grateful for that or not.

–

Ben looked at Daniel Porter in amazement. 'Are you sure of that?'

'Oh, aye. It wouldn't take much doing, either.'

'And Ross approves?'

'He does. He'd have told you about it himself this morning but his wife sent word he was feeling poorly again.'

'Well, then, you'd better show me exactly what you mean.'

They spent a happy hour getting their hands thoroughly dirty as Daniel demonstrated a type of guard cage he'd designed for one of the new machines; a cage which not only kept the young workers' fingers out of a danger area, but also trapped some of the cotton fluff that was always drifting about the mill and clogging up the machinery and lungs alike. And it would be safe to clean out, too, an important point when children were the ones who'd be cleaning it.

Ben helped him attach a roughly-made version to one of the big spinning machines to test it out, glad to have an excuse to spend time with his new employee and get to know him better. Noll Brindley had stopped Ben in the street the previous day to warn him that Porter was a trouble-maker, but by now Ben had realised that Daniel wasn't interested in much except machinery, whatever his father had been like. In fact, when this new employee was thinking about machinery or had his hands on a piece of equipment, you sometimes had to speak to him twice to catch his attention.

'I believe you saved Miss Penelope Merridene from trouble during the riots,' he said casually after they had finished and were washing their hands.

'How did you know about that? I didn't tell anyone because I didn't want Brindley thinking she was friendly with me.'

'Someone saw you helping her climb the back gate.' Ben couldn't hold back a grin. 'I'm surprised a lady would do something like that, actually. She must have shown her legs and ladies don't usually admit they've even got them.' He couldn't imagine his step-mother climbing a gate, however urgent the need.

Daniel grinned. 'I was surprised, too, but she was nimble enough.' And had very trim ankles and calves. He'd tried not to stare, but you couldn't help seeing them when you were giving someone a boost. The grin faded as he thought about the aftermath of the riot.

'Are Brindley's men still annoying you?' Ben asked suddenly.

'I can manage.'

'Tell me the truth.'

'Well, they're trying to. I take a different route home each night to avoid them.' But he was afraid they'd catch him one day and beat him up so badly he wouldn't be able to work. 'Someone threatened my mother t'other afternoon. If they lay one finger on her I won't be answerable.'

'I'll speak to Mr Harmer about it. As our local magistrate he can drop a word in Brindley's ear.'

'I doubt it'll do any good.'

'I think it will. Harmer may sit out there on his estate looking down his nose at people like myself and complaining about the ruination of Tapton village, but he does care about keeping the peace. If he won't help, we'll have to think of something else.'

He sighed, speaking mostly to himself as he added, 'I don't think our troubles have subsided yet. Owd Noll never gives up easily. I'm going to keep on the extra night watchman. If anyone tries to damage my machines, I'm the one who won't be answerable. But you're right: we don't want the Merridene ladies brought into this.'

'Yes, but will they be sensible? When I told Miss Penelope not to speak to me if she saw me in the street, she said she wasn't going to be frightened off by men like that. "My father brought us up not to give in to bullies," were her exact words.' Daniel smiled, remembering her eyes sparkling with indignation as she'd spoken. He could still remember every single thing she'd said to him. 'She's a fine woman, that. Pity there aren't more like her.'

'Her sister's another.' Ben wondered what he was doing exchanging confidences with one of his workmen, but then this man wasn't like any of his other hands. Engineers often were a law unto themselves and so far Ross was very pleased with Daniel, said he had the makings of a first class engineer. 'Well, we'd better both get back to work now. You continue making those guards and install them as you find the time. But your main job just now is to make sure those new machines are running properly and to train our people to look after them.'

Daniel hesitated, then said in a burst, 'I just want to thank you for taking me on and giving me this chance, Mr Seaton. At the last town we lived in the owner treated my father and me like slaves and when he died, they threw me out of a job and the family out of a home because there was only me working in the mill and they wanted big families living in their houses who'd all work for them. I wouldn't let our Meg start there, you see, and Mam couldn't because the fluff makes her breathless.'

He drew in a breath still shaky with anger at the unfairness of it. 'So I came back to Tapton because Mam has relatives here, but I could only get taken on at Brindley's, where it was more of the same. Then I found that Owd Noll still held a grudge against my father an' I reckon he was planning to take it out on me, only he found me too useful.'

He looked his new master steadily in the eyes, as one equal to another. 'You'll not regret taking me on, sir. Let alone I'm a hard worker, I'm only just beginning to learn about machines an' I'll get better at it.'

'I'm sure you will.'

When his employer left, Daniel didn't move for a minute or two, then went back to work, soon forgetting everything except a machine that needed attention. He was fascinated as always by the beautiful way the parts moved together when running properly and the wonderful smell of hot lubricating oil.

–

The following morning the three ladies went to the house again and when Hepzibah arrived to see if there was anything she could do to help, the sisters left her alone with Sally.

'Let's go for a walk and explore a bit,' Martha said. 'The snow's all melted now and it looks like it'll be fine for a while. I'm going mad just sitting around. I do wish the furniture would arrive.'

They set off at their usual brisk pace, exploring all the streets leading off the square. As they got further from the centre of town, they marvelled at the way the workers' dwellings were built up the steep sides of the hills, often with a high wall at the bottom and the streets running parallel to the valley floor, except for an occasional track that sloped at an angle up towards the moors. They asked an old man standing on a corner the best way out into the countryside and followed his directions. A short walk up the hill brought them to the end of the terraces and a lane leading up towards the moors.

'We'll just go up to the first decent view this time,' said Martha eyeing the gently rolling expanses of land beyond the terraces longingly. She was missing her father dreadfully today, for she'd often tramped through the countryside for hours with him. Indeed, she still couldn't understand how a man so hale-looking and vigorous could be struck down so abruptly. She pushed that thought and the pain it still brought hastily aside. No use dwelling on what couldn't be changed.

They passed four older houses set half-way up the hill, three-storey places built of creamy stone with the third floor having a whole row of windows set in adjoining oblong stone frames.

'How pretty they are!' Penelope exclaimed. 'I'd love to sketch them.'

A blast of icy wind made them both glance up at the sky, in which clouds were piling up fast.

Martha grimaced at them. 'We'd better turn back, I suppose. It looks like it's going to rain.'

But as they turned towards the lower terraces, two men came round a corner and barred their way.

'Well, look at the pretty ladies,' one of them said, giving them a mocking bow. 'What are you doing here, I wonder?'

'None of your business. Kindly let us pass,' Martha snapped, amazed at his impudence.

'How are you going to make us?' He raised his voice. 'Jack! Come and see what I've found.'

A third man came round the corner, older, with a hard face and eyes that seemed to have no light in them at all. 'Who are you?' he asked in a hoarse, scratchy voice.

'That's none of your business,' Martha repeated, exchanging quick glances of dismay with Penelope, who was clutching her arm and staring at the third man as if he had two heads. She didn't like to push past them and was starting to wonder what to do if the men attacked them. Would anyone hear them if they called for help—or come to their aid?

The one called Jack studied them for a moment or two longer then asked, 'What's your name, miss?' He spoke civilly enough but there was something about him that worried her, though she tried not to let that show.

'Miss Merridene.'

'Ah. Sorry you were troubled.' He stepped aside and dragged one of the other men with him, gesturing with his free hand for the ladies to pass. The third man moved hastily away without prompting.

As they were walking on Martha heard a cry and turned to see one of the two men who had stopped them lying on the ground, groaning. The words 'Didn't t'master tell you not to cause any trouble, 'specially with them two?' floated back to her.

'Let's walk more quickly,' she said in a low voice.

'Yes, let's.' Penelope glanced over her shoulder, than whispered, 'Martha, I'm sure that man was one of those causing the riot. I recognised his voice. It's so hoarse you can't mistake it.'

'We'd better let Mr Wright and Mr Seaton know what happened.'

They had to run the last few yards and even so, only just managed to reach their new home before the rain began pounding down. They watched it for a moment or two from the hall—it was falling so heavily it seemed to cloak everything in grey mist—then closed the front door and went to join Sally in the kitchen.

'How did you go on with Hepzibah?' Penelope asked.

'She's a very decent body and I was pleased to make her acquaintance.'

The sisters exchanged satisfied glances.

'And what's more, she knows of a little lass who's looking for a place in service, so she's sending her round to see us this afternoon, if that's all right? Oh, and she sent down some cups and a teapot, so that we can make ourselves a hot drink when we're here, just till our own stuff arrives. They're a friendly lot here, aren't they?'

'Some of them.' Penelope remembered the riot and today's incident with a shudder. Who was 't'master' and why didn't he want anyone upsetting her and her sister? Could it possibly be Mr Brindley causing trouble again? Well, who else could it be? She had heard nothing good about that man.

She supposed they should be thankful they'd helped his son, or perhaps he might have sent his men after them as well.

—

That afternoon a knock on the kitchen door heralded the arrival of a scrawny girl of about twelve with ginger hair, a bright expressive face and vivid blue eyes. She was wearing rather ragged clothes but they were clean and well-mended, as Sally didn't fail to note. The ladies left their housekeeper to speak to her first and went to stand in the front parlour, looking out of the window.

'I like having something to watch,' Penelope said. 'Don't you?'

Martha considered this, head on one side. 'No, I think I'd rather have a garden than a street outside my parlour.'

'We'll have to agree to disagree, then.'

A few moments later Sally joined them. 'I think she'll do. She's called Meg Porter and she's twelve. But she won't be able to provide a proper outfit because—'

'Meg Porter? Daniel's sister?' Penelope exclaimed before she could prevent herself. 'Oh, then we must definitely employ her. Her brother saved my life, after all.' Well, perhaps not her life, but he'd prevented her getting hurt, that was sure.

Meg Porter was brought to meet her two employers. She was not, as Penelope didn't fail to notice, struck dumb by their questions, but informed them in a clear voice that she could read and write a bit, thanks to Grandma Binns, who ran a little school in her front room. Her brother Daniel had paid the school sixpences, she told them proudly, well he had until he'd lost his job. From her tone, she obviously adored her brother.

The two ladies had trouble understanding some of her expressions, not yet being used to the local dialect. They explained that she would be expected to live in and would earn five pounds a year, paid quarterly, as well as her board and keep.

Beaming, she promised to come to live here and work for them as soon as their furniture arrived.

After that they went back to the hotel to sit and make plans for their school.

—

That afternoon, just as dusk was falling, the two sisters returned to the house to collect Sally, who had been putting away in the pantry some more purchases of household necessities, delivered with flattering promptness by the grocer. Their housekeeper seemed to prefer to spend her time in the empty house to sitting around in the inn.

Suddenly there was the sound of vehicles drawing up outside and Martha raced to the window, to shout, 'It's them! The drays have arrived!'

Jem Saverby knocked on the door and informed them that he and the lads would prefer to unload the furniture that very night, if the ladies didn't mind. 'It'll be better kept in your house than in our storage area, because we get a lot of mice an' blackbeetles. Mr Wright is sending some men down from the mill to help. For tonight we'll just set things down anywhere, then tomorrow he'll send a couple of men to help you put the place to rights.'

'We'll need some lamps then,' Martha reminded him.

'They'll be here soon,' said a voice behind her and she turned round with a start to see Ben Seaton standing in the doorway, smiling at her. 'We'll show you now how efficiently our Lancashire lads can work.'

She found herself returning his smile then felt a warmth steal into her cheeks and could only hope the dusk hid her blushes—though why she should be blushing she couldn't imagine! She made up for that lapse by speaking especially briskly. 'Good. Let's get started then. I think you'll find Leicestershire ladies are not afraid of hard work, either.'

Penelope watched this interaction with great interest, then turned to find that Daniel Porter had joined them as well. That easy, lithe body and those bright, observant eyes had the same impact as before, and she was surprised at how very pleased she felt to see him. She hoped she had hidden her reaction to him, however. It would never do to set people gossiping and friendship could so easily be mistaken for something else.

'It seems we're bound to keep meeting, Miss Penelope,' he said with a smile.

'Yes, it does.' Such a stupid answer, she thought as he turned away. He'll think I'm a fool.

The men worked quickly and by eight o'clock everything was unloaded. Daniel was the last to leave, apart from Ben, who had stayed to supervise.

A minute later, Ben snapped his fingers in irritation. 'I forgot to ask Daniel something. I wonder—would you ladies stay here while I run after him, then I'll come back and escort you to the inn?'

'We can find our own way there, surely? It's not far.'

'I'd prefer you to stay here till I return. Things *are* settling down again in the town, and I promise you it's not the normal state of affairs for Tapton streets to be unsafe, but there are still a few troublemakers around.'

'Very well.'

When he had gone running down the street, Martha went to the open door, muttering, 'Oh, I do wish women weren't so helpless.'

'Do they need to be?' Penelope asked from beside her.

'Shh! Did you hear something? Oh, my goodness!'

–

As Ben rounded the first corner he came across three men attacking his Assistant Engineer and without hesitation launched himself into the fray. It had been a long time since he'd been involved in a fight, though he could usually count on giving a good account of himself, but didn't like the odds this time, especially as Daniel was already down on the ground. He grabbed one man's jacket, yelling for help at the top of a very powerful voice, then found himself trying to fight off an assailant experienced in rough street fighting.

When he heard footsteps behind him he let out a growl of relief, but as he cast a hurried look over his shoulder, hoping someone was coming to their help, he saw to his horror that it was the Merridene ladies and their maid, armed with a rolling pin, a walking stick and a warming pan.

'Get back!' he yelled, but then had to turn to give his full attention to his opponents again as a punch narrowly missed his chin.

Daniel grabbed the foot that was moving to kick him again and twisted it sharply. As his opponent crashed to the ground, he rolled out of the way, knowing he was still disoriented, but determined not to give in as long as there was breath in his body.

'It's them ladies again,' one of the attackers called. 'Back off, lads!'

With a suddenness that took everyone by surprise, the men moved away, two of them dragging their half-conscious comrade with them.

Panting from his efforts Ben turned to face the three women. 'I thought I told you to stay in the house!' The fear he had felt for their safety made him speak sharply.

'When we heard you shouting for help, we naturally came after you and it's a good thing we did,' Martha said coolly.

'Why did they run away when they saw us?' Penelope asked. 'I think they're the same men we met when we went for a walk, and they left us alone when they recognised us.'

Ben hauled Daniel to his feet then stared at the ladies. 'What do you mean? What men are you talking about?'

She explained.

'That makes me even more certain it's Noll Brindley behind these disturbances. He has a grudge against Daniel, but owes you two a favour for bringing his son here, so must have told his bullies to leave you alone. If he doesn't stop attacking my men, he'll get more than he bargained for, however. I'm not standing for this sort of thing and shall report the attacks to the local magistrate first thing tomorrow morning. And—'

Penelope pushed past him as if she hadn't heard a word.

'Take your time, Mr Porter?' Without thinking she put an arm round Daniel for support as he swayed dizzily. 'How are you feeling?'

'I've been better.' He gave her a lop-sided grin. 'I think this makes us even, miss. You saved me this time.'

'You'd better come back to the house and let us look at you. There's a cut on your forehead that needs bathing and you seem dizzy to me.'

Ben moved to Daniel's other side and put an arm round him to support him, so she had no choice but to move away.

'Lead the way, ladies.'

At the house they found that Daniel had a big lump on the back of the head, a cut on his forehead and, he said with a wince, bruises in places he'd rather not show the ladies. It didn't seem serious enough to call in a doctor, so Penelope, always the nurse of the family, bathed the cut and worried about how safe he would be getting home.

Ben took charge again. 'Once we're sure you ladies are safe at the Dragon, I'll make sure you get home, Porter, though I think I'll call in a couple of the men to accompany us. And first thing tomorrow I'm going to see Harmer.' He caught an inquiring look from Penelope and added, 'He's our local magistrate, lives just outside the town on his estate and looks down his nose at mill folk. If he won't do something about Brindley, I will.'

'I never heard the likes of it,' Sally said once they were back in the inn. 'Are you sure this doesn't happen often?'

'So Mr Seaton tells me,' Martha replied.

Sally grimaced. 'I hope he's right. That was Meg's brother, I gather?'

Penelope took it upon herself to answer. 'Yes. Daniel's the Assistant Engineer at Seaton's. He's self-taught, but he must be good or he'd not have been given such a responsible job. He's the one who saved me the day of the riot.'

She went to her room, but couldn't sleep for a while because she kept seeing Daniel's face, a little battered this time, but still with that bright, intelligent air she found so attractive.

What had got into her to react to the man like this? she wondered sleepily, but fell asleep before she had time to work out an answer.

–

Late that night Peter heard his father going down the stairs muttering to himself. What was the old man up to at this time of night? he wondered. Not really sleepy after a day spent sitting around in boredom broken by a slow and chilly stroll round the town centre, he suddenly decided to see what his father was doing. He could always plead hearing a noise and worrying about burglars.

Taking great care not to make a noise, he crept down the stairs and turned towards the kitchen, where a light was showing under the door. As he got there, he heard a rap on the back door and the sound of the bolt being drawn back.

'You're late,' his father said in that harsh, carping tone he used with underlings and employees.

The man who replied had a very hoarse voice. 'Had to wait till it was safe, Mester Brindley. Didn't want anyone seeing us.'

What was his father plotting now? Peter moved closer to the door and didn't scruple to listen to what they were saying.

'Tried to get Porter tonight, as you wanted, but Seaton came after him an' we had to leave things be. He's a good fighter, for a mill-owner, and Porter's not bad either.'

'Damn him! Will that fellow never stop interfering in my business?' After a pause Noll added, 'I'm not best pleased by your efforts this time, Jack. You failed to stop Seaton's new machines getting here and you can't even kill one man for me. What do you think I'm paying you for?'

Suddenly, things his father had muttered fell into place in Peter's mind. Oh, hell! As if it wasn't bad enough to have a grasping mill-owner for a father, now he found the old man was engaged in criminal activities. He shivered, wishing himself anywhere but here and with any other father on earth.

Then he heard the sound of the back door opening again and hurried back up to his room, his bare feet making no sound on the carpeted stairs.

It was a long time before he got to sleep. He didn't want to get involved in what sounded like murder. What the hell was he to do? Should he write to his uncle, try again to get some help there? But even as that thought occurred to him, he shook his head. His uncle was a skinflint who had declined to help in no uncertain terms because his nephew had a father with plenty of money.

Without thinking he rolled over on to his bad arm, let out a low groan and tried to move to a more comfortable position. It was a long time before he managed to get to asleep.

Chapter 7

The following morning, the ladies moved out of the inn as soon as they'd eaten breakfast. Delighted to be in their own home and determined to set it to rights as soon as possible, Martha and Penelope put on their oldest gowns, enveloped themselves in aprons and covered their heads with mobcaps, laughing at their reflections in a mirror propped against one wall. They decided to start with the parlour, so that they would have somewhere comfortable to sit in the evenings or when receiving visitors, and managed to rearrange all the furniture except for the piano.

'It's just too heavy to pull across the carpet!' Martha said, after it had defied all their efforts to move it more than an inch or two.

Penelope flung herself down in a chair, fanning her red face and panting from her exertions. 'Oh, bother, there's someone knocking at the door.'

'I'll go.' Martha pulled off her mobcap and stuffed it into her apron pocket, oblivious to such details as ruffled hair and whether there was a smut on her nose—until she opened the front door and discovered Mr Seaton standing on the doorstep. Only when he grinned at her did she realise that she hadn't checked her appearance, by which time he'd stepped inside without waiting for an invitation.

'You find us still in chaos, Mr Seaton,' she said pointedly, not moving from the hallway. 'What can we do for you?'

He moved forward until he was standing very close and brushed one fingertip gently against her nose. 'Smut,' he offered by way of explanation.

The touch, gentle as it was, set off a current of warmth that hummed through her body and the familiarity startled her so much she could only stare at him in shock.

He looked almost as disconcerted as she was feeling. 'I'm sorry. I wasn't thinking. I shouldn't have—um—touched you like that.'

Her voice came out too high-pitched. 'That's all right. You were only trying to—um, help. Let me show you into the parlour.'

He didn't move. 'I came to see if you were all right, not pay a social call and also to ask if there's anything I can do to help you settle in. I'm sending some men to help move the heavier furniture but they can't come until the early afternoon, I'm afraid.'

Penelope came to the parlour door, having overheard the whole conversation, including the intriguing silences between the bursts of speech. 'Good morning, Mr Seaton. If you really mean your offer of help, there is the piano. It's too heavy for us to move, but with your help we might just manage it, then we can finish off this room.'

'Show me.' He entered and glanced round the parlour, making no attempt to hide his interest. 'You've got some nice things.'

Martha stiffened. Not only had he caught her looking like a housemaid—why had she answered the door at all?—and touched her as if she was a housemaid, too, but he was now commenting on the quality of their furniture.

Perhaps these were northern manners, but she wasn't sure she liked them.

He moved across to the piano and looked back at her. 'Where do you want this?'

Martha said nothing, just continued to scowl, so Penelope jabbed an elbow into her sister's side and said, 'Over there.'

He was already eyeing the path along which they had to push the piano. 'I'll just move this chair. Right. If you two get to that end and push, and I pull from here, we should be able to move it without too much trouble.'

After that task had been accomplished he hesitated then said, 'I also came to ask a favour of you.' He hesitated again, biting his lips as if uncertain how to start.

'Do sit down and tell us what we can do for you, Mr Seaton,' Penelope prompted when her sister continued to stare at him in that strange, puzzled way.

'To be frank, I need to keep Georgie occupied. Can I send her across to you while I'm at the mill from tomorrow onwards? I know the school isn't open yet, but she's upsetting the servants and they don't have the authority to keep her in order. She and Hepzibah had a big quarrel yesterday about the state of her bedroom, but I'm on Hepzibah's side about that.' He scowled at the memory of Georgie's subsequent tantrum.

'Of course you can send her. Can't he?' Penelope glanced sideways at Martha for confirmation.

'Yes, certainly, Mr Seaton.'

'Thank you. I'm grateful to you.'

Penelope watched in fascination as the other two gazed at one another and the silence lengthened again. She couldn't believe what she was seeing. Martha was definitely reacting to him, growing flustered when he spoke to her—Martha of all people! She had always felt a great sense of pity that her practical and loving elder sister should never have experienced what it was like to love someone. Was it possible that the attraction that was so obvious between these two might develop into something more enduring? Oh, she did hope so. She could imagine nothing that would make her happier than to see Martha get married.

In the end he stood up and broke the spell. 'I must go now.'

Penelope murmured something she was sure neither of them heard and made no attempt to escort him to the door.

Martha followed him down the hall, then realised suddenly that she was alone with him once again. Why had Penelope not come with her? She took care to keep her distance from Mr Seaton as he opened the front door himself.

'I'll bring Georgie round tomorrow morning, if that's all right? Don't hesitate to set her to work helping you. I suspect it's boredom that's making her so cross. It's been like living with an angry wasp.'

Martha nodded, watching him stride down the path, nod to someone in the street and disappear from view. Not until she shivered in the chill breeze did she remember to close the door again. When she turned round, she saw her sister standing in the parlour doorway watching her with a quizzical expression on her face.

'Why is that man always so rude?' Martha demanded, hands on hips. 'Just tell me why!'

'You bristle at the mere sight of him and I think he can't resist teasing you. He's been extremely kind to us, actually. And if he does speak rather brusquely at times, I believe it's only his way, not a sign of rudeness.'

'Well, *I* think his manners are appalling!' declared Martha, tossing her head. 'Telling me I had a smut on my face. A gentleman would have ignored it.' And no gentleman that she'd ever met would have removed it without her permission. Though his touch had been very gentle, very… She went back to work in the parlour, using excessive energy as she polished the furniture with beeswax.

Penelope smiled at her own reflection in the hall mirror then paused for a moment to listen to the sound of Sally's voice uplifted in song coming from the kitchen. And one of her more cheerful hymns too. Another excellent sign.

She returned to the parlour, added more coal to the fire and watched Martha for a minute or two, then said quietly, 'I'll make a start on the schoolroom, then, shall I?'

Since the bookcase there was in the position they wanted it, she began to unpack a box of books, humming the same tune as Sally under her breath. It was good to be busy, good to have an aim in life again.

But what she wanted most of all from this move was Martha's happiness. Her sister had given so much to others and now deserved something for herself.

Surely fate would be kind to her?

–

In the mill office at the end of the day Noll and Gerry shared a glass of gin, his favourite tipple, though his son considered it a low and vulgar drink. 'Had a visit from bloody Harmer today.'

'Oh, aye?' Gerry knew that perfectly well, since he'd seen the magistrate's carriage standing outside the mill house and a maid come scurrying across to fetch her master.

'He came to warn me to stay away from Porter. Said I'd be the first person he came hunting for if anything happened to the fellow.'

'Probably as well to back off for now.' Fighting and riots didn't get the spinning done. In fact, Gerry couldn't see that they'd done anything useful at all.

'It was Seaton as came to Porter's rescue, so it must be him as called in Harmer.' Fuming, Noll drained his glass and poured another. 'He should mind his own business, that one.'

Gerry refrained from commenting that it *was* Seaton's business now Porter was working for him. He eyed the decanter longingly.

'Pour yoursen another,' Noll said, reverting to the speech of their childhood as he often did when they were alone together.

'Thanks.'

'I shan't forget about Porter, though. I'll let him be for now, but one day I'll make him regret crossing me.' He scowled darkly at the fire, seized the poker suddenly and broke apart a large piece of coal with a quick thump. 'That's better. Bloody cold out.'

'How's that son of yours going?'

Noll rolled his eyes. 'How should I know? I never could understand what goes on inside his head. He spends half his time fiddling with his clothes and hair, too bloody much time. He looks like a man-milliner to me. Eh, I've got to find the stupid bugger a wife because he's not shaping up to do owt else for hissen.'

'That shouldn't be too hard. After all, he's your heir.'

'Not if I can get me some grandsons, he isn't.' Noll glanced at the clock and drained his glass. 'I suppose I'd better go back to the house and get mysen summat to eat. Told 'em to keep dinner waiting till I was ready.' He grinned. 'Peter will be famished by now. He has a decent appetite for one as does no work. You lock up here, Gerry lad.'

His friend watched him go, sat on for a few minutes longer sipping his gin, then checked that everything was settled for the night and the watchman in place in his little room near the gate. He walked home in a thoughtful mood, wishing Noll wouldn't get het up about things. So what if he couldn't buy Seaton's mill? He already had one of his own. Most folk would think that more than enough.

If he didn't watch out, Noll would be getting into trouble with nobs like Harmer and who knew where that would lead? And what for? Money, that's what, when he already had more than a man needed to live comfortably.

Gerry only wished he owned a tenth as much as his friend did. He'd not waste his time on getting his own back on folk, nor he wouldn't work as hard as Noll did, either. He'd enjoy himself, that's what he'd do, and make sure his wife did as well. She always worked hard and been a good wife to him. There were the grandchildren too. He wanted better for them than to toil in a mill as he'd done during his childhood, much better.

–

On their third day in the house the sisters were sitting in the parlour enjoying a rest between labours and chatting lazily to Georgie, who seemed desperate for conversation.

Once she'd realised they didn't intend to treat her as a child, she'd relaxed her guard a little.

Someone hammered on the door so loudly that Martha felt annoyed even before Meg hurried to open it. But Sally had made it very plain to them that she considered it wrong for 'her ladies' to answer their own door, so she sat waiting to be enlightened. Who could it be? She could hardly go and peep out of the window with Georgie sitting there, so had to contain her impatience.

'Are your mistresses in?'

What a harsh voice it was! And so loud they could hear it all too clearly in the parlour. Martha frowned, not liking the sound of it.

Meg answered in a scared, breathless voice. 'Yes, Mr Brindley. I'll see if they're receiving visitors.'

'Just show me straight in, girl. If they're there, why would they not see me?' There was a silence, then he added, 'Don't I know you?'

'I don't think so, sir.'

'It's Mr Brindley,' Georgie whispered. 'He's a dreadful man. Mama would never receive someone like him. Why does he think he can push in here?'

Penelope stood up. 'I'd better go and stop him questioning Meg.' If Mr Brindley had a down on the Porters, there was no need to tell him who Meg was.

She opened the parlour door to reveal a man already standing in the hall handing his outdoor things to Meg. He looked much older than she'd expected, appearing closer to seventy than fifty, and was short with a distinct paunch and a harsh face in which age had engraved deep lines. A scar on one temple ran right up into the thin grey strands of hair that covered only the rear half of his scalp.

He looked her up and down. 'I'm Oliver Brindley. You'll be the younger sister, from my son's description. Miss Penelope, isn't it?'

'Yes. Won't you come in.' She nodded dismissal to Meg, who cast a scared glance back over her shoulder as she hurried away, then led the way into the parlour. 'This is my sister, Miss Merridene, and you've probably met Miss Seaton already.'

He went across to shake Martha's hand, then stood staring at Georgie as if he had never seen her before. She blushed under his scrutiny, but that only made him give the slight twitch of the lips that was his nearest to a polite smile. 'Quite the young lady now, aren't you, Miss Seaton? I remember when you were a scrawny little lass always trying to tag along after your big brother.'

Seeing that Georgie was embarrassed by his remarks and seemed for once to have lost her voice, Martha interrupted. 'Perhaps you'd like to take a seat, Mr Brindley?'

'Aye. Just for a minute. Though I'm a busy man so I can't stop for long. But I don't forget my obligations.' He took the chair Martha had indicated and wasted no more time on civilities. 'I gather my son is in your debt, ladies. How much do I owe you?'

Martha decided to answer such curt remarks in like manner, though it went against her upbringing. 'I paid the doctor half a guinea on your son's behalf.'

'And for bringing that young fool of mine back to Tapton?'

'Nothing. We were coming here anyway and it was our cousin's carriage so cost us nothing.'

He scowled at them so blackly that Penelope intervened. 'It was no more than anyone would have done. We were glad to be able to help your son.'

'Peter was lucky he met you. The young fool had nothing left in his pocket. I'll make sure he doesn't get near the place again, that I will!' He threw five guineas on the small table between him and Martha. 'This should pay for your trouble.'

Colour heightened, she pushed four of them back to him and went to fetch her purse from the mantelpiece, fumbling in it for change, so angry at this insult that her hands were shaking. 'A half guinea will be quite sufficient, sir.'

'I prefer to reward them as have done me a service.'

'And we, sir, prefer to be reimbursed only for what we have expended. It wouldn't be right to accept more.'

'Suit yourselves, but they tell me you've to earn your own bread, ladies or not, so you're fools to refuse money!'

'And it's just because we *are* ladies, sir, that we wouldn't dream of accepting.' She was aware of Georgie's gaze moving from one to the other and wished their pupil hadn't been there to see this scene.

He scooped up the coins then snapped his fingers. 'Meg Porter, that's who the maid is, I'll be bound! Same colour of hair as her brother. Eh, you'll be sorry for taking *her* on. They're all trouble-makers in that family. I had to sack the brother because he doesn't know his place and dares to tell his betters how to run their businesses. I'd advise you to find another maid for yourselves.'

Martha's face was so rigid with the effort it was taking to control her temper that Penelope held her breath as her sister spoke.

'I believe, sir, that we can be trusted to choose our own servants.'

'Well, don't say I didn't warn you. Any road, it won't be long before that brother of hers leaves town and she'll be going with him, then you'll be short of a maid.' He thrust himself to his feet, staring round with a sneering look on his face. 'I've not got all day to spend gossiping.' He stared at Georgie again, head on one side, making no attempt to hide his interest, pleased when she blushed.

'Let me show you to the door, sir.'

When he'd gone, she returned and blew her breath out with a whoosh. 'Well!'

Penelope shuddered. 'What a dreadful man!'

Georgie chimed in. 'Mr Brindley's not liked in the town and I can see now why Mama said he wasn't to enter our house. The Wrights don't receive him, either, and they didn't even before Mrs Wright became so ill.'

'He frightens me,' Penelope said slowly. 'There's a ruthlessness about him, as if he cares for no one and would...' She broke off, not wanting to say in front of Georgie that she felt Mr Brindley wouldn't balk at murder if it suited his purpose.

Martha let out an unladylike snort of disgust. 'He doesn't frighten me but he made me very angry today. How dare he throw money at us like that? And what business is it of his whom we hire?'

Penelope couldn't forget the expression of undisguised hatred on Brindley's face when he'd spoken of Daniel. 'I do hope Mr Porter will take care. He's made a dangerous enemy in that man.'

'My brother says Daniel Porter has the makings of a good engineer,' Georgie volunteered. 'Why does Mr Brindley hate him so?'

'Who knows?' Martha looked round the room. 'Well, this isn't getting the work done. We need to get that schoolroom sorted out. Georgie, come with me and we'll start unpacking those other boxes.'

With a long-suffering sigh, the girl pushed herself to her feet and trailed out of the room into what should have been the dining room but had become the schoolroom instead.

'Do you always sigh and scowl so much?' Martha asked as she stood contemplating the room.

Georgie looked at her in puzzlement.

'It's just that it seems to make you look less pretty and usually girls your age want to look as attractive as possible.' Hiding a smile at Georgie's look of horror and refusing to listen to her conscience about this unorthodox way of treating the young woman's sullen behaviour, Martha studied the room. Her next remark concerned how best to arrange the furniture.

She couldn't help noticing that Georgie glanced at her own reflection in the mirror a couple of times when she thought Martha wasn't watching. The girl scowled, then smiled in turn, and Martha nearly betrayed herself by chuckling.

She'd been watching Georgie more carefully than she showed, however, and had noticed how unhappy the girl's expression became when she wasn't chatting. It must be very lonely for her with her brother working such long hours, and if the mother was as indifferent to her needs as she sounded, that would only add to the girl's unhappiness.

From what Georgie had said, her father had been the centre of her universe and his death had torn her life apart. Well, Martha could understand and sympathise with that. She still missed her own father so much it was like a physical pain.

-

That evening Noll looked across the table at his son, who had recovered enough to make a hearty meal, though he still needed help cutting up his food. 'I went to see those ladies of yours this morning. They'd only take half a guinea from me, the fools, though I offered them five.'

Peter stared at him in horror. 'You should have asked me first. I could have told you they'd turn any extra payment down. In fact, I could have saved you the trouble and gone in your place.'

'I wanted to see 'em for myself. Not bad looking for a pair of spinsters, but you're right. They're too old for you.'

'Well, of course they are.'

'I doubt they'd have you, anyway. They look like they've got a bit of sense in their heads.' He ignored his son's expression of outrage and shovelled in more food, chewing it noisily before adding, 'Seaton's sister was there too. She's pretty enough, though a bit plump, and looks as silly as they come. That one would make a much better wife for you. It's more than time you provided me with a grandson or two.'

Peter choked on his food and only the knowledge that he hadn't a penny to his name kept him silent. It was a minute or two before he could speak calmly enough to say, 'Seaton would never let me near her. And anyway, isn't she too young to marry?'

His father ignored the interruption. 'Seaton might not let you near her, but if you got in well with those two spinster ladies, you could do the pretty, flatter the chit and catch her interest before her brother could stop you. She looks old enough to marry to me, though I'll find out how old she is, and I gather old Seaton left her a nice little fortune, which is why young Seaton's a bit short of the ready.'

After that they both ate in silence. Peter could see that his father was hell bent on marrying him off to someone and actually, he wouldn't mind finding himself a wife with some money of her own. Perhaps that way he could escape from Tapton for good.

But he couldn't see Seaton allowing a Brindley to court his sister, let alone marry her, not the way things were between the two families, so it seemed a waste of time even thinking about it.

He tried to remember Georgie as a child, but couldn't. 'Perhaps I should call on the ladies and inspect her for myself,' he said lightly.

His father nodded approval. 'That's the ticket. Call round to offer them your thanks and get your feet under the table.'

Chapter 8

The next day being Sunday, the sisters were spared the presence of their alternately sulky and voluble pupil. They got ready for morning service at the small parish church, certain that, like any newcomers, they would be stared at by the rest of the congregation.

'I shall be interested to see what the minister is like,' Penelope said as they walked across the square. 'I hope he's not too high church.'

They stopped just inside the entrance to study the building, which was very plain inside, but with nicely carved pews and pulpit.

The service was conducted at a brisk pace, with a mere fifteen-minute sermon and only two hymns.

When they came out, they encountered Mr Wright in the churchyard, with his daughters clustered around him, and he introduced them to some of the other local families. They agreed that the girls could start coming to them immediately after Christmas and sent their regards to Mrs Wright, but it was too cold to linger so they soon set off on the brief walk home.

'Thank goodness there was no sign of the Brindleys today,' Martha said as they opened their own front door.

'I wish I need never see old Mr Brindley again,' Penelope said with a vehemence unusual to her. 'There's something truly evil about him and we already know he's a bad employer.'

'We've been *told* that. We haven't seen it for ourselves,' Martha corrected.

'I believe it—and anyway, we both saw those three men, didn't we? Who else in this town could have hired them?'

After luncheon they sat in the parlour, allowing themselves a quiet hour or two's relaxation, Penelope with her embroidery and Martha writing a letter to Jenny Barston, their governess friend in Woodbourne, who had begged for early news of them. Almost as an afterthought she penned a few lines to Edward and Rosemary, but this letter was short and contained far less personal information.

'There! That's Edward out of the way for a while,' she declared as she set her quill down and flapped the piece of paper to and fro to dry the ink. 'I think I'll go up now and finish arranging my bedroom.'

Left on her own in the front parlour, Penelope went to stand by the window and watch the passers-by. It had already become a habit about which Martha teased her but she'd always loved watching people. When she saw Daniel Porter walking along the street, laughing down at his little sister, who had had the afternoon off to visit her family, she decided now might be a good time to speak to him about helping with his reading. She went into the kitchen to catch him before he left.

'Did you need something, Miss Penelope?' Sally asked.

'Mr Porter's just bringing Meg back. I saw them go past the front and they'll be here in a minute. I want to ask him something.'

The housekeeper looked at her in surprise, but said nothing. When Meg came in, her cheeks rosy from the cold air, Penelope went to the back door just as Daniel was turning to go out of the rear gate.

'Mr Porter!'

He turned. 'Miss Penelope?'

'I wonder if you could spare me a few moments? I want to ask you something.'

She brought him into the kitchen, where Sally was stirring something in a pan and telling Meg to hurry up and change so that she could see how to cook this dish. It would obviously be difficult to talk here. 'Would you come through into the parlour, please, Mr Porter?'

He frowned at her. 'Me?'

'Why not?'

He gestured to himself. 'You can see why not. I'm not fit to be seen in a lady's parlour.'

'Well, we can't talk here, so if I think you're fit, I'm sure you could humour me.'

He hesitated. 'All right, then.'

'Will you bring us in some tea and cake?' she asked Sally, knowing how cold it was outside. Ignoring their housekeeper's barely hidden surprise, she led the way into the parlour. 'Let me take your hat. Do please sit down.'

Daniel sat on the edge of the chair opposite hers, holding his hands out involuntarily to the blazing fire.

'It's a chilly day, isn't it?'

'Aye, but then you'd expect that in winter.' He looked at her inquiringly, waiting to hear what she wanted.

She was having trouble finding the right words and as she hesitated, couldn't help noticing that his hands had been scrubbed red in an effort to get them clean. She saw that he'd realised what she was looking at and blushed.

His tone was sarcastic. 'I do try to get the oil out of my nails on Sundays.'

'Mr Porter, we will get nowhere if you take offence so quickly.' She was amazed at her own temerity in confronting him with this—but John had always said that one should never try to fool the poor, because they only lacked money, not wits.

He looked at her, a long, thoughtful stare, then nodded. 'You're right there. Though I'm not sure where we want to get.'

'I want to help you with your reading.'

Another stare, then, 'Why?'

'Because I believe education is important—and—and because it's what John would have wanted. It's the last thing I can do for him, carry on his work. Don't you wish to improve your reading?'

'Of course I do! And I may not always sound it—well, I know I'm too blunt sometimes—but I'm right grateful to you for offering me the chance, Miss Penelope.'

A knock on the door heralded the arrival of Sally with a tea tray. With instinctive courtesy Daniel stood up and took it from her as she began to manoeuvre through the furniture.

'Put it on this side table, if you please, Mr Porter. Now, Miss Penelope, you ate practically nothing at lunch time, so I've cut you some of my fruit cake. And I'll be obliged to you, Mr Porter, if you'll make sure she eats it.' She fixed him with a gaze slightly less hostile, but still with something of a warning in it.

Penelope was glad to have something to occupy her hands, because she still felt a little tense, as if all her senses were heightened. 'How do you take your tea, Mr Porter?'

He looked puzzled. 'What do you mean?'

'Do you have both milk and sugar in it?'

The smile he gave her was laced with grimness. 'I "take my tea", Miss Penelope, as it comes, an' grateful to get it. No milk, plenty of sugar if I've got the choice.'

He watched her pour the amber liquid, enjoying the sight of her hands moving so surely among the delicate china. Eh, what pretty hands ladies had, not red like his mother's from taking in washing! When she passed him a cup, he set it down to offer her the plate of cake. 'I daren't start drinking my tea unless I do as Mrs Polby ordered.'

Smiling, she took a piece and laid it on a small plate, then said, 'You must join me, or I shall feel uncomfortable eating alone.'

He drank the tea with obvious appreciation and demolished the piece of cake in a few bites. She offered him another piece.

'Would a *gentleman,*' his tone was slightly sarcastic, 'take another?'

She couldn't hold back a gurgle of laughter. 'I've frequently seen my father—and John too—take three or four slices of Sally's cake. She's an excellent cook. And they usually took several cups of tea, as well, so I'll pour you another one, shall I? Gentlemen, Mr Porter, are allowed to have hearty appetites. It's we ladies who must eat like birds.'

The tension between them eased a little. 'Then I don't mind following their example, Miss Merridene. It's the best cake I ever tasted.'

She allowed him to take another bite before asking, 'Do you like reading?'

'Aye. When I can get something to practise on. Mr Seaton lets me have his newspapers after he's done with them and there's a group of us who go through them together.'

'Would you like to borrow one of our books?'

'I wasn't hinting!'

'I know. But friends usually lend one another books.'

'Friends?'

She looked at him defiantly. 'Why not?'

'You know why not.'

'No, I don't.' The silence that followed was longer than it should have been as he continued to stare at her. For the first time he was looking at her openly, as a man looks at a woman, and she was responding to that as a woman too, feeling herself soften and warm to him.

'You're playing with fire, lass,' he said quietly.

She didn't pretend not to understand. 'I know. But some fires go out and others blaze up.'

'This one can't blaze. There's too much difference between us.'

She could feel her cheeks getting warm as she answered him. 'We don't know that.'

'But you wouldn't... you couldn't...'

She flushed even more hotly but was determined to be honest with him because she knew he wouldn't make any moves unless she did. 'Only time will tell. I'm prepared to give the fire a chance to burn brightly. Are you?'

He jerked to his feet and went to stand by the window, his back towards her. 'If you're playing with me...'

'I'm not! I'd never do that.'

Martha came in just then and the moment of honesty was over. And perhaps it was a good thing, Penelope decided. It was early days yet, after all. Only she did like him and admire the way he was making a life for himself against great odds—and she did find him very attractive. He was the first man to stir her senses since John.

Her sister greeted him civilly and demanded a cup of tea from her because it was cold upstairs and she was frozen.

'You'll have another cup, too, Mr Porter?' Penelope poured him a third one without allowing him time to refuse. 'And do have another piece of cake. Martha, you'll bear witness that I've eaten a piece, won't you? Sally was scolding me for not eating my luncheon and ordered Mr Porter to see that I made up for it.'

He ate the cake and drank the tea mostly in silence, listening to Martha talk about her plans for the school-room. When he'd finished, he looked at Penelope and gave her another of his wry smiles. 'How do gentlemen take their leave after this sort of thing.' He waved one hand at the tea tray.

'They thank their hostess for her hospitality, then she shows them to the door. Or she calls the maid to do so. Only we don't often bother with that, because Sally and Meg have enough to do.'

He stood up and said with a grin, 'Then I thank you kindly for your hospitality, Miss Penelope.'

She stood up and moved towards the door. 'You must come again, Mr Porter. But before you leave, if you'll come into the schoolroom, I'll find you that book I prom-ised.'

He nodded a farewell to Martha and followed Penelope along the corridor, saying, 'You're a determined lass, aren't you?' as she handed him a book.

'Sometimes. Let me show you to the door.' She took him to the front door.

'Wouldn't it be better if I went out the way I came in? What will your neighbours think?'

'I shan't care what they think. My friends always leave by the front door.' She held out her hand to him.

He surprised her by taking it in both his and holding it for a moment, saying in a low voice, 'Eh, I don't know how to deal with you, lass.'

'Honestly, if you please.'

He kept hold of her hand and she stared into his eyes, wondering what had driven her to behave so forwardly with him. She didn't pull her hand away, however, because she enjoyed his touch. When he let it drop and said a quiet farewell, she stayed at the door, watching him walk down the short path to the gate. He turned there and stopped for a moment, his eyes meeting hers again. With another of those puzzled shakes of the head, he went through the gate and strode off down the street.

When she got back inside, Martha looked at her quizzically. 'Found yourself another protégé, have you?'

Penelope looked at her anxiously. 'You don't mind, do you?'

'I don't mind at all, but you don't usually bring your protégés into the parlour to take tea—and you were on your own with him. You should have called me down. We don't want to give people any cause for talking about us.'

'He was a perfect gentleman. I'd expect nothing less of Meg's brother.'

'He has a very intelligent face.'

'He's hungry to learn.' She gave her sister an apologetic smile. 'To me, educating working people is more important than teaching little girls, though I shall no doubt enjoy that as well. And as to Daniel Porter, he *is* very intelligent. It shines from him. Your Mr Seaton recognises that or he wouldn't have let him work as an engineer. He only—'

'*My* Mr Seaton? Why should he be mine, pray?'

Penelope realised she'd made a serious error here and said hastily, 'Because you met him first, of course. I'm going to speak to him and Mr Wright tomorrow about arranging some reading classes. After all, they said they wanted us to help their workers.'

'Hadn't we better wait until we've settled in with teaching the girls? It's why we came here, after all.'

'Why can't we do both?' She got up and began to pile things back on the tea tray, putting an end to this conversation before it took them down awkward tracks.

Later as she got ready for bed Penelope's thoughts returned to Daniel Porter. He already felt like a friend, which was strange when she had known him for such a short time and there were such great differences between them. She very much wanted to get to know him better, wherever that might lead. Then she dismissed such thoughts, trying not to remember the warm look in his eyes, or her own reaction to that look—and completely failing.

In the bedroom next door, Martha was also lying awake. She was thinking that the old Penelope had returned with a vengeance, ready to take on the world for something she believed in, just the way she had been with John Medson.

Only this time there was no gentleman to protect her, so Martha would have to do her best to fulfil that task. It would mean getting involved in teaching some of their employers' workers to read, which she found rather daunting, but it was better to have too much to do than too little and if Penelope could teach these men, so could she.

—

Ben leaned back in his chair and smiled at his sister who had been a little easier to live with in the past few days, thank goodness. 'How are you enjoying being with the Merridene ladies?'

Georgie shrugged, not returning his smile. 'It's someone to talk to.'

'Good. Look, it's fine today so I thought we'd go for a tramp up on the moors.'

'No, thank you. You walk too fast for me. Besides, the wind's getting up and my bonnet will blow off.'

'You need something simpler to wear for walking on the moor—and some good stout boots, too. Haven't you got any? You used to go walking with Dad.'

She elevated her nose. 'I was much younger then. Now I'm grown up and Mama says a lady tries to appear elegant at all times.'

He'd had enough of her scornful answers and assumption that he knew nothing about ladies. He knew one thing for certain: what she was wearing didn't flatter her. 'Then if you want to appear at your best, why are you wearing all those frills and bows?'

She looked down at herself then across at him, her brow wrinkled in puzzlement. 'What do you mean? These are the very latest fashion. Mama always made sure I was well turned out.'

'You're too short for so many frills. They make you look fat.'

She glared at him. 'What do *you* know about that? You spend all your time in that dirty mill and never meet real ladies.'

'I meet the Merridenes. They're undoubtedly *real ladies*!'

'They're teachers, which isn't the same thing. And they're in mourning, so they're not wearing fashionable clothes.'

'Whatever they wear, they'll always look like ladies to me.' He decided to go and work in his office for a while. Every time he tried to talk to Georgie he came close to quarrelling with her and that was no way to live together. He was at his wits' end sometimes as to how to deal with her, how to make friends again.

She watched him go, then sighed and began to trace the pattern on her dress with one fingertip. After a minute or two she stood up, shook out her skirts and looked down. There were rather a lot of frills... but surely Mama knew best what suited her?

She turned slowly round in a circle, seeking something to do and not finding it. Life here was so boring and there was no one in the town of her own age and class! It was a sad state of affairs when it was more interesting to go and help two teachers set up their school than it was to stay in her own home. Perhaps she should write to her mother and ask to go there for a visit? No, her mother didn't want her. She'd only say no again.

An hour later, driven by frustration and boredom, Georgie put on her bonnet and went for a leisurely stroll round the square, lingering to look in the windows of the drapery, though she knew the contents of the displays by heart.

If things went on like this, she decided as she walked, she'd be driven to reading books or embroidering, two occupations of which her mother approved for young ladies. Georgie detested embroidery but did occasionally read a novel. Only Ben didn't have any novels, just dry old books about people who'd travelled to other countries or, even worse, about cotton. As if she didn't hear enough about cotton living in this dreadful town! Mama had always hated Tapton and had only lived there for Papa's sake.

Georgie wished she lived somewhere else now that Papa was dead. Anywhere but here! She kept expecting to see him coming towards her down the street. She blinked furiously to get rid of the tears and turned towards home.

–

The following day, just as the ladies were settling down to take afternoon tea following another hard day's work, there was a knock on the front door and they heard a man's voice in the hall. 'What now?' Martha muttered, setting her plate down.

Sally appeared at the door of the parlour. 'Mr Brindley to see you, miss, the one we brought to Tapton, not the old one. Are you at home?'

The two sisters exchanged glances. 'Oh dear! I suppose we must receive him,' Martha said in a low voice.

Georgie looked from one lady to the other. 'He was the scrubbiest young man, very thin and had dreadful spots.' She giggled. 'He was always tripping over his own feet. My Mama wouldn't let me even speak to him, but I used to see him in town sometimes and—'

She didn't get a chance to say anything more because Mr Brindley was shown in, no longer spotty but a well turned out and romantic figure with his arm in a sling. Brightening, Georgie sat up straighter, more aware than her companions that their visitor was dressed in the very height of fashion and impressed by that.

'Your servant, ladies.' He bowed to each of the sisters in turn then looked thoughtfully at the third lady, guessing who she was, but pretending not to know.

She gazed back at him limpidly, then lowered her eyes in assumed modesty. Who would have thought that Peter Brindley would turn out like this? He was the first person she had met since returning to Tapton who had the slightest pretension to being fashionable. Those peg-top trousers were all the crack, for the son of one of her mother's new friends had a very similar pair. And if his father wasn't a gentleman, all she could say was that the son had somehow transformed himself into one.

Her self-righteous brother might not associate with the Brindleys, and indeed she had always been afraid of old Mr Brindley when she was a child and found him only slightly less fearsome now, but she didn't intend to let that hamper her with regard to the son.

'Have you met Miss Seaton?' Martha asked.

'Not for many years. I doubt I'd have recognised you, you've changed so much, Miss Seaton.'

Georgie simpered at the obvious admiration in his expression and gazed at him through her eyelashes.

Watching her antics made Martha feel quite nauseous. This pose made Georgie hold her head at a very odd angle, however effective a way it might be of showing off her fine blue eyes.

Mr Brindley noted his hostess's scornful expression and hastily abandoned Georgie. He had to keep the older women on his side or he'd not get near the younger one. 'I came to say a proper thank you for rescuing me.'

'Your father already did that.' Martha stared at him coolly.

'That was the reason I had to come. He told me about offering you money and—well, I wished to apologise. He didn't mean to insult you, I'm sure, but he has no idea of how to go on in genteel society.'

Martha could not prevent herself from snapping, 'I don't like to hear a son criticising his father.'

'I just wanted to explain.'

'May I offer you a cup of tea, Mr Brindley?' asked Penelope, seeing no way out of extending this courtesy to him.

'That would be most kind. As long as someone will sweeten it for me. I'm not yet very proficient with my left hand.'

'I'll do it!' Georgie put down her own cup so quickly she splashed tea into the saucer.

'You'd be better seeing to your own cup,' said Martha sharply, 'or you'll spill the rest. My sister is quite capable of adding sugar to Mr Brindley's tea.'

Twenty minutes later, just as their visitor was very correctly standing up to take his leave, the doorknocker sounded again. Georgie looked up expectantly, not at all averse to more company, but sagged back in her chair when she saw it was only her brother.

At the sight of the other man, Ben's expression became chill and disapproving. He made the tiniest possible inclination of his head. 'Brindley.'

'Seaton.' Peter bowed himself out as quickly as he could.

The appearance of her brother brought the sulky expression back to Georgie's face and she turned ostentatiously away from him to study the ornaments on the mantelpiece as if she'd never seen them before.

Once the door had closed behind the unwelcome guest, Ben said in tones of strong disapproval, 'I didn't think to find you entertaining that worthless fribble.'

'He called to thank us for helping him,' Penelope said. 'We could scarcely turn him away. And he's not that bad. He has excellent manners, at least.'

'And he dresses well,' Georgie couldn't help saying.

Martha didn't mince her words. 'Clothes don't make the man. And personally, I'd still have liked to turn him away. I don't like the connection with his father. I shall tell Sally we're not at home if he calls again.'

Ben regarded her with warm approval. 'You're a woman after my own heart, Miss Merridene.'

Which brought more colour into her cheeks. 'What can we do for you, Mr Seaton?'

'Miss Penelope left a message that she wished to speak to me and I thought I'd escort my sister home afterwards.'

Georgie stood up. 'I'll go and get my outdoor things.'

When she was out of hearing, he looked pleadingly at the two women. 'I wonder—could you help me do something about Georgie's clothes? The ones she's wearing are surely not suitable for a girl of her age, and correct me if I'm wrong, but they don't even flatter her.'

Martha didn't try to hide her delight at this request. 'We'd be happy to. Indeed, I was going to speak to you about that myself. When we open our school we'd prefer her to dress more simply.'

'There's a dressmaker in town—Miss Briggs—all the ladies seem to patronise her. Perhaps she could alter

Georgie's clothes or make her some new ones? The cost is irrelevant. I just want her to look her age.'

Footsteps heralded the return of his sister so he changed the subject. 'What did you want to see me about, Miss Penelope?'

'Daniel Porter—and men like him. I'm eager to help him and his friends with their reading.'

'I thought you'd be doing that later after you'd settled in with the school.'

'Why wait? It's so important for everyone to be able to read fluently.'

'I agree. Very well, we'll start as soon as we can arrange it. Jonas and I will select the men and you can hold the classes in the old mill house behind my residence. We only use it for storage nowadays and some of the men eat their midday meals there. I could send Daniel Porter over to escort you there after work, since you know him already. We don't want you walking through the streets on your own after dark. I'll escort you back home myself.'

Her face lit up. 'That'd be wonderful! I'll be happy to start as soon as it's ready.'

'I'll let Jonas know. He'll be pleased, I promise you. You must tell us what materials you'll need.'

She was very pretty when she smiled like that, he decided, and seemed to have more character than he'd first thought, but somehow he preferred her sister's looks. He turned to look at Martha, admiring that strong face and stubborn chin, then realised he was staring again and looked away hurriedly.

He and Georgie walked home so briskly she was out of breath even going that short distance.

'You're getting fat and lazy, Georgie,' he said as he opened the front door.

'I'm not fat!'

'Not yet, no, but you will be if you go on at this rate, sitting around all day. You're definitely plump.'

'Well, there's nowhere to go for walks in this stupid town, except round and round the square.'

'You could try going up on the moors. I'd be happy to take you on Sunday. I did offer last week.'

'No, thank you. I don't enjoy your company.'

She was very cool to him all evening, which was nothing new.

Not for the first time he wondered what the hell he was going to do with her after this last year of schooling ended. He didn't intend to send her back to Belinda, who seemed to have brought her up to think of nothing but frivolities and fashion. And anyway, his step-mother didn't want her and sounded from her two brief letters to be enjoying her new married status hugely and to have little thought for what her daughter was doing, for she had only enquired about Georgie as an afterthought at the end of the letter.

Belinda hadn't written to Georgie this time, which had upset his sister, he knew. Sometimes she looked as if she'd been crying, only she denied it when he asked. He wished there was some way he could do more to help her—only she wouldn't accept his help.

And he had other troubles taking up his time. He still kept a guard on the mill, and had men watching over Daniel Porter, who was doing a grand job with the machinery.

–

The following day Georgie worked sullenly, staring at herself in the mirror whenever she could. In the end

Martha grew tired of her half-hearted efforts and said roundly, 'What on earth is the matter with you today? I swear you haven't heard a word I've been saying.'

'Ben says I'm getting fat.'

There were tears in Georgie's eyes and Martha didn't fall into the error of making light of this worry. She'd been plump at that age, too, and had once cried herself to sleep when Edward teased her about it.

'Ben says my clothes make me look fatter.' She waited, eyes fixed pleadingly on Martha's face. 'He's not right, is he?'

'The clothes aren't as flattering as they could be, I'm afraid.'

Georgie looked down at herself in bewilderment. 'But Mama said they were the latest fashion. She had them made specially so that I'd look nice when Ambrose came calling.'

Was it possible that the mother had been making Georgie look plump deliberately in order to make herself look more attractive in comparison? Or did she just have appalling taste in clothes? Martha knew she shouldn't make judgements about people she'd never met, but Georgie's mother sounded to be an extremely selfish woman and if she'd been doing this on purpose to her daughter, it was cruel.

'Those clothes are the latest fashion for ladies of more mature years, perhaps, but they're not really suitable for girls of your age.' She saw the tears overflow and roll down Georgie's cheeks and couldn't help putting an arm round her. 'Shh now. Don't cry. We can easily do something about it.'

'I'm not going back into children's clothes! I want to look grown-up. I don't like being a child. No one talks to you and you can't go to parties and there's nothing to *do*!'

What hours of loneliness did that outburst reveal? Martha wondered. 'Well, you've got me and Penelope to talk to now. And I do understand how you feel because I was plump myself at your age, but grew out of it.'

'You did? Truly?'

'Yes, truly. The materials of your clothes are pretty and they could probably be altered quite easily.' She realised Georgie wasn't listening and was still sobbing quietly and despairingly against her about nobody loving her, so held her close.

'No wonder you're upset.' Martha stroked the soft, dark hair. 'Men aren't always tactful, even when they're trying to help, but I'm sure your brother didn't mean to hurt you.'

'Ben wasn't trying to help. He doesn't c-care about me. He didn't want me here. No one wants me. You're the first person to cuddle me since Father died.'

'Of course Ben wants you. Why else would he bring you back here to live?'

'Because there was nowhere else to send me and he's my guardian.' More sobs shook her.

Martha began patting Georgie's back and rocking her slightly. 'Shh, now. He does care, I'm sure. Look, why don't we visit the seamstress and get your clothes altered?'

'What does a seamstress in a small town know about fashion?'

'If we went to see her, we could find out, couldn't we? I have to go shopping this very afternoon, so why don't we call on her then?' She pushed Georgie to arm's length and smiled at her. 'I used to like pretty clothes too, but we didn't have much money so I've always had to be very practical.' She looked down at her dark skirts and pulled a wry face. 'Don't tell Penelope I said that. I'd much rather spend the money making sure she looks her best than on myself.'

Georgie was leaning against her once more, as if desperate for the contact. As she listened an occasional hiccup shook her. 'Why?'

'She's young enough still to find a husband. I'm not.' Then Martha realised she'd been exchanging confidences with one of her pupils and bit off more words. 'Don't tell anyone what I said, please, Georgie. I shouldn't have told you, only you're almost grown-up and I wanted you to know that I do understand how you feel.'

'I promise I won't tell anyone.'

Martha pulled out a handkerchief. 'Here. Wipe your eyes and then you can go home and fetch one of your other day dresses. We'll take it to the seamstress later and see if she can alter it to make it more flattering. If that one turns out well, we'll take your other clothes to her.'

Georgie plied the handkerchief, then handed it back with a gruff, 'Thank you. I'll go home right away for the dress, if you can manage without me.'

'That's a good idea.' Martha watched her go, thinking how much prettier the girl looked without that sulky expression.

As the front door banged shut, she smiled wryly and continued her work, getting on much faster on her own. Once she stopped to look at her own dark-clad figure in the mirror and sigh. Perhaps Pen was right and she should wear her hair in a softer style. Why not? It never did any harm to look your best.

But it was still Pen who mattered, pretty Pen, who surely still had a chance to marry.

As Georgie walked along behind the church, she was so lost in thought she nearly bumped into a gentleman who had stopped to bow to her. 'Oh, I'm sorry, Mr Brindley. I was thinking about something.'

Peter smiled. 'I hope they were happy thoughts.'

She shrugged and gave him a half-smile.

'May I escort you somewhere, Miss Seaton? I'm finding time hanging a bit heavily on my hands at the moment and would enjoy some company.'

She hesitated but couldn't resist that appeal, since loneliness was her own problem. 'Just to the end of the street. I don't think my brother would like me to walk with you.'

'Yet I would love to walk with you.' He smiled at her, surprised to find that this was the truth.

'Oh.' She blushed and stood feeling flustered.

'Anyway, you're surely old enough to decide for yourself who your friends are, Miss Seaton? Or am I mistaken and do you look older than your years?'

'I'm seventeen,' she said at once. 'And you're quite right. My brother has no right to tell me who I may talk to. Mama never did so.'

He walked along beside her, speaking cheerfully of London and when they got to the end of the narrow street behind the church, she stood there as if unaware that time was passing. Eventually he judged it best to leave her in case anyone saw them together and tattled about it to Seaton. 'Sadly, we're at the end of Church Lane, so must part company. Perhaps we'll meet again from time to time?'

'Oh, I do hope so.'

He walked off, whistling cheerfully. Seventeen and a charming companion. Quite old enough to marry—and an heiress to boot. The whistling faded to nothing as he suddenly realised that he didn't want to do things his father's way. She was a pretty little thing, or would be if she knew how to dress. It'd be unfair to treat her as if she didn't matter personally. That was the way his father treated him.

When she got home, Georgie hummed as she sorted through her clothes, leaving the ones she'd rejected piled on her bed and stuffing her chosen dress into a bandbox. She couldn't be that fat and ugly, whatever Ben said, if a gentleman like Peter Brindley, who had lived in London and dressed so fashionably, wanted to walk and talk with her. And fancy Miss Martha liking pretty clothes too! Who'd ever have thought it? Georgie well remembered her own year of wearing black for her father. It had made her feel very low in spirits and not been at all flattering.

Perhaps going to the school wouldn't be as bad as she'd expected. Her teachers had treated her kindly so far and they didn't leave her on her own with nothing to do, something she hated. They were talking about teaching her how to manage a household, which might be quite interesting, not stupid things like copying maps of countries you'd never visit. And Miss Penelope had promised to teach her to draw better, which would be a useful accomplishment for a lady.

She looked at the framed sketch on the wall of her bedroom. It was one of the few things she'd ever done that she was proud of, a likeness of her father. She still missed him dreadfully, wept for him at night, longed to be able to confide in him. Only *he* had truly understood her, taken her walking, talked to her, teased her. Why did he have to die? She had no one who cared about her now.

Chapter 9

Martha and Georgie set out after their midday meal to visit the seamstress, who lived in the west end of town. It was a longer walk than they usually took, but for once Georgie didn't complain at that prospect. Instead she chattered on happily, pointing out which were her family's terraces and which belonged to the other mill owners. 'Father had to build the houses or the workers wouldn't have had anywhere to live, because at first they came from other places to work here. This was quite a small village when he was younger, you know.'

Brindley's houses looked markedly inferior to Seaton's and Wright's, with sagging doors, tiles missing off the roofs and broken windows stuffed with rags. Thin children or worn-looking women stood outside some of them, arms huddled around themselves against the cold and Martha could feel their hostility as they passed.

Even Georgie commented. 'They get upset sometimes because Mr Brindley treats them so badly. Ben said they'd settled down again after the riots, but I'm glad I'm not on my own today. They look hungry, don't they, poor things?'

They did indeed, Martha thought, feeling pity surge through her.

The seamstress was a cheerful woman of middle years, who spoke with a broad Lancashire accent and was not in the least servile, treating them more like old friends than customers. She was wearing a dress which Martha considered well-cut and flattering, and that spoke volumes for her ability as a seamstress.

Miss Briggs tutted at the mere sight of the dress they showed her. 'Far too fussy,' she said disapprovingly, holding it up, 'but lovely material.'

Georgie was torn between annoyance at the woman's criticism of her mother's choice of style and hope that maybe Miss Briggs did know something about making dresses that were more flattering.

'What do you advise?' Martha asked, careful to bring Georgie into the discussion while at the same time guiding her choice. To her relief the girl agreed with everything suggested.

When they came out, Georgie asked, 'Will it really make me look less fat?'

'I'm sure it will. And it'll be ready by tomorrow, so you won't have long to wait, will you? If this one's all right, you should take your other dresses to her.'

'Perhaps they don't suit me because I've grown. I'm sure Mama would never choose something unflattering for me.'

Martha was touched by the girl's faith in her mother and by her general vulnerability. She had never had time to become deeply concerned about clothes because at that age she'd been running a household and had had more important things to deal with. She felt a dampness on her face and looked up to see that black clouds had blown up to cover the sky and more rain was threatening. 'Oh, dear. It's done nothing but rain lately and I'm longing to go for a tramp up on the moors.'

'I used to go with my father. Ben offered to take me on Sunday, but I didn't want to go with him.' Georgie looked sideways at Martha and added, trying to appear casual, 'Anyway, I haven't got any proper walking shoes and I'd get blisters because mine are too small now. And I'd need a simpler bonnet than this one, as well.'

'The bonnet's easy. Penelope is a dab hand at trimming them—or in your case un-trimming them. We could make that a needlework lesson for you. A lady should always be able to sew, don't you think?' She was glad to see the girl's face brighten. 'Isn't there a shoemaker in town? We could visit him on the way back and order some sturdier shoes for you. I'm sure your brother would be happy about that.'

'I suppose it wouldn't matter if my walking shoes weren't in the latest fashion,' Georgie allowed.

We've got to give that girl something to think about besides fashion, Martha decided, already heartily sick of the word. It was one thing to appreciate pretty clothes, quite another to talk about nothing else.

The shoemaker was all attention and promised a pair of half-boots within days. He studied Georgie's feet and nodded. 'You've got a neat little foot there, Miss. I remember making your shoes when you were a child. Don't cram yourself into shoes that are too small and narrow, like those.' He indicated the shoe she'd taken off, his expression scornful. 'Whoever made that pair didn't look at the shape of your foot. I should be ashamed to turn out ill-fitting rubbish like that.'

'We'd better check with your brother,' Martha said as they continued on their way. 'It seems to me you need several pairs of shoes, not one.'

'He won't care.'

But Ben did care, showing a keen interest in all his sister had to tell him about her outing with Miss Merridene and approving her visit to the shoemaker's. 'I should have thought of that myself. You're at an age where you're still growing. Last spurt into womanhood, probably. I've seen it with lasses at the mill. They suddenly shoot up and almost overnight they're women, not girls.'

He couldn't have said anything which pleased her as much and she was more affable that evening than at any time since she'd come to live with him.

Martha Merridene had worked miracles with Georgie, he thought as he got ready for bed. He smiled as he pictured her brisk, no-nonsense ways. Strange sort of miracle maker! He was very grateful to her, though surprised that she was the one who'd been able to help his sister. He'd expected it to be the younger teacher, who was more softly pretty and looked elegant.

–

Georgie's dress turned out so well, a clever rearrangement of trimming hiding the fact that it had been altered, that Martha did a few calculations and decided to visit Miss Briggs on her own account. Her clothes were getting very shabby and although it was a little early to stop wearing mourning for her father, she didn't want to order more black garments. Perhaps a soft grey or lilac? What did Penelope think?

'I think it's about time you got something new for yourself. It's been years. You even had your old things dyed for mourning. I told you when I bought my last dress length that you should do so too. And if this seamstress is as good as you seem to think, I've a mind to have a new dress made for myself soon as well.'

'Come with me, then. We could go and buy a dress length now. You haven't been out all day and I'm tired of that schoolroom.'

'I'd love to. And we'll invite Georgie to go with us to the seamstress tomorrow, perhaps? She'll love that.'

They enjoyed their small outing, returning with some soft blue material for Martha, which brought out the rich colour of her hair. She had demurred, worried about breaking their mourning, but as Penelope pointed out, she'd still be wearing her dark clothes most of the time and keeping this for best.

But the following day Penelope came down with a slight cold, enough for Martha to insist she stay indoors. And Georgie was limping badly, admitting that her shoes had been hurting for a while and had rubbed up blisters, so she couldn't go far until they were better and she had her new boots.

'I'll go on my own, then,' Martha decided.

'Should you, dear?'

'It's only a few streets away, for all Georgie makes it sound like half-way to London. Miss Briggs lives at the west end of town, just beyond Brindley's mill. To tell you the truth, I shall be happy to stretch my legs. We've done far too much sitting around lately.'

She set off briskly, wondering if she could find a longer way back because she was enjoying striding out at her own pace, for once.

It was as she was passing some of the less salubrious terraces belonging to Brindley that she heard the sound of voices shouting. Not more troubles! she thought, pausing to listen and try to work out where the sounds were coming from. They were to her right and ahead of her, she decided, and quickly came to the conclusion that it would be prudent, if disappointing, to return home. After the riots they'd had in the town lately, it was better to be safe than sorry.

But then more shouting erupted, seeming to come from behind her this time, and she stopped again, beginning to feel worried now for her own safety. The only thing she could think of was to hurry to Miss Briggs' house and take refuge there.

As she was passing the end of the next narrow street, which was at a right angle to this one, she saw men running along it towards her and abandoning dignity and ladylike behaviour, she picked up her skirts and ran on, her boots thudding on the earth with a dull sound that seemed to beat along her veins.

To her horror, two men erupted from a street ahead of her, facing the other way and yelling obscenities at someone still hidden from her. She stopped dead, shrinking closer to the high wall that ran along the lower edge of the hill on her left. Perhaps they wouldn't see her.

Unfortunately one of them did and nudged the other, who swung round to stare. They strode across to her, stopping a few feet away to look at her in an assessing way that made her shiver. Some women who were following them began to shout insults, though no one actually touched her.

'Rich bitch!' one shrieked. 'What do such as you care if my childer go hungry?'

'Who is she? Has Brindley brought in a whore in now? He hasn't been near any of his operatives since last year when we showed him we wouldn't stand for it. Or is this one his son's fancy piece?'

Other men and women gathered, shaking their fists at her, their voices swelling into a crescendo of anger. They were so loud she couldn't make herself heard when she tried to tell them who she was.

Then a woman bent and picked up a stone, throwing it at her and catching her on the upper arm. There was a roar of approval from the crowd.

Another woman came right up to her, grabbing her skirt and rubbing the material between her fingers. 'My childer ha'nt got enough to wear an' look at her! She's got enough in this skirt alone to cover three.'

'Let's take it off her then,' one of the men said.

'I'll do that for you, lad.' The woman reached out again, grabbing Martha's sleeve and tugging. 'And we'll see what she's got in that parcel, too.'

As Martha slapped her hand away and began to struggle to keep both her parcel and herself intact, there was a roar from the crowd.

'You show her!'

'Get her clothes off!'

When someone came up behind her and pulled her backwards by the shoulders, Martha spun round, terrified she was being attacked by more than one person.

'What's got into you, Mary Dixon?' roared a man's voice from close to her ear.

Ben Seaton! Martha stopped struggling and when he pushed her behind him, she went willingly, leaning against the wonderful strength of his powerful body for a moment and trying not to shake with sheer relief. There were still only the two of them and a crowd of angry operatives, so she said nothing, waiting to see what would happen.

The woman had stepped back, panting, her face and body so thin you could see the bones beneath the grimy skin.

'He's making us work longer hours for the same money,' she said sullenly. 'We're not having it.'

'That doesn't give you the right to attack ladies passing by.'

'We thought she was one of his son's grand friends. Why else would she be in this part of town?'

'She's one of the new teachers who've come to work for me and Mr Wright. You'd better learn who your friends are, Mary.'

Ben turned and pulled Martha forward to stand beside him, putting his arm round her shoulders, feeling her tremble as he shouted, 'This is Miss Merridene. She's a teacher and she works for me and Mr Wright. If anyone harms her, I'll come after them and make them regret they were ever born.'

They had stopped shouting now, a few looking ashamed but others scowling.

'She's got a sister, too,' he called. 'Tell folk that these ladies are under my protection.'

Martha knew she should pull away from him, for he was holding her so close it was almost an embrace, but she couldn't. She was still shuddering inside, trying to overcome her fear of these ragged, almost feral creatures. Then she saw Mary brush an arm across her face and step back, sagging with weariness and despair, and felt a surge of pity for the emaciated woman.

'You'll do no good by this sort of behaviour,' Ben warned as some of them began to move away.

'What will do good, then?' a man asked, one who'd stood scowling with his hands shoved deep into his pockets. 'My childer go to bed hungry as often as not, an' so do I.' He pulled his pockets inside out as he added, 'I've got nowt left to buy food, not one penny, because he fined me for being late. Put his clock forward, he did, the sod.'

Ben's voice softened just a little. 'I don't know the solution. Brindley goes his own way. I wish I could help you.'

'Aye, well, you can't, so we shall have to help oursen, shan't we? We s'll not stand for him making things worse. We might as well line up outside the poorhouse now. At least in there they feed you enough to keep you alive.'

Ben fumbled in his pocket and tossed a coin to the man. 'Here, buy your children some food.' Then he produced some more money and offered it to Mary. 'Share it out, will you, lass? You'll know who's most in need.'

She nodded.

The crowd gathered round the woman, as orderly now as they'd been unruly before, waiting patiently as she counted the coins and frowned in thought. Once Mary had shared the coins out, they began to disperse.

Martha let out a great shuddering sigh. 'Thank good-ness you came along. I don't know what they'd have done to me if...' She couldn't even finish the sentence, her voice was shaking and she was having trouble not bursting into tears.

'You were a brave lass,' he said gently. If Georgie had been in this situation, he was sure she'd have been in screaming hysterics by now, too terrified even to try to fight back. Facing an angry crowd was daunting to even the bravest of men, as he knew from experience.

He had meant to smile at Martha in a reassuring way, but suddenly became aware of her body pressed close to his, a woman's body with all its delightful curves and hollows. Her eyes were raised to his in a trusting way, beautiful blue eyes. And her hair, ah, that was indeed her crowning glory. In the scuffle it had tumbled from its pins and was spread over her shoulders, a mass of wavy brown with a hint of auburn in it. Why did she screw it up into a tight bun and hide its beauty?

Her eyes were over-bright with unshed tears and he put one fingertip out to brush away a gleaming drop that was about to roll down her cheek. She drew in her breath in a long sobbing gasp and said nothing, only breathed deeply and continued to stare at him. He had enough experience with women to realise that she was reacting to him physically, though he doubted she understood that.

'Are you all right now, Martha?'

Neither of them noticed that he'd used her first name.

'Not really. I still feel shaky. I thought they were going to k–kill me.'

Her voice broke on the last words and he pulled her right into his arms, holding her tightly and marvelling that she was still fighting against the tears, still desperately trying to regain her self-control. Hating to have her do this publicly, for he could see faces still peering at them round corners and through windows, he drew her along to where there was a low wall at right angles to the street, running along beside the steps leading up to the next row of houses. This little indentation in the wall was the nearest thing he could find to privacy. 'Here. Let's sit down for a minute or two while you recover. And let's put that parcel down.' He guided her there, his arm still round her shoulders, and sat down beside her.

He wondered about taking his arm away, but it seemed the most natural thing there was to continue holding her, so he left it where it was.

Martha leaned against him with a sigh. 'I hadn't expected anything like that to happen.'

'It was partly because they didn't know you. We're not on any main roads in Tapton and we don't get many strangers coming into town. Those who do certainly don't walk through these streets. Why were *you* here?'

'I was going to see Miss Briggs. This is the way Georgie showed me.'

'Hah! Trust her to seek a short cut. But neither of you should use these streets after what's been happening during the past few months. I'll show you another way to get to Miss Briggs'.' After a further few moments' thought, he added, 'And I think, if you agree, I'll take you and Miss Penelope on a tour of my mill, and ask Jonas to do the same. When quite a lot of people are able to recognise you in the street and know you're not connected to Brindley, you should be much safer.'

'Whatever you think best, though I doubt I shall feel safe for a while.'

Her hair was tickling his nose. He closed his eyes for a moment and breathed in. 'You smell of lavender. My mother used to put it among her clothes and it always makes me think of her.' The simple fragrance pleased him far more than his step-mother's expensive perfumes ever had.

'We used to grow it in Woodbourne and we still have the dried flowers among our clothes. I brought a cutting with me and if it survives, I'll plant it in the garden next spring.'

He could see that her expression was sad as she said that. 'You must be missing your old home.'

'A little. I miss my father most. And the walks. He and I used to go for long tramps together and fond as I am of Penelope, I have to admit she's not a vigorous walker.'

'I could take you up on the moors on fine Sundays,' he offered.

She'd have loved to but didn't dare. 'Thank you for the offer but that might not be—appropriate. Us walking alone together, I mean.' She smiled wryly. 'Teachers have to be very careful not to do anything people might gossip about.'

'We could take Georgie with us as chaperone. She used to be a good little walker.'

Martha couldn't help it. She laughed out loud at that. 'Georgie! A chaperone!'

He loved her rich chuckle and smiled with her. 'Wouldn't she serve?'

'She might. If we can persuade her to go once the new boots are ready.' Abruptly Martha became aware that his arm was still round her shoulders and his warm body was pressed against hers. Then she realised that her hair had come down. What was she thinking of to sit here like this? She must look a hoyden. Colour flooded her face and she edged away, 'I think I'd better put my hair to rights. I'll come back to see Miss Briggs another time.'

'I'll send someone to escort you tomorrow morning if you like. Today isn't a good day to be out and about.' He scowled as he added, 'If Brindley really is going to make working hours longer, it's an inhuman thing to do. His operatives can't really manage on what he pays now and they're exhausted when they finish work.'

'Do you pay more?'

'Yes, indeed. We feel people who're not hungry work better. And we'd not dream of making the hours longer.' Her fingers had been busy and he was sorry to see that glorious hair pulled tightly back again. He noticed with a wry smile that when his companion stood up and brushed her clothes down, she once again became 'Miss Martha' the schoolteacher. He picked up her parcel and offered her his arm most correctly. 'I'll escort you home.'

'Thank you.'

They hardly said a word as they walked back.

Martha could feel herself blushing all over again at the thought of how strong and safe he had felt when he held her in his arms. She also couldn't help noticing how well their steps matched.

–

The sisters had a very quiet Christmas and both felt sad to be without their father, who had always made a big fuss of them both at this time of year, buying presents and brewing his own hot punch.

On Christmas Day they went to church, then were invited to have luncheon with the Seatons. Even Sally was invited to join Hepzibah in the kitchen there, which Martha felt showed great thoughtfulness on Ben Seaton's part.

Georgie wasn't sulky that day, but said very little.

'It's been so quiet,' she confided in Martha at one point, 'that it doesn't feel like Christmas at all. Last year we had all sorts of parties and Mama let me stay up for some of them and drink champagne.'

'Your brother must have been on his own last year, then. He'll be happy to have your company this time.'

The girl looked at her in surprise. 'That didn't occur to me.' She pulled a wry face. 'Well, you don't think of parties when you think of Ben, do you? This is the first time I can remember him inviting people round.'

'Penelope and I are very grateful. We have each other, of course, but it's nice to enjoy the company of friends as well.' She smiled and whispered, 'How about playing charades? Do you think we could persuade Ben to join in? We'd only have two people in each team, but it might work.'

Not only did they persuade him to join in, but he did so with such enthusiasm that they were all laughing and a little breathless by the time they'd stood up and sat down, trying to act out the various syllables.

Georgie whispered to Martha as they left. 'Thank you. It's been lovely.'

Martha hugged her, not caring whether that looked strange.

As they sat quietly together in the evening, Penelope said, 'I like Ben Seaton, don't you?'

'Yes. I didn't the first time I met him, but I know him better now and hope I value him as he deserves. He's been very kind to us and I was never so glad to see anyone as the day he saved me from attack.'

Penelope said nothing about the way Martha's cheeks had gone a little pink when talking about him. What exactly had happened between the two of them on the day he had saved her from the rioters? Martha had blushed about it several times, but her account of the incident seemed to show nothing to be embarrassed about. And what had the two of them been talking about tonight while planning their charade? They'd seemed quite at ease with one another and her usually staid sister had laughed and smiled the whole time.

So had he! Even Georgie had commented on how well the two of them got on.

'Are you glad we came here or are you regretting it?' Penelope asked suddenly.

Martha looked up, an expression of surprise on her face. 'I'm glad, of course.'

'So am I.'

–

On the other side of town, Oliver Brindley celebrated Christmas in a less lavish manner, fretting that his workers had to have a whole day off work, which they didn't deserve, and be paid for doing nothing.

'What do you do with yourself all day?' he grumbled, scowling at his son who was all dressed up like an actor in a pantomime. He answered his own question. 'You do nothing, that's what, except eat me out of house and home. And I don't know why you bother to dress up like that when you're not going anywhere.'

Peter tried to fend off his father's ill humour. 'I like to dress well because I sometimes meet Miss Seaton when I go out. I think she's glad to see me, in spite of her brother, and we've had some very pleasant chats.' More pleasant than he had expected, actually. He found her charming.

His father's scowl lessened. 'That's more like it.' Noll looked at his son, sucking thoughtfully at a hole in one of his rear teeth while he considered this development.

'She'll be back at that school after Christmas,' Peter went on, 'so I can start meeting her by accident on the way home again. She uses the lane behind the church and I wait inside the church porch till I see her coming.' Heaven help him, it had become the highlight of his day! He was meeting her now for his own pleasure, not to follow his father's orders, though it wouldn't be politic to tell the old man that.

Noll nodded and stared into the fire as he thought about the situation. As soon as he found out whether the girl was worth the marrying, he'd do something about getting his son wed to her. He grinned as he considered this. No use asking Ben Seaton for permission. The fellow would never allow her to marry a Brindley and he guarded his sister rather carefully, apart from that short walk to and from school. It might be best just to snatch her and then make sure she was well and truly compromised before anyone found her again.

'The only way you'll get the Seaton lass is by compromising her.'

Peter looked at him in dismay. 'Compromising her? You can't mean it!'

'Don't be such a sap-head. What other way is there when a girl's guardian refuses to give permission? I'll arrange to have her kidnapped and then *you* can spend a night or two with her. That should do it.'

'I'm not going to *force* her.'

'You'd be a fool not to, but from what I hear of *polite* folk, just spending a night or two with her should do it. They'll soon have you two wed then.'

Peter saw the expression on his father's face and cut off what he was going to say. He couldn't believe his father really would kidnap her and if he tried, it should be an easy matter to warn her. He picked up the wine glass and studied the port against the light of a candle, more to deflect attention from himself than because he cared about the colour. 'This is rather a nice port.'

'I asked that wine merchant fellow for a good one, an' I'd have give 'em what for if they hadn't found one for me. I don't mind a glass of port now and then but I'd rather have gin.' He tapped his glass.

Peter nodded but didn't comment. Surely his father hadn't meant that? He couldn't help picturing Georgie

Seaton, young and puppyish, far too trusting. No, he definitely didn't want to see her kidnapped or hurt in any way. And wished he wasn't so cowardly about telling his father that.

Noll lifted his own glass. 'Here's to your marriage! However we get you to the altar.'

As soon as he could, Peter excused himself and went up to bed, feeling totally despondent.

Oh, hell, things were getting worse, not better! was his last thought as he drifted into sleep.

Part Two

January 1829

Chapter 10

As soon as the festive season was over, lessons started. The four Wright children were escorted to and from school by Mrs Wright's maid, an elderly woman who had been with the family for as long as Sally had been with the Merridenes.

The children were a delight to teach and even Georgie was slightly less abrasive these days. She was wearing her altered clothes, and not only looked slimmer, Martha thought, but prettier, too.

They spent the morning finding out what the four girls knew, but as it was a crisp, sunny day, Martha decreed that they should all go for a walk in the afternoon. Mr Wright had made it plain that he wanted the girls to start getting more exercise as well as receiving a decent education. She had already asked Georgie to be their guide and since the new boots had been made and pronounced comfortable, the girl led the way cheerfully up to the edge of the moors, happy to be in the role of expert, for once.

'They're delightful children, aren't they?' Penelope murmured, watching as the Wright girls began to throw a ball to and fro. Even Georgie condescended to join in, then took over the management of the game, helping little Alice, who was at a disadvantage.

'I'm beginning to think Georgie has hidden talents,' Martha said. 'Look how well she's organising the others and how they mind what she says.'

'She's not stupid, though I think that mother of hers sounds to be very silly and has taught her to hide her talents, not display them.'

'I agree!'

Martha began to walk up and down, watching the children play and smiling at their pleasure and high spirits. But her own spirits weren't as high as theirs because she hadn't realised how much being with the children would rouse the old longing for a family of her own. She had never talked about this to her sister, pretending she was happy with her single state, but now she asked quietly, 'Do you ever wish you had children of your own?'

Penelope looked at her in surprise. 'Of course I do. Don't you?'

Martha could only nod, because if she spoke she might give away how emotional she was feeling. But she saw that her sister understood. They knew each other all too well.

–

Ben saw them coming down from the moors, Georgie in animated conversation with Beth, the oldest Wright girl, Penelope walking with Helen and Jenny, the middle girls, and Martha holding Alice's hand as the child skipped along. Both teachers had cheeks as rosy as their charges and when Martha bent down to listen to something Alice was saying, he found the picture they made very touching.

It was only as he was going back to the mill that he realised he'd hardly noticed how Penelope looked. Strange, that.

Then he forgot about everything as his two engineers brought him into a discussion about the steam engine and the new machines, which were proving their value.

'Daniel's got an idea for getting some more of the fluff out of the air,' Ross said, smiling benignly on his assistant. 'It sounds feasible and you must admit not only would the operatives benefit, but we'd have less cleaning up to do. He needs to draw his idea up properly, though, if we're to have parts made, and I'm no better than him at drawing— worse in fact.'

Nor had Ross ever been an inventive engineer, Ben thought, unlike Daniel, though the older man understood machines and how to maintain them, and did a very competent job. After they'd finished discussing the idea, Ben took Daniel aside and said quietly, 'If this works, you'll get five guineas for your idea and an increase in wages.'

Daniel stared at him in open-mouthed astonishment.

'We're not all like Brindley, you know,' Ben said mildly, then carried on making a round of the mill, something he did several times a day. He reminded the men he'd chosen for the reading classes that they were staying behind the following day and promised them a meal at his expense before the class. This had been Penelope's idea and he thought it a good one, a small reward for the extra effort they were making. Hepzibah had agreed to provide the food and Jonas had offered to pay his share of the costs.

In fact, things were going so well Ben could hardly believe it after the rioting and other troubles of the previous year. Maybe Noll would admit defeat now and leave Seaton's mill alone.

But that still wouldn't solve the problems caused from time to time in the town by the unhappy workers from

Brindley's. He and Wright would like to do something about that, for the sake of their fellow citizens, but neither of them wished, or could afford to buy the other man's mill, even if Brindley would sell it.

The man seemed impervious to reason and bent on working his operatives to death. This couldn't go on, surely?

–

Late that evening Sally answered a knock at the front door to find Daniel Porter standing there.

'Could I see Miss Penelope, please?'

'It's getting a bit late for callers.'

'It's urgent or I wouldn't disturb her. Please, Mrs Polby. I've only just finished work and I had to have a wash and change my clothes before I came here.'

Her eyes softened as she took in his reddened, scrubbed hands and threadbare but neat clothes. 'Come in, then, and wait in the hall. I'll go and fetch Miss Penelope.'

While he was waiting, Meg peeped out of the kitchen door and waved to him, her face rosy and cheerful, which did his heart good. When Sally returned a moment later, Meg vanished.

Penelope came to greet him at the door of the parlour and offered her hand, which he took very briefly. 'Mr Porter. Do sit down. You know my sister.'

He nodded to the other woman, but it was to Penelope that he addressed himself as he sat on the edge of a chair, clutching some papers and looking thoroughly uncomfortable. 'I'm sorry to disturb you so late, but I wondered if you could spare the time to help me with these?'

'You know I'm happy to help you in any way I can. What are they?'

'Drawings—well, just rough ones. I've had an idea about changing our machinery to take some of the fluff out of the air. It gives folk working in the mill bad chests an' it's not good for the machinery, neither. Only I need to draw it up neatly to get the parts made and I can't do that well enough yet.'

'How interesting! May we see your drawings?'

The two women studied Daniel's sketches, which were smudged and crossed out, made on scraps of paper picked up in the mill. Martha found them hard to understand and soon resumed her seat by the fire, but Penelope had a better eye for diagrams and after a few questions had soon worked out what Daniel was trying to show.

The two of them sat close together on the sofa, heads bent over the pieces of paper, discussing how best to show what was needed so that the owner of a nearby foundry could make the parts.

Watching them, Martha was surprised at how easily they seemed to understand one another and how animated her sister became as the two of them discussed the diagrams. She hadn't seen Penelope glowing with life like this since she'd been betrothed to John Medson. On that thought Martha became very still and stared across the room in shock. Surely Pen couldn't have fallen for this fellow? John had been a gentleman, however reduced his circumstances, while Daniel was a working man, with no money and no education—definitely not a proper husband for a Merridene.

No, it couldn't be, she must be mistaken. It was just Pen's love of helping others that was driving her. That was all it could be.

When Penelope had perused the last piece of paper, she smiled at Daniel, quite unaware of her sister's scrutiny. 'How exciting all this is!'

'It's amazed me how well you understand it!' he exclaimed. 'There's not many as would, you know, let alone a lady like yourself. But can you teach me to make proper drawings? I'll pay you whatever is usual.'

'Oh, yes. I'd enjoy it. And I wouldn't dream of taking payment. But we'll need to go and make a start on them in the schoolroom. It's lucky I've got some bigger sheets of paper for my sketching. Come and see them.'

Before Martha could protest, they had left the room. She wondered whether she should accompany them then leaned back against her chair with a tired sigh. What need was there for chaperoning when Penelope was only just across the corridor? Anyway, she was quite sure Mr Porter would behave himself. Meg's brother was full of enthusiasm, not mischief.

In the schoolroom Daniel looked round and said teasingly, 'Another of your grand rooms?'

'Not grand at all and it'll soon look shabby, I'm sure, with the girls coming and going.' Penelope got out the bigger pieces of drawing paper and spread one on the table. 'Here, this is the size I think we need.' She found a ruler and they measured it carefully, then, as she was putting the ruler down again, their hands collided.

Warmth flooded him and he stopped moving. 'Eh, lass,' he said softly. Unable to help himself, he took her hand in his, marvelling at how white and soft it was. Without thinking he raised it to his lips.

She made no attempt to pull away, just sat smiling slightly, remembering how it had felt when John touched her, wondering that this man should have the same effect.

Abruptly, with a wordless exclamation of annoyance at himself, he put her hand down and withdrew his own. 'Sorry!'

'It won't go away,' she said, her voice as soft as his had been.

He didn't pretend to misunderstand what 'it' was. 'It *can't* happen between us.'

'Why not?'

'You know very well why not! I haven't two pennies to rub together, let alone you're a lady and I'm a working man who doesn't even speak proper.'

She gave one of her quiet chuckles. 'That only means we must wait until you're established as an engineer and earning more money, not that we have to ignore our feelings. John would only have earned four pounds a week, you know, as a curate. I don't need to be rich to be happy.'

'But I can't even read properly! How can you think of a man like me in that way?'

'It happens like that between two people sometimes. And since I know you'd never speak out without encouragement, I make no bones about admitting my attraction to you.'

'Your sister would have me out of that front door in an instant if she knew.'

'Well, I shan't tell her anything yet—and there isn't really anything to tell, just the prospect of it. And anyway, she can't prevent me from seeing you. I'm twenty-four and in control of my own life.' She took hold of his hand again, loving the roughness and strength of it against her skin. 'Besides, I think Martha has an interest in someone too, only she won't let herself see it. I'm going to have a lot of difficulty in marrying my sister off, for she's convinced herself she's a born spinster.'

He tried to pull his hand away, but when she wouldn't let him, asked, 'Are you quite sure, Penelope lass?'

She liked the way he pronounced her name with that slow northern accent. 'Oh, yes. And you?'

'You know I am. Except I can't believe this is happening to me.'

'I have an advantage over you. It's happened to me before. You'd have liked John.' Her smiled wavered for a minute.

'He must have been a grand chap to win a lass like you—lady, I should say.'

'No, call me lass. I like it. No one else has ever called me that before. It's early days yet, Daniel, but let's give our feelings a chance to grow. And in the meantime, I'll help you improve yourself so that you can read easily and draw up proper sketches.' She smiled warmly at him. 'So if that's all that's stopping you…'

'Eh, I think you're the bravest lass I've ever met. The whole world would disagree with your choice of me.'

'Then they must disagree.' She looked up at the clock on the mantelpiece. 'It's time for you to go home now, though.' She took him to say goodbye to her sister, then walked with him to the front door. Only then did she whisper, 'I'm not pushing you too hard, am I, Daniel?'

'Nay, lass.' He raised his hand and brushed his fingertips lightly against her cheek, then left without a backward glance.

Penelope stood for a moment, still feeling his touch. Such a small thing, that light butterfly caress, yet it lingered on her skin. She had been very forward tonight while he had been trying to be sensible. Only she didn't want to be sensible. She knew how rare and precious was that rapport between two people, and how abruptly it could be terminated. Life was, at best, a very chancy thing. And Daniel wasn't dull or brutish, only uneducated. He was also kind and responsible and intelligent. His little sister adored him.

And she was falling in love with him—had already fallen, Penelope acknowledged to herself. How wonderful!

When she went back into the parlour, she kept her smile as serene as she could while she talked about the drawings she would be helping with. She didn't want Martha to realise how she felt about Daniel yet, didn't want to give anyone the opportunity to trample on their fragile shoots of happiness.

–

That same evening, Noll scowled at Gerry, who had come to tell him that Seaton and Wright were paying the Merridene sisters to teach their overlookers and Assistant Engineer to read and write better.

'Have they run mad to spoil their men like that?' he spluttered. 'Why do workers need to read and write? The best thing is to keep them ignorant.'

'You learned to read and write,' Gerry said mildly. 'So did I.'

'Aye, because my mind were set on mekkin' summat of mysen. But if everyone is reading the newspapers and such, they'll all want to better their lot and then who'll we get to work in our mills?'

'Ah, they're mostly women working there nowadays. They won't want to read the newspapers.'

But Noll wasn't to be appeased. 'Next thing we know, those buggers will be putting on classes for women as well.'

'Never. What would they do that for? Women will only go off and have babbies, then it'll all be wasted. Even Seaton's not that daft.' Gerry judged it prudent to change the subject. 'How's your Peter coming on, then? He's got his arm out of that sling, I see.'

'He's getten friendly with that Seaton lass, done summat right, for once. Meets her behind the church. We'll give him a few weeks to sweet talk her, then we'll act.'

Gerry rubbed the side of his nose thoughtfully. 'I still don't see how you'll get 'em wed.'

'Ben Seaton will be glad to get her wed to my Peter when I've finished with 'em. I'll snatch her and send the two of 'em away together for a few days. If we shut 'em up together day and night, whether he touches her or not, even her bloody brother will want her wed.'

Gerry could see that his employer expected praise for this, but he was shocked. He managed to say, 'You're a cunning old devil,' and was relieved when Noll took it as a compliment, but he was thoughtful as he walked home. It seemed unfair to little Georgie Seaton to treat her like that. He remembered her as a child and had seen her in the street since her return to Tapton. She looked very young to him, even if she was seventeen. He'd a daughter that age. Dilly was already expecting her first babby and right pulled down by it she was, too.

And what if Peter wouldn't take part in kidnapping the Seaton lass? The lad seemed decent enough at heart, more like his mother in nature than his father, and decent men didn't abduct innocent young women.

But he daren't tell Noll what to do. When his employer had set his mind on something, that was that, and if you had any sense, you said yes and did as he ordered. Well, you did if you wanted to keep your job, as Gerry did. He'd grown used to the comfortable life he could lead on an overlooker's wage, and had accepted that the price he had to pay for it was working for a man like Noll. But he sometimes regretted the things he had to do.

–

Penelope tidied her hair with hands that fumbled more than usual. For all her confident words, she was nervous about tonight's class. She'd only ever taught such groups with John beside her leading the proceedings. Now, she must lead them herself. Oh, Martha would be there—of course she would!—but her sister had no experience of this sort of teaching and little interest in it, either. What *she* cared about was children. Already the Wright girls were devoted to her and ran to do her bidding and she seemed to get on well with Georgie, too.

It suddenly occurred to Penelope that she'd be less nervous if she didn't have Martha watching what she was doing and she pulled a face at herself in the mirror. It wouldn't be seemly to be there on her own. 'Stop thinking about yourself and start thinking about them,' she scolded her reflection.

There was a knock on the door. 'Are you ready, Pen? Mr Wright is here to escort us to the mill. I thought Mr Porter was coming for us, but apparently Mr Wright wants to be there this first time.'

Penelope took a deep breath and opened the door.

They walked to the mill through a frosty evening, their feet making a crunching sound on the hard earth of the lane behind the church. Both ladies were carrying papers and books and had refused to give them to Mr Wright, since they were arranged in careful order, with loose markers for the pages they intended to use.

'I wanted to come myself tonight to show the men how important I think these classes are,' he said. 'And we haven't discussed payment for this extra work, either.'

'We can do that later.' Penelope's voice came out sounding a little breathless.

He looked at her. 'You're not nervous, are you? I can promise you the men will be very respectful.'

She hesitated then said in a rush, 'Yes I am nervous, just a little. I've never even met your workers and they're grown men, not children.'

'They're eager to learn, that's what counts, or they'd not be coming to the classes. They can all read a bit already, some quite well. It'd help if they could write neatly, too, and be able to do simple arithmetic.'

He ushered her through the small doorway in the larger mill gates and left the night watchman to lock it carefully behind them. Both he and Ben were still taking precautions against attack, though there had been no signs of that sort of trouble for weeks. The yard was lit by lanterns hanging on the wall and was still and silent, so different from the daytime bustle both sisters had noticed around each mill. He led them round to the rear of the big building, where a single-storey structure stood on its own.

'This was the original mill, built by Ben's grandfather.'

Martha stopped to stare back at the modern mill and then again at the original one. 'Goodness, it's so much smaller, more like a house!'

'That's progress for you.'

She could hear the satisfaction in his voice. She wasn't sure it was progress to shut children up inside a grim-looking building all day so that they never saw daylight in winter, but she knew he was an enlightened employer, who treated his hands well, and that most children needed to earn what they could to help feed themselves and their families.

'Right then, let's go inside.' He pushed the door open and gestured to them to lead the way. Faces turned and three rows of men stood up as soon as they saw who it was.

Taking a deep breath and trying to summon up a smile, Penelope led the way to the front of the room, where Ben Seaton was waiting for them. What helped her most was to see Daniel standing at the end of the front row, his bright hair shining in the lamplight and his smile holding true warmth and understanding, as if he at least understood how she was feeling tonight.

When they had been introduced to the men, she turned to Ben and said in an undertone, 'I think we'll do better without you and Mr Wright here.'

He nodded. 'Send someone for me if you need anything. I'll be working in the mill office, just round the corner.'

When the ladies were alone with their eleven pupils, Penelope said, 'I just want to say before I start how happy I am to be able to help you. I believe everyone should have the opportunity to learn to read and write.'

Eleven heads nodded approval of this statement.

Daniel added, 'We're grateful for your help, Miss Penelope.'

'Right, then, let's start.' She gestured to the pile of books. 'Tonight we'll just read and leave the writing for next time. I hope you won't feel insulted that these are children's books, but I need to know how well you can read. We have enough books for you to work in pairs, except for one group of three. Mr Seaton is going to buy some more books, but I didn't want to wait for that to start the classes. I'd like to listen to you reading one by one. Please don't be embarrassed if you're not very good. My sister and I will make sure you improve.'

To Martha's surprise some of the men immediately began to look apprehensive. They weren't as tall or strongly-built as she'd expected and a couple of them were distinctly undersized, like many of the ordinary folk in Tapton, but their faces shone pink with washing and their hands were also well scrubbed, even if their clothes bore the marks of their day's toil.

'I'll ask Mr Porter to read first,' Penelope went on, 'because I've met him before and know his name.' She glanced quickly in Daniel's direction and he gave her a quick nod and smile. 'As I don't know the rest of you, I'd be grateful if you'd each tell me your name before you start reading.'

Here among his fellows Daniel was more confident than in the alien territory of Fern Villa. He opened the book, a geography primer which the Wright girls used, and read slowly, stumbling over a couple of longer words and turning to her for help, so that she found herself standing beside him, looking down on that unruly amber hair.

When she asked him to stop, he nudged the fellow beside him. 'Your turn, lad.'

The man, balding and at least forty, swallowed hard, as if facing a huge ordeal. 'I'm Fred Cruckley, Miss Penelope, and I'm not near as good a reader as Daniel here.'

By the time they'd gone round the room, she had some idea of what she was facing. As John had done, she rearranged the men, making sure each pair was led by one of the better readers and explaining what she was doing as she asked them to change places.

'Now, if you'll read on at your own pace, helping one another, my sister and I will come round and listen. It's practice that does it with reading, you see, and someone to help you with the harder words. If you need help from us, just raise your hand.'

The men settled at once to reading, clearly not wanting to waste a second of these precious two hours, spelling out the words earnestly, some with a work-roughened finger travelling beneath each line. The two women moved round the room, quietly explaining or correcting the harder words.

Everyone was surprised when the door opened and Ben came back. 'Time to stop, lads.'

'Nay, it's not two hours gone already, is it?' one exclaimed.

'It feels like nobbut a few minutes,' said another.

Before they filed out, each man came and thanked the ladies.

'Soon I shan't be shamed by my childer reading better nor me,' one said with a twinkle. 'They're getting on that well at Sunday school, I'm downright ashamed of mesen.'

When only Daniel and one other man were left, they began moving the tables and chairs swiftly into another arrangement. 'This place is used for the charge hands and engineers to eat their midday meals, miss,' Daniel explained when he saw Martha watching them.

Penelope went over to the pile of books and papers on the table she had used. 'I've brought you one of our old newspapers to read, Daniel. There's an article in it on the spread of railways and the opportunities this has brought to ordinary people to see something outside their own parish. I think you might find it interesting.'

'I'll do my best to read it then.'

'And if you'll come round to our house tomorrow evening, we'll work on those plans again.'

Ben came up as she spoke. 'What plans?'

'For the modifications to your machinery. I'm helping Daniel draw up the plans.'

'We're working you too hard, I think.'

She laughed. 'Not at all. I'm enjoying myself.'

Ben moved on to speak to Martha and Penelope turned back to Daniel. As their glances caught, both stopped speaking to stare at one another.

Daniel took a deep breath. 'I lay awake racking my brains last night and I couldn't see what future we'd have together. It'd not be *fair* to you, so we shouldn't even think of it.' His voice grew suddenly harsh. 'You deserve a gentleman, not a common chap like me.'

She smiled serenely. 'If this—*feeling* keeps happening between us, then we'll have difficulty ignoring one another, shan't we? Anyway, I don't want to ignore you and I refuse to even try.'

'Are you allus this stubborn?'

'Yes.'

He muttered something under his breath, snatched the newspaper from her and stalked out of the room.

When he'd gone, Penelope stood lost in thought, completely unaware of the other two.

Ben looked at Martha. 'Am I imagining it or is there something going on between those two?'

'If you're imagining it, I am too.' She had seen the glances pass between them tonight and couldn't dismiss her suspicions.

'Shall I have a word with him, tell him to stay away from your sister?'

'That's more likely to drive Penelope into spending time with him. She can be very stubborn.'

'But she's a lady... and he's only...' He shook his head. 'Mind you, he's a clever fellow and I think he'll go far, given the chance. He has a feel for machinery that even Ross doesn't. But still, I feel responsible.'

Martha could see that Penelope was lost in thought. 'Don't try to interfere. She's a grown woman and has always made her own choices. Father didn't approve of her previous fiancé, you know, but she insisted it was John or no one, and in the end Father had to give in. She looks gentle and easy-going but she's one of the most stubborn people I've ever met once her mind is fixed on something.'

He looked down at her with a slight frown. 'I'd have thought you'd be the stubborn one.'

'Because she's prettier? Even the most beautiful roses can have thorns, Mr Seaton.'

The words were out before he could stop himself. 'I don't think she's prettier than you.'

Martha stared at him in shock and colour flooded her face.

Ben was upset to have embarrassed her. Yet he did think her the more attractive of the two sisters, especially now that he'd seen her with her hair loose. He'd remembered that moment several times and the strong desire he'd experienced to run his fingers through that shining mass. Which was stupid, really. He wasn't in the market for a wife, any more than she was looking for a husband. She wore the plainest gowns, pinned her hair up to hide its beauty and made no attempt to flatter him, as other young women had done. Yet, somehow, she eclipsed them all in his eyes.

When her sister didn't move, Martha went across to her, glad of an excuse to leave her present companion, who was still studying her in that disturbing way. 'Surely you're ready, Pen? Mr Seaton is waiting to escort us home.'

'What? Oh, sorry. I was just thinking about something.'

None of them said much on their way back across town.

When the two sisters got inside the house Martha said firmly, 'We need to talk, you and I.'

Penelope sighed but went with her into the parlour. 'About what?'

'You and Mr Porter.'

'Oh. Is it so obvious? I didn't think you'd notice.'

'Well, not only did *I* notice how friendly you were with him but so did Mr Seaton.'

'That's all there is at the moment, Martha dear, just friendliness and the possibility of something more. Daniel is very adamant that it isn't possible, but I don't happen to agree.' She looked at her sister. 'It was the same with John. I knew at once that I was attracted to him.'

'But John was a gentleman and Mr Porter is a poor man! He's not even properly educated!'

'At the moment. But he has excellent prospects, Mr Seaton tells me. This town and the rest of Lancashire are full of self-made men living in comfortable circumstances after a poor start. Why should Daniel not be another? And why should I not help him?'

Martha couldn't find an answer to this. 'You won't— do anything rash, will you?'

'No, of course not. We can't. He has no money and I'm not a fool. Now, I want to go to bed. I'm tired and those children are full of energy.' And Daniel was coming round again the next evening. She wanted to look her best for him.

'I worry that you're taking on too much.'

Penelope shook her head. 'I'm doing what I was meant to do, helping my fellow human beings. It makes me feel alive again.'

Martha watched her go, thinking how happy her sister looked, then went to sit beside the fire for a few minutes longer and try to work out what to do about Daniel Porter. But she kept thinking about Ben Seaton instead, so in the end gave up trying to make any plans and went to bed.

Chapter 11

'I heard tell as how Porter has some ideas for improving the machinery and cutting down the fluff,' Gerry said as he joined his master for their usual evening chat once the operatives had gone home.

'I heard the same thing.'

Gerry often marvelled at the way Noll picked up information about things that were going on. 'They say that schoolteacher, the younger one, is helping him with the drawings for the new parts.'

'Is she, now? I hadn't heard *that*!'

Gerry hid his satisfaction at knowing more than Noll. 'He goes round to their house at night after work.'

'You'd think a lady would know better than to entertain a chap like that. She'll be causing talk about the two of them.'

They both laughed heartily at the mere idea of a lady dealing with Porter in that sense.

'She'll be doing it to please Seaton,' Gerry said comfortably. 'Maybe she's setting her cap at him.'

After a short pause, Noll said thoughtfully, 'I'd pay a bit to see those sketches. Maybe I'll send for Jack and ask him to find me a burglar.'

Gerry scowled. Croaky Jack had caused altogether too much trouble last time he was in town and Gerry didn't trust him an inch. Those riots did no one any good, just slowed down the production of thread, and then Noll got angry with him as if it was his fault. In fact, Noll got angry quite often these days. He'd always been sharp, but now you had to watch your step all the time. 'Is that a good idea?'

'Do *you* know someone as'll break into their house?'

'I daresay I could find someone, if you insist, but I reckon it's best to leave them ladies alone. They've got Seaton and Wright on their side and we could stir up a lot of trouble for nothing. Besides, that Farrell you've hired as engineer won't know how to do owt about it, even if we do get the diagrams. He's not near as good as Daniel Porter with machinery.' He saw Noll drumming his fingers on the desk, a sign of a rising temper, and shut up.

'Why did Porter not come to me with them fancy ideas when he was working here?'

Gerry didn't attempt to reply to that, because he knew how Noll would have greeted any ideas that cost money and didn't increase production.

And since the guards had been removed from some of the machines by James, they'd had a couple of accidents. Minor ones, luckily, but Gerry prayed nothing worse would happen. Them childer got tired after a hard day's work and grew careless. He was wondering whether to tell the overseers to strap them, to keep them safe, but some of them looked as if a breath of wind would knock them over and he didn't like to make their lives even harder. He realised Noll was speaking again and banished his worries to listen.

'See if you can come up with someone to break in an' get them plans, lad. We'll keep Jack for that other little plan of mine.'

Two nights later, a man climbed the back wall of the Merridenes' house once all the lights had been out for a while. He kept careful watch over the lantern he was carrying, its front panel closed across the horn pane that allowed light out at one side only to guide one's footsteps in the dark. If the flame went out, he'd not be able to find his way around inside the house.

Pausing to open the panel on his lantern, he pulled out a piece of paper spread with treacle, unfolded it carefully and stuck it over the scullery window. After licking the mess off his fingers, he broke the pane with one quick, expert tap, making hardly any sound because the broken glass mainly stuck to the treacle. When he'd pulled away enough pieces of glass to make a hole big enough for his hand, he reached in to unscrew the latch and then slid the lower window frame up on its sash, grinning at how easy this was proving.

Using the lantern to scan the interior, he moved forward cautiously, letting the light play ahead of him. It was a rum thing when someone paid you to break into a house and all for some papers with drawings on them. They'd told him which room to look in and said to find big pieces of paper with sketches of machinery on them. He might not be able to read but he reckoned he'd recognise a drawing of machinery when he saw one.

And if he saw owt else worth taking, he'd lift that, too. No use wasting this night's work on some damned bits of paper.

Penelope couldn't understand what had woken her. She listened but the night was quiet. Then, just as she was settling to sleep again, she heard a noise and opened her eyes. She hadn't been mistaken the first time! A window was rattling downstairs and this didn't usually happen because the window frames in this house were well made and none of them were loose. What's more, Sally usually locked them all before she went to bed, because she reckoned in a town you were more at risk than in the country.

Perhaps Sally had forgotten a window tonight? Penelope slipped across the room to open the door and listen. Nothing. She was about to shut the door again when she heard the rattling from downstairs. Definitely a window and it was going to keep her awake if she didn't do something about it.

As she was going down the last few stairs she noticed a faint light coming from beneath the schoolroom door and froze. They definitely hadn't left any lamps burning in there. She listened intently and heard someone moving about. Someone must have broken into the house. Anger surged through her at the thought of that person stealing their things and she had an urge to run in and stop him, but held her temper back. She had to be sensible about this. It'd be better to go and fetch the others before confronting the burglar. Three women could surely deal with one man, however strong, or at least chase him away.

But even as she was turning to creep back up the stairs, the schoolroom door opened and the intruder moved down the hall towards her, shining a shuttered lantern ahead of him.

She shrank back against the wall, but as he played the light to and fro, he caught her skirt in its beam and raised it to reveal her face. At once she began to scream for help and heard a thud from upstairs and her sister's voice calling her name.

He muttered what sounded like a curse and turned to leave, but she could see that he was clutching something to his chest. She couldn't bear him to take their things, so launched herself after him, trusting that Martha would soon be joining her. She caught him at the open window and for a moment grappled with him, but he was stronger than she'd expected and threw her off. As she fell she hung on to his coat for dear life, regardless of her own safety. She wasn't going to let him take their things.

Then the world exploded in pain and darkness swallowed her up.

–

Penelope woke to find her head thumping. She opened her eyes cautiously and discovered she was lying on the sofa in the parlour, with Martha beside her and several other people in the room. The light hurt her eyes, so she closed them again.

'Don't try to do anything, Pen.'

It was Martha's voice, calm and reassuring.

With her eyes still closed, she asked, 'Did the burglar get away?'

'Yes.'

'What did he take?'

'Nothing.'

'Don't believe you.'

Martha patted her hand. 'Shh. You're supposed to be resting. Stop worrying.'

'Where's that doctor? He should be here by now,' a male voice said.

Penelope risked another glance and saw their neighbour, a robust man of about fifty, standing nearby, wearing an overcoat, but with bare ankles showing beneath it and feet thrust into house slippers.

There was the sound of the front door opening and someone came hurrying into the room. 'What happened?'

Several people tried to tell him at once.

Ben Seaton, Penelope thought gratefully. Now they'd be all right. He'd help Martha sort things out. She closed her eyes and let herself drift. So much easier than trying to work out what to say or do.

Ben ignored the neighbours and moved across to Martha. 'I gather you had an intruder.'

'Yes. A man broke in through the kitchen window. Penelope must have heard him and gone downstairs. She was unconscious when we found her and had received a nasty blow to the head. A few minutes ago she opened her eyes and spoke to me, made sense, so I think she'll be all right.' She lowered her voice to a near whisper. 'Can you please get our neighbours to go home? There's nothing they can do now.'

He nodded and turned to face the group of men and women. 'You can leave this to me now.'

'What if the intruder is still around?' one woman asked fearfully.

'He'll not be that stupid. He'll be miles away by now.'

The man standing next to her put his arm round the woman's shoulders. 'We'd better go back home, dear, or we'll get no sleep this night.'

'How did the neighbours know what had happened?' Ben asked once they'd left.

Sally replied. 'It's my fault, Mr Seaton. I was that overset to see Miss Penelope lying there I just opened the front door and screamed for help.'

He could see she was still upset and decided it might be best to keep her occupied. 'Perhaps you and Meg could go and make us all a cup of tea?'

'You won't leave?' Sally asked. 'Not till it's all secure again, at least?'

He moved across to take her hand and pat it. 'No. I'll stay here till morning, Mrs Polby, then we'll get that window mended for you.'

'Thank you, sir.' With little sign of her usual crispness, she turned to Meg. 'Come on, child, I'm going to need your help.'

He turned back to see that Penelope still had her eyes closed and Martha was standing looking down at her. He saw a tear roll down her cheek and without thinking, walked across the room and put his arm round her shoulders. With a sigh she leaned against him. 'It's all right now,' he said quietly.

'If I can only be sure Pen's all right.'

He tried to distract her. 'Is that what you call her—Pen?'

'Mmm. It was all she could say when she was a tiny child and it sort of stuck, just in the family, you know.'

She was so close he could have kissed her. He saw her hand shaking as she tried to brush her hair out of her eyes and spoke without thinking. 'Leave it.'

She looked up at him in puzzlement. 'Leave what?'

'Your hair. Leave it hanging loose. It's beautiful.' The look in her eyes changed to shock and he realised he shouldn't have said that. He was always speaking out of turn with her and couldn't understand why he kept doing it. 'I beg your pardon, only it *is* beautiful. I thought so when you confronted the mob.'

'You're always catching me at a disadvantage, Mr Seaton.'

'I like to think I've managed to help you once or twice.'

She knew she should move away from him, but couldn't. 'You have helped. I don't know what we'd have done without you.'

'Or I without you. Look what a difference you've made to Georgie.' Then there was a knock on the front door and he had enough sense to pull away from her, though it was the last thing he wanted to do. 'I'll answer that.'

By the time he got back, crisp Miss Martha the schoolmistress had returned and the unruly hair had been tied back with a crumpled piece of ribbon. Ben left the doctor and Martha to attend to Penelope and went into the kitchen, where he accepted a cup of piping hot tea, which he was very glad of, and one of Sally's scones, which he could have done without, only it seemed to help the elderly maid to have someone to fuss over and feed.

'I shan't be able to sleep at night from now on, for fear of another intruder,' she said, sinking down on a chair opposite him.

'You will, because I'll have bars fitted to your rear windows and make sure the watch keeps a better eye on this house.'

She sniffed. 'That's as may be, but if someone wants to get in, they will.'

'Do you know what was taken?'

'Nothing. But he dropped these.' She picked up some crumpled pieces of paper from the dresser top and handed them to him. 'What did a burglar want with Miss Penelope's drawings?'

Ben spread them out, feeling equally bewildered. He soon concluded that no one but another mill owner would be interested in drawings of improvements to machinery. And since there were only three mill owners in the small town and he trusted Jonas Wright absolutely, that left Brindley. *Again!* The man had caused nothing but trouble in the past two years and something needed to be done about him. But without proof, what?

He kept his thoughts to himself and when he heard the parlour door open, went out to ask the doctor how Penelope was.

'She'll be all right. It was a nasty blow, though, so keep her quiet for a few days.' The doctor looked over his shoulder, then asked in an undertone, 'What's the world coming to when a scoundrel breaks into a lady's house? We'll have to look into the watch we're keeping on our town.'

Ben, who like him was a member of the Watch Committee, nodded. 'I mean to increase the number of watchmen and I'll pay for it myself, if I have to.'

'Oh, I think this will make everyone on the committee agree to spend a little more. We have to protect our homes and families, after all.'

Ben escorted the doctor to the front gate, then went back inside and tapped on the parlour door.

Martha opened it, trying to look as dignified as possible, but not feeling it when wearing her dressing gown in front of a man who wasn't even a relative.

'How is your sister now?'

'She's gone back to sleep again.' Her crisp tone became a little gentler as she admitted, 'I don't know whether to get her to bed or leave her where she is.'

'If you'd like to warm her bed, I'll carry her up for you.'

She blinked up at him. 'Can you do that? She's not a small woman.'

'Oh, I'm sure I can manage.'

'Well, maybe that would be best.'

'And afterwards, if you can let me have a blanket and pillow, I'll sleep on the sofa in here until it's light, when I can send some of my men to make the house safer. I feel responsible for this.'

He was standing too close again, she decided, edging back a little. 'It's not—um, not your fault.'

'I brought you and your sister to Tapton, I own this house and I employ you, so it *is* my responsibility. I intend to make very certain that you're not troubled again.'

She nodded. 'I'll go and see Sally, then when we're ready, you can carry Penelope upstairs. And Mr Seaton—'

'Yes?'

'—thank you. For all your help and support tonight. I wasn't myself, I'm afraid. I don't usually fling myself into men's arms.' She could feel her cheeks going warm at the memory.

'You didn't fling yourself and everyone needs comforting from time to time.'

But even after they'd got Pen to bed and Martha had slipped in beside her, just to be there in case her sister needed help, she couldn't banish the memory of how it had felt to be held in Ben Seaton's arms. He was a very strong man, the only one who had ever made her feel helpless and small. It was such a strange feeling. That must be why she felt rather—disturbed when he was close by.

And he'd said again that her hair was beautiful. Perhaps Penelope was right and she should start taking more care how she arranged it. No, what was she thinking of? She was a teacher, a spinster, past the age for trying to attract a gentleman. She wasn't going to make a fool of herself trying to look... to look like...

Her thoughts faltered to a halt and lying alone in the darkness, she blushed hotly. *Attract!* She wasn't trying to attract Ben Seaton. Certainly not. That would be ridiculous at her age.

Wouldn't it?

–

Ben went home once the workers started making their way towards the mills, mingling with his people as he strode along the street and accepting their cheerful greetings. One or two stared at his odd assortment of clothing, for he'd not had time to go home and tidy himself up before the mill opened.

When he saw Daniel Porter ahead of him, he quickened his pace and tapped him on the shoulder.

'Can you come to my office?'

'Aye.' Once inside, Ben shouted at the office lad to fetch him a cup of tea and be smart about it, then gestured to a seat. 'Have you heard about what happened to Penelope Merridene?'

Daniel sat bolt upright. 'Happened to her?'

'A burglar broke into their house last night and knocked her unconscious.'

'She's all right?'

'Yes.'

'What was he after?'

'Your drawings, it seems.'

Daniel gaped at him. 'My drawings? Why would anyone want to steal those?'

'I can think of only one reason and one person.'

It took only a second, then, 'Brindley.'

'I'd guess so. Did you ever make any modifications to his machinery?'

Daniel let out a scornful snort. 'It was all I could do to keep them old things running. It was cobble things together, not improve them.'

Ben frowned and tapped the desk with his forefinger. 'It's not like Brindley to show his hand.'

'Those who've worked there for a while tell me he's getting chancier to deal with and you never did know where his temper would lead him, so I don't envy them. If it wasn't for Gerry Cox, I reckon there'd have been some damned stupid things done at that mill.'

'I thought Cox was as bad as his master.'

Daniel frowned, thought for a moment, then shook his head. 'No. I can only speak as I find, but although he's a hard man and does as his master wants, it sometimes seemed to me that Cox didn't like what he was doing and tried to soften his orders, especially where the children were concerned. He'd deny that, of course.' Another pause, then Daniel added, 'They're also saying Brindley's been looking old and tired lately, though that doesn't stop him trying to take every farthing he can away from his operatives. They fine you for breathing too loudly in that place. It's a shame to treat decent folk like that.'

'I agree.'

'Are you going to do anything about Brindley and this break-in, Mr Seaton?'

'Not yet.' He saw anger still glowing in Porter's eyes and added quickly, 'Nor are you. We need to obtain proof that he's behind all these troubles or we'll get nowhere. I want your word that you'll say nothing, do nothing.'

'As long as he doesn't hurt her again.'

Definitely fond of her, Ben thought as he watched Daniel leave. But Martha had asked him not to interfere.

The thought of Martha leaning against him for comfort last night popped unbidden into his mind and he smiled involuntarily. She was a cosy armful—whether she meant to be or not!

—

Two days later Georgie tripped along towards school, all agog to see poor Miss Penelope, who was to resume giving lessons today. The whole town was still buzzing with wild conjectures about the burglary.

She didn't expect to see Peter Brindley so early in the morning, but there he was, clearly waiting for her, something which gave her a great deal of pleasure. She might not be seventeen yet and might be treated as a child by her brother, but this man recognised that she was a woman grown in every way that mattered.

'Miss Seaton.' He tipped his hat.

'Mr Brindley,' she replied demurely, but couldn't hold back a smile.

'I woke feeling restless,' he said, 'so I thought I'd start my day with a sight of you to cheer me up.'

'Dear me, sir, I can't think how I cheer you up.'

'In many ways. I like to chat to you. You and I have so many things in common.' He smiled at her, surprised to find that he'd spoken the absolute truth. She *was* the only person in Tapton whom he wished to see, and when he didn't see her for a few precious minutes of conversation, he felt as if something was wrong with the day.

'Georgie Seaton, what do you think you're doing?' a voice roared from the end of the narrow street.

She spun round to see her brother striding towards them. 'Oh, drat!'

Peter stood his ground but when Seaton came up to them, he swallowed and wished he were anywhere else. Apart from being a very large man, this was a furiously angry one.

'Get off to school at once,' Ben snapped to his sister.

She scowled at him and turned to Peter. 'Goodbye, sir. I apologise for my brother's rudeness.'

'I'll speak to you tonight,' Ben snapped, then as Peter turned away, he moved swiftly to stand in front of the fellow. 'A word, if you please, Brindley.'

'Certainly.'

'I'll thank you not to accost my sister in future.'

'Accost!' Peter stared at him. 'I wasn't *accosting* her, merely exchanging a few words of greeting as I would with any acquaintance.'

'Acquaintance, is it?' Ben's voice was a low rumble, like a volcano about to erupt. 'How did *you* become acquainted with *my* sister?'

'At the school, of course, when I was calling on the Misses Merridene to thank them for helping me. In fact, you saw me there yourself. It isn't my habit to walk past a lady of my acquaintance without a word or two of greeting.'

'Then make it your habit where my sister is concerned!'

'I cannot possibly promise to be so impolite.' Peter walked away slowly, half expecting the other man to come after him, but there was no sound of footsteps, so he could only assume that Seaton was standing watching him. He didn't turn round at the corner to find out if this was so, but continued on towards the square at his usual walking pace.

But several times that day he remembered the sight of Seaton in a rage and shuddered. What would happen if his father carried out the plan he had broached only the day before? It'd be Peter that Seaton came searching for, not his father.

And anyway, he didn't want to be involved in kidnapping Georgie and ruining her reputation, he definitely didn't—only his father had made it plain that he'd throw him out unless he played his part.

How was he to find a way out of this dilemma?

–

Once Brindley was out of sight, Ben made his way to the school and hammered on the front door, still in a towering rage.

Sally opened it, starting to smile when she saw who it was until she realised how angry he was.

'I wish to see Miss Merridene,' he snapped. 'At once, if you please.'

'She's teaching, sir.'

'Then bring her out of the schoolroom. It's urgent.' He walked into the front parlour without an invitation, too upset to sit down.

When he heard her come in, he swung round.

Sally had warned her that he was annoyed about something, but Martha hadn't realised how angry. 'How may I help you, Mr Seaton?' she asked in her coolest tone.

'I just came across my sister having a tryst with Peter Brindley on the way to school.'

'A tryst?'

'What else would you call it? They'd met behind the church and were having a cosy gossip together. So I'd be grateful if you'd take particular care not to let her out of your sight while she's here.'

His tone was so sharp she began to feel a little angry herself. 'We try to take care of all our pupils, Mr Seaton, but it's not possible to keep watch on one who hasn't yet arrived at school.'

'Well, from now on you're not to let Georgie go home alone. I'll send someone to escort her back and she's to wait here until that person arrives. And she's not to go out alone during the day, either, as you've allowed her to do before.'

Martha raised her eyebrows. 'The only time she went out alone was to fetch a dress when *you* had asked us to do something about her clothing. As your house is only two streets away, I could see no harm in that.'

'Let me make it very plain that she's not to so much as poke her nose out of the door without someone watching. I'm *not* having her associating with young Brindley. I give you good day, Miss Merridene.'

She watched him swing round and fairly stamp out of the house. She could understand his anger with his sister, though meeting Peter Brindley in the street could hardly be counted as a tryst, but she was upset at the tone he had taken with her. She hadn't deserved that.

When informed that she was not to leave school that afternoon until someone came to escort her home, Georgie flew into a tantrum and spoke her mind on brothers who interfered with their sisters' lives and treated them like criminals if they so much as stopped to chat to an acquaintance.

Martha pulled her up short at the way she was speaking and Georgie burst into tears, so overwrought she couldn't stop crying for quite some time.

Penelope peeped into the parlour, but Martha gestured to her to leave, looking meaningfully at their pupil to indicate the delicacy of the situation.

When the tears had more or less stopped, Martha went to sit beside Georgie on the sofa. 'Here.' She offered a handkerchief to replace the sodden mass the girl was wielding.

'Thank you.'

'This isn't the end of the world, you know. When you're a little older, you'll be able to make all sorts of new friends and—'

'In Tapton? Who, pray? There *is* no one of my own age in this horrible town, no one Ben would approve of for a friend, that is. The county gentry consider folk like us beneath their touch. The doctor's children are grown up. The parson isn't married. And my mother doesn't want me to live with her. I'm doomed to be a friendless spinster for the rest of my days, with my brother acting as gaoler.'

In spite of the gothic language and tone, Martha felt sorry for the girl, but couldn't think of anything she could do to help. 'What actually happened this morning?'

'On my way to school I met Peter Brindley and we stood talking for a few minutes. That's all.'

'Have you met him before?'

The words were hesitant. 'Once or twice.'

'By arrangement?'

'No, never!'

There was no mistaking the sincerity in her voice.

'It's not so bad, then.'

'You'd think I'd committed murder to hear Ben talk. My brother has no polite conversation, none whatsoever. He doesn't read poetry or novels, or care about the theatre. He doesn't even *talk* to me in the evenings, let alone take me out anywhere. Mama used to let me go with her to the theatre until she met Ambrose, you know, and I loved it. Or we'd go shopping, or to visit her friends, some of whom had daughters of my age.'

Martha knew it was wrong, but she couldn't help herself. She gave Georgie a big hug, and although the girl was stiff and unyielding at first, she suddenly hugged her teacher back and then wept again on her shoulder. But for all her sympathy, Martha could think of no way to lighten the girl's loneliness when she wasn't at school.

That evening, she said thoughtfully to her sister, 'I'm going to speak to Ben Seaton about Georgie.'

'What has she done now?'

'Done? She's done nothing. Why does everyone always think the worst of her?' She saw Penelope's look of shock at her sharp tone and took a deep breath before saying, 'Sorry. Didn't mean to snap your head off. I'm just worried about her, that's all. She's a very lonely girl with no friends of her own age in the town and *we* are hardly able to be her friends, are we? I think Ben needs to find a way to give her a more interesting life. And if I ever meet that mother of hers, I'll be very tempted to tell her what I think of a woman who abandons a girl of that age.'

'She's hardly abandoned her. Ben Seaton *is* her guardian and brother, after all.'

'It's as good as abandoning her. What does an unmarried man know about a girl of that age and her needs? And look at what happened today. When she stops to speak to a young man in a public place—and she assures me she didn't arrange to meet him—Ben thunders and roars at her as if she's committed a crime. It's not good enough.'

Penelope was surprised at this outburst, but held her tongue.

–

That evening Daniel once again came round after work and Martha tried to talk her sister out of over-exerting herself. It was a waste of words. Penelope had recovered quickly from the blow to the head and had fretted at being kept in bed even for a few hours. She always had hated playing the invalid and was far stronger than she looked.

Daniel came into the parlour to greet Martha, then followed Penelope to the schoolroom. She spread out the crumpled sheets of drawings and they discussed various details, then she showed him some techniques for getting a good perspective and accuracy in detail, inviting him to try for himself.

'I still can't understand why a burglar would want to take these,' she said a little later, as they both worked on their drawings.

He hesitated.

She looked at him sideways. 'You know something, don't you?'

'I can guess. I don't know whether Mr Seaton would want you to be involved, though.' Her smile was his undoing. 'It's probably Brindley, seeing if he can gain some advantage from what I'm doing for Mr Seaton.'

She sat there, brow wrinkled in thought, then nodded slowly. 'I can believe that. He's a horrible man.'

'Worse than you know. It's like working for the devil being in his mill.'

'Tell me.'

He shook his head. 'You don't need to know the details.'

'Because I'm a lady? I sometimes wish I weren't.' Her tone became mocking. 'I'm supposed to behave this way and not that, wear this sort of dress, not that, walk sedately, never be alone with a man... The list is endless, Daniel.'

'Eh, lass, I didn't know it fretted you. Is that why—?' He broke off and bent over his work again.

'Is that why I'm interested in you? Out of rebellion? No, Daniel. I like you because of who you are and who you could be, given even half a chance. And I hope you like me for the same reasons, not because I'm a *lady*.'

He looked up and forgot to be sensible. 'Oh, I do. For me, it happened that first day I rescued you. I should be more sensible, though, and stay away from you. Seaton won't like it, I'm sure.'

Her eyes flashed. 'Just let him dare interfere in *my* life!'

Their glances caught, held and for a moment or two it was enough for them simply to be together. Then Penelope gave him a quick smile, before bending her head over the drawings again.

His smile was particularly warm and then he followed suit.

Chapter 12

A few days later at lunch time, Hepzibah banged a plate down in front of Ben so hard that he looked up in surprise.

'What's wrong?'

'That sister of yours is what's wrong.'

'What's Georgie done now?'

'She hasn't done anything, but she's moping—and she's not eating like a lass that age should. You're fair keeping her a prisoner, Mr Ben. It's not right.'

'I know she's unhappy and I don't like to keep her so confined, but what else am I to do? I'll not have her associating with Brindley and he seems to be seeking her out.'

'He's not like his father, Mr Peter isn't. Weak, perhaps, but not evil, that young man. You'd no need to stop him speaking to Georgie. Girls that age need admirers, even when nothing's going to come of it.'

Ben was astonished. Hepzibah didn't usually criticise her employer.

'You need to do something about her, Mr Ben, something different from locking her up.'

'Everyone keeps telling me that, but no one tells me *what* to do.'

She looked at him indulgently, as if she were an adult and he a particularly stupid child. 'Find yourself a wife, of course. If Georgie had a woman to talk to and people visiting the house regularly, she'd cheer up in a minute.'

He gaped at her, then snapped, 'I'm not interested in finding myself a wife, as you well know.'

'Well, you should be. Let alone that sister of yours needs a mother, *you* need a proper family. What sort of life is it you lead, sitting on your own at night and working till all hours?'

'Hepzibah, please.'

'I must speak out when I see things that need mending and could be mended quite easily, for your mother's sake and for the love I bear you, lad. Who else is there to tell you, now?'

His voice was gentler when he answered. 'Even if I agreed with you, where would I find a wife?'

She smiled at him, a knowing smile. 'You've found one already, if only you'll admit it to yourself. That school-teacher, the older one. I've seen you looking at her—and her looking at you. She'd suit you down to the ground, that one would. No nonsense about her, yet she's bonny enough to tempt a man.'

Shock made it difficult for him to answer her. Were his reactions to Martha so obvious? 'While I respect Miss Merridene greatly, yes, and like her too, I'm not intending to court her, Hepzibah, because I'm *not* looking for a wife.'

'Well, you should be. But I've spoken my piece now so I'll hold my tongue.' She picked up the tray and stalked out of the room, radiating disapproval.

He shook out his newspaper and tried to take what she had said with a pinch of humour, but somehow he couldn't. Find himself a wife indeed!

But the thought of what his housekeeper had said came back to him again and again, and his employees found him very absent-minded that day, as did his sister during the evening.

He lay awake for a long time in his comfortable bed, unable to sleep, thoughts twisting round and round in his brain. Find a wife indeed! And fancy Hepzibah suggesting Martha Merridene? Why, if ever he'd seen a confirmed spinster, it was she.

But even as he turned over and punched his pillow, which seemed unaccountably hard tonight, he remembered how pretty Martha had looked with her hair loose, or how her face glowed with happiness when she was playing with the Wright children. He'd seen the small group several times, because they often walked past his mill to get out of town and up to the freedom of the moors.

Martha was good with Georgie, too, but that was no reason to consider marrying her. He'd vowed when Amanda jilted him that he'd never give himself into a woman's power again, and he'd meant it.

Besides, you didn't marry to get a keeper for your sister. You married because you wanted the woman.

Hepzibah was wrong. Definitely wrong. He liked Martha, but that was all. And he liked her sister, too. Both ladies were hard workers and you had to admire that.

But he dreamed of Martha that night, a wonderful happy dream in which they were married. It wasn't the first time she'd entered his dreams, but it was the first time she'd figured there as his wife.

And it was a long time since he'd felt so happy in his personal life.

–

A few streets away Noll ate his last bite of cake and looked at his son over the dinner table. 'You've been in a miserable mood today. What's up?'

Peter glanced quickly sideways, trying to estimate his father's mood. 'You may as well know. Seaton caught me talking to Georgie this morning behind the church and has forbidden me to speak to her again. He's having her escorted to and from school by that old maid of theirs from now on, so I'm afraid I've lost my opportunity to win her trust.'

'Hmm. Well, we'd better think what to do next, then. It's about time we made a move any road. I'm sick of hanging about, letting Seaton get ahead. It'll be good to take him down a peg or two. How's that arm?'

'Better. Just aches a little at times.'

'Good, because it's about time we made our move.'

'I really don't want to kidnap Georgie.'

'Don't want! *Don't want!* You'll do as I damned well tell you.'

'But I—'

'Not another word! I want this settled.'

Peter shook his head, but said nothing more. However, he had no intention of treating Georgie like that and if he found out any details of his father's plot, he'd warn her. He pushed the rest of his breakfast around the plate, but couldn't eat it. What was he to do with himself today? And tomorrow? And all the weary days that stretched ahead of him?

He couldn't go on like this. But every time he tried to make plans to leave, it came back to the same thing: he hadn't a penny of his own, had no way of earning any money and his father refused to give him even the smallest allowance.

The following morning when Georgie arrived at school, Martha gave Hepzibah, who had accompanied her, a note for her master.

Georgie watched this in apprehension and as soon as the housekeeper had left, blurted out, 'What have I done now?'

'Nothing at all, dear. I just want to speak to your brother about something, that's all.'

Which left the girl wondering and worrying all day.

That evening after their meal Martha sat in the parlour, waiting for her visitor. She asked Penelope to stay with her because she wanted no more of those embarrassing moments when the world seemed to stop moving around her and Ben Seaton. She hadn't even confided in her sister about these incidents, because she found them so disconcerting.

Just before eight o'clock there was a knock on the front door and Sally appeared to say that Mr Porter had arrived.

Penelope stood up. 'Would you mind if I just took him through to the schoolroom and settled him down, Martha dear? I'll be back in a few minutes.'

'Don't be too long. It wouldn't look right for me to receive Mr Seaton on my own.'

Penelope smiled as she led Daniel along the corridor and when they got into the schoolroom, she shut the door and went to put some more coal on the fire. 'I'm not going back to join them,' she announced.

He looked at her in puzzlement.

'Martha's expecting Mr Seaton and I think she's attracted to him—and he to her. Who knows what will happen if they're left on their own together?'

He grinned. 'I think if you make up your mind to it, you'll have them getting wed whether they want to or not.'

She shook her head very decidedly. 'No, I won't. If there isn't that spark of affection between two people, it's wrong to marry, I'm quite sure of that.'

'And if the spark flies between the wrong people?' he asked.

'It's up to them to decide what's right and wrong.'

He let out a growl of exasperation. 'Every time I come here, I'm resolved to tell you it can't work between us, for your sake.'

She moved across to lay her hand on his arm. 'If you're not attracted to me, Daniel, you have only to say so and I'll leave you alone.'

And heaven help him, he couldn't resist pulling her towards him and kissing her soundly, which seemed a better answer to her question than mere words could ever be.

When he drew away from her, she linked her arms round his neck and pulled him closer again, savouring the feel of his skin, his lips, his lean body against hers. Neither heard the front door knocker when it sounded.

'You're a witch,' he said hoarsely when the kiss ended.

'Ah, Daniel, for once let's meet without agonising over this,' she murmured, leaning her head against his shoulder.

They stood like that for quite a while before settling to work on the drawings, which were nearing completion. She found herself finishing sentences for him, understanding instinctively what he needed, and he was doing the same with her.

'We work well together,' she said at one point.

'Aye.' He allowed himself a lingering glance then forced himself to concentrate. If he was to have any chance of winning her, he must make something of himself.

For the first time he allowed himself to hope—or maybe dream was a better word.

—

That morning Ben had an encounter with Noll Brindley, who stopped him in the street to ask why he was trying to prevent Peter from so much as passing the time of day with Miss Georgie. 'I take exception to your attitude, Seaton, I tell you frankly. There's nowt wrong with my son. He's been brought up a gentleman an' has excellent manners.'

'I shall do as I see fit with my sister.'

'I pity that lass. You're keeping her a prisoner.'

Ben was furious to hear Noll echoing Hepzibah's words. 'How I treat my sister is none of your business. Just tell your son to keep away from her, that's all.'

Noll's expression turned ugly. 'Think you're better than the rest of us, you Seatons, don't you? Your father was just as toffee-nosed. Well, you're no better than us Brindleys and I'll tell our Peter no such thing.'

'Then I shall continue to take my own measures to protect Georgie. Now, I have work to do.' Ben walked away and when he glanced back at the corner, saw the other man still scowling in his direction. What had got into Brindley, who normally passed by with the slightest of nods? Surely the fellow hadn't cherished any hopes for his son and Georgie? The very thought of that disgusted Ben and made him even more determined to keep Peter away from his sister.

He went home to find a letter from Belinda regretting that she would have to postpone having Georgie over to visit her in York. They were busy redecorating the house and all was at sixes and sevens. He knew his sister had been eagerly anticipating the visit, which had been arranged a while ago, and his heart sank at the thought of telling her.

What next?

When he opened the final letter in the pile, which had been hand delivered, he found out: a summons from Miss Merridene, no doubt to complain about Georgie's behaviour. What else could she want to see him for?

He worried about it all day, but as Miss Merridene had asked, said nothing about it to his sister.

–

When Sally showed a dour Ben Seaton into the parlour, he sat down with such a grim expression that Martha looked at him in surprise and forgot what she had been going to say.

'You wanted to see me about Georgie?' he prompted.

'Yes.' Taking a deep breath, she tried to speak calmly, but however much she'd rehearsed what she wanted to tell him, she'd not found a way that pleased her, so in the end said baldly, 'I'm worried about her.'

'What has she been doing now?'

'Nothing. Why do you automatically think she's been misbehaving?'

'Because that's what she keeps doing.' He rubbed his forehead, which was aching.

When he looked across at her, Martha was staring down at her lap, pulling the material of her skirt into more even pleats. She glanced up and caught his eye, taking a deep breath before she spoke. 'I think the only reason Georgie misbehaves is to get people's attention. She's very lonely. And she gets angry when you treat her as a child, because she isn't really a child any more.'

'I know she's lonely. I do care about my sister, you know. I've tried to talk to her, take her for walks at weekends, share my work with her, but she's not interested.'

'At her age, Mr Seaton, she isn't likely to be interested in what's happening inside your mill, though you may get her to go for walks with you now that she's got proper shoes, especially once the weather improves. What she does care about are the same things as other girls of her age: young men—only there aren't any suitable ones to practise on in Tapton; clothes—but obviously you can't share that interest; and social life—only there are no girls of her own age and class here for her to make friends with and you have no social life of the sort she's used to.'

He shook his head, grimacing a little at this all too accurate summary of the situation, but didn't say anything, waiting to see what Martha would suggest as a solution.

'From chance remarks she's made, I gather Georgie's mother has hurt her greatly. She tries to hide her feelings, but sometimes I catch a look of sadness on her face.'

He folded his arms and scowled at her, not needing this rubbing in. 'What do you suggest I do, then?'

'She needs female friends, so I wondered if perhaps—well, maybe you could find a school for young ladies and send her there, just for a year, so that she could make friends of her own age?'

'That's the last thing I'd have expected you to say! You'd lose half your income, and what about this house?'

She was startled. 'Would you turn us out?'

'No. Of course I wouldn't. But I don't want to send Georgie away, either. Let alone she'd feel I didn't want her either, I don't trust her out of my sight at the moment.'

'Then at least let her walk to school on her own.'

'And continue to meet young Brindley? Definitely not.'

'But she was only chatting to him in the street. What harm can there be in that? At her age, she feels humiliated at being escorted to and from school.'

He was disappointed that she had no better suggestion to offer and still felt angry at all the people trying to interfere in the way he looked after his sister. 'Then she'll just have to feel humiliated, Miss Merridene, because I shall continue to do as I see fit. I protect my own. And if you'll confine yourself to your teaching from now on, we'll both be a lot happier.'

She drew herself up, amazed at the harshness of his tone. 'I shall say no more, then.'

'Is that all?'

'Yes.'

He stood up. 'Then I'll get off home.'

After she'd showed him out in a heavy disapproving silence, he strode down the dark street without a backward glance. She whisked inside, resisting with great difficulty the temptation to slam the door behind him.

A murmur of voices coming from the schoolroom reminded her that Penelope hadn't returned to join her and she moved in that direction. But through the half-open door she saw her sister casting a laughing glance sideways at Daniel Porter and there was something so intimate and cosy about the picture they made that Martha froze, then tiptoed back to the parlour.

What was Penelope thinking of? He wasn't at all suitable for her.

Martha sat staring into the fire. Should she raise the matter again? No, better not. Pen only became more stubborn when someone tried to tell her what to do.

It seemed a long time until Martha heard voices in the hall, then the sound of the front door opening and closing.

Penelope came into the room, smiling, then noticed Martha's stormy expression. 'Is something wrong?'

'Only Mr Seaton being rude and autocratic. The man has no manners. He's the last person who should be left in charge of a girl that age.'

'Oh, dear.' She went to sit in her usual armchair and picked up a piece of embroidery. 'Well, now you can forget him and we'll have a comfortable half-hour together before we go to bed.'

But Martha hardly said a word and although she had a book on her lap, she made no attempt to read it, but spent most of her time staring into the fire.

–

The following day Daniel showed the drawings he and Penelope had made to the engineer, then Ross took them and him to Ben's office, pausing to knock on the door, but not waiting for an answer before he opened it.

Ben waved them to chairs and set his pen down carefully before leaning back and asking, 'Is something wrong?'

'Nay. We've come to show you the drawings. The lad's shaping up nicely.' Ross bobbed his head in his assistant's direction. 'He's not feared of hard work an' got these finished in his own time, with that teacher lady's help.'

His protégé blushed slightly, but his expression was pleased.

'Show me.' Ben gestured to the desk.

Daniel unrolled the drawings and spread them out. He quickly lost his diffidence as the three men studied them and discussed materials.

'I'll take him out to Lumbley's, shall I?' Ross asked. 'He might as well start making the acquaintance of our suppliers.'

'Yes. When shall you go?'

'Tomorrow's as good a day as any. The new machines are working well and if you're going to be here, you can be the engineer for the day.' He grinned at his employer, whom he had known as a lad and who had always been fascinated by machinery, often to the detriment of his clothes. 'I doubt you'll be needed, though. I make no bones about it: Daniel here is an engineer to the bone and those new machines'll do owt he asks 'em to.'

Such high praise was unusual from Ross. Ben looked thoughtfully at Daniel. If he had a treasure here, it behoved him to make sure the man wanted to stay. 'We'd better raise his wages then, to a full Assistant Engineer's rate. We don't want anyone tempting him away from us. All right with you, Porter?'

Daniel stared from one to the other, open-mouthed in surprise.

Ross nudged him. 'Stop fly-catching and say thanks. He'd not have offered that if you didn't deserve it.'

Daniel gave his employer one of his quick smiles. 'Then I thank you, Mr Seaton.'

When he left the office, he looked sideways at Ross as they walked back to their own office cum workshop. 'I'm grateful to you as well.'

Ross grinned at him. 'I'm relieved to have found you. I'm getting on a bit and when the time comes for me to step down, I'll be glad to see someone capable of taking my place here. I helped Ben's father build this place an' I'd hate to see it go downhill again.'

'I've never worked for anyone as *raised* wages,' Daniel said wonderingly. 'He's just *doubled* what I get.'

'You've never worked for anyone as could see what a man had in him like Ben Seaton does. It's only with women he can't see his nose on his face.' He didn't explain this cryptic remark caused by a recent conversation with his cousin Hepzibah, but went on briskly, 'Now, we'll have to catch the early stage coach into Manchester tomorrow, so you'd best be up early. Lumbley's makes our special parts for us and well worth the trip, because they know what they're doing, none better.'

Daniel wished he could tell Penelope what had happened. He didn't wish Ross Turner ill, but if there was a prospect of him becoming engineer at Seaton's when the other man stopped working, then a future for him and Penelope was also possible. Surely it was?

Ross clapped him on the shoulder. 'Come down from them clouds, young fellow. We've still got work to do.'

–

In the slums of Manchester, a stone's throw away from the River Irwell, the man known as Jack to his face and Croaky Jack behind his back, opened a letter and read its contents, smiling as he did so. 'Thought he'd come back to me for more help.' His companions looked up as he spoke. 'We're off to Tapton again,' he told them.

'Sodding place. They give me the creeps, those moors do, all that bare space an' no people.'

Jack stopped smiling to study him. 'Are you saying you won't go back there, Hobb?'

'A'course I'm not. Just sayin' I don't like it, that's all.'

'Well, I'm not interested in what you like and don't like. I'm interested in making money out of that old rogue.'

He grinned as he stared into space for a moment, relishing the thought of squeezing a few bright gold sovereigns out of Noll, and the other men kept quiet. You didn't upset Croaky Jack, if you could help it.

'We have some work to do before we go back, lads. I need to find a house to keep some prisoners in for my friend Noll. A comfortable place but on its own, a farm house out on the moors, maybe. And we'll need a woman to cook and wash for 'em, because they're to be well looked after. The folk we're capturing may need to stay there for a few days or even longer. I wonder…'

The men stayed silent. Born of the slums, they knew little of life outside Manchester.

'The place needs checking out personally. Hobb, you and me can do that.' He grinned as his henchman scowled. 'Cheer up. You were getting better at staying on horses by the time we got back from Tapton. Riding is just a matter of practice.' He swung round to the other man. 'Your job, Dirk, is to find me a carriage and horses.'

'To buy or hire?' Dirk asked.

'Neither, if I can help it. Why spend money if you don't need to? I want a carriage we can pinch from someone and then not bring back again, something very ordinary, that folk won't look at twice.'

'Bit hard, that.'

'Well, you'd better start working on it, then. We'll need some horses too. Might have to buy them.' He sucked thoughtfully on a gap in his teeth and decided that was the main needs covered for the present. Waving one hand in dismissal, he waited till they'd left then fumbled in the drawer he called 'my desk' and pulled out a piece of paper with a couple of grimy fingerprints at the top. As he began to draft a letter, he chewed on his thumb from time to time, considering what he should charge.

Noll was going to find this more expensive than he'd expected and he wasn't going to wriggle out of paying handsomely.

–

A few days later Noll scowled out of his office window at the weather. Black clouds were scudding across the sky and even as he watched, fat drops of sleet began to rattle against the panes of glass. Within seconds it was pouring down so heavily you couldn't see across the mill yard. He went to hold his hands out to the fire.

When there was a knock on the door, he yelled, 'Come in!' and Gerry peered inside.

'Well, are you going to let all the warm air out? Come inside, man, and quick about it.'

The overlooker did as ordered, sinking down thankfully on to a chair because his feet hurt after being on them for several hours. 'There's someone to see you.'

'Oh? Why didn't you bring him in?'

'It's the fellow as helped out when we were after Seaton last time. He's round at my place, like you arranged. The wife sent our youngest over to tell me.'

'Make sure she doesn't say anything about him to your neighbours. He's her cousin as far as they're concerned.'

'She knows that.'

'You can bring him round here once the mill's shut.'

Gerry nodded.

'Why the sour face?'

'I don't trust him.'

'He's all right, Jack is. Did me a favour or two when I was starting up, so if I can push a bit of work his way, I do. He won't try to diddle me like some might.'

Gerry refrained from saying that last time Croaky Jack had let his master down good and proper, allowing Seaton to get his machinery in under the cover of darkness. It didn't do any good reminding Noll of things that had gone wrong. In fact, nothing did much good with him lately. He'd turned into a right cantankerous devil and Gerry was the one who usually bore the brunt of his ill humour.

But what was a man to do? You had to eat, didn't you. There were no other jobs like this one available in Tapton.

Chapter 13

On the final Sunday in February, Martha and Penelope enjoyed a brisk walk to church, while Sally went there shortly afterwards with Meg by her side.

Ben escorted his sister to church. He hadn't been a regular attender until Georgie came to live with him but now considered it his duty, though truth to tell the service bored him to tears. One of the main benefits was that it got his sister out of the house and gave her an excuse to dress up, so she was usually in a better mood on Sundays.

He felt a bit down-spirited today, however, conscious that he had been far too sharp with Martha the other evening and unsure how to set things right with her. Her good opinion had come to mean a lot to him and… he cut his musing off short, not wanting to pursue that avenue of thought. He had enough on his plate trying to deal with Georgie.

As he sat down he noticed Peter Brindley across the aisle in the pew Noll paid for but rarely used, and his bad humour surged back with a vengeance. You couldn't go anywhere without tripping over that damned popinjay. He scowled across the aisle and Brindley smiled at him, inclining his head slightly as if Ben were a friend.

Georgie flopped down beside her brother in the pew, straightening her clothes then sighing as she stared round at the congregation. She didn't know why she bothered to come here, but at least it was something to do. Then she saw Peter gazing steadily at her from the other side of the aisle and felt a warmth creeping through her. She couldn't help stealing a few more glances in his direction. To her surprise, he was looking thinner and when he looked down at his hymn book, letting his guard drop, it seemed to her that he had a weary air to him, as if something was preying on his mind.

Then he raised his head, saw her looking at him and nodded a greeting. Deciding on outright rebellion, she raised one hand in response. After all, he'd once said it brightened his day to talk to her and she felt the same about him. He was so easy to be with and he made her laugh, unlike her solemn brother who was always giving her lectures or scolding her, and who usually treated her like a child.

She hadn't felt like a child since her father died.

Ben nudged her. 'Stop staring at him!'

She pulled away. 'How are you going to prevent me? Cover my eyes as well as tying me to your side?'

Jonas Wright, who was sitting in the pew in front of theirs, half-turned his head and gave Georgie a stern look. She scowled at him as well, for good measure. He was as bad as her brother, always looking at her disapprovingly.

From a few rows behind them Martha saw the sudden rigidity of their backs and the way Georgie edged along the pew till there was a two foot gap between her and her brother. It wasn't hard to guess that there had been some disagreement between them and she hadn't missed the lowering look on Ben's face as he walked into church. She wished he would be kinder to that poor girl, but it wasn't her business, as he'd made only too plain, so she didn't intend to interfere again.

But he was heading for trouble if he didn't change the way he was treating Georgie, she was quite sure of that.

After the service the two sisters lingered in spite of the chill wind, exchanging greetings with the parson's wife, then the doctor and his wife. They were beginning to know a few people now, Martha thought with satisfaction, which made her feel more at home in Tapton.

She watched Mr Wright send his children home in the elderly maid's care then come across to them with his wide smile.

'Libby asked me to thank you, my dear ladies, for doing exactly what we wished with the girls. They need a carefree time away from home.'

'How is your wife?'

His smile vanished abruptly. 'Sadly her incapacity is increasing and it casts a shadow over us all. She would have liked to ask you to visit, but hasn't been well enough to leave her bed.'

'Is there nothing to be done for her?'

'We can find nothing.'

'I'm so sorry.'

'Mmm. Thank you.' He was silent for a moment or two, then went on in a brighter tone, 'She's very pleased about the girls, though. We haven't seen them look this rosy-cheeked for a long time.' As Ben happened to be passing just then with Georgie, he stopped his friend to say, 'I was just complimenting the ladies on the way they run their school. We did ourselves a favour bringing them to Tapton, did we not?'

'Indeed.'

Georgie went over to Martha, turning her back on her brother. 'Your new dress looks pretty, Miss Merridene.'

Ben looked at the dress, which had been the cause of another incident he couldn't forget. It was blue, almost the colour of Martha's eyes, though not as bright as they were, and it had sleeves which were wide at the top, but not ridiculous like Belinda's. The whole was finished with a neat lace frill at neck and wrist and her bonnet was trimmed with matching blue ribbon and lace. He thought it very becoming after the blacks he'd seen her in so far.

And the girls weren't the only ones to be rosy-cheeked. The Merridene sisters were also the picture of health. They'd been a good influence on Georgie and it was churlish of him not to admit that, but before he could speak, they'd begun to take their leave, so the opportunity was lost.

'Please give your wife our regards, Mr Wright.' Penelope took her sister's arm and nodded farewell to Ben, since Martha had been avoiding even looking at him.

After they'd gone, Jonas frowned at his friend. 'What's the matter? Have you and Miss Merridene quarrelled about something? You're as surly as a bear and she was obviously keeping her distance from you.'

'Um, nothing important. Just a small disagreement. I probably spoke too strongly.'

Jonas couldn't hide his surprise and Georgie looked at her brother in disgust. He'd been quarrelling with everyone lately and even Hepzibah seemed annoyed with him. And what a fuss he'd made and was still making about Peter Brindley! It was ridiculous.

If only her mother would let her go back to York on a visit! She had nothing to look forward to, nothing! She might as well be dead as living like this. And if *he* thought buying her a few novels made a difference, he was wrong!

Ben watched the Merridene sisters walk away, chatting animatedly as usual. Their fondness for one another seemed to emphasise the way he and Georgie hardly knew one another. He'd tried to do his best for her and watch over her, but the way they were living wasn't making either of them happy. What he wouldn't give to enjoy such easy relations with someone!

Suddenly he noticed Brindley standing to one side, staring at Georgie longingly, damn his eyes! And she was smiling at him again. Taking her arm, he said abruptly, 'We have to get home now.'

She shook his hand off. 'I can walk without your help, thank you very much. You take far too long strides for me to be comfortable on your arm.'

They made their way back in silence and she went up to her room at once, leaving him alone in the parlour. In the end he went for a walk round the silent mill, so different from the clattering, noisy place of weekdays, then sat in the chilly office, thinking how much he disliked Sundays. To hell with having a day of rest! If you had nothing to do, you only started worrying and that was no help to anyone.

But he would have to apologise to Martha, he decided, and try to explain what was upsetting him. Only that was going to be a little difficult because he didn't really know himself whether he was doing the right thing by Georgie.

When his sister came down to the midday meal, it was obvious that she'd been crying.

'What's wrong, Georgie?' he asked gently. 'Can't we talk about it?'

She scowled at him. 'Everything's wrong, but most of all *you*! I hate you, Ben Seaton!' Tears welled in her eyes and she flung down her napkin, shoving her chair back so violently it fell over.

He heard her sob as she ran out of the room, then her feet pounded up the stairs. He followed her, heard the key turn in the lock of her bedroom door and knocked. 'Georgie, open the door, love. We can't go on like this.'

'No, I won't open it. I don't want to talk to you. Go away and leave me alone!'

She didn't answer again, though he tried hard to persuade her to come out.

That put an abrupt end at his efforts to get closer to her. He finished his own meal, then told Hepzibah to keep something for Georgie and try to tempt her to eat later. After fidgeting round for a few minutes, he put on his boots and greatcoat and went out for a long tramp across the moors, not caring that it was a cold day and his face growing numb from the biting wind.

–

On the Tuesday morning Noll said to his son over break-fast. 'Better pack your things this morning. It's all arranged for this afternoon.'

Peter took a deep breath. 'I'm sorry, but I just can't do it to her.'

Noll choked on a piece of ham and when he'd finished spluttering, leaned forward and said in an ominously quiet voice, 'You'll do as we planned.'

'You can't make me.'

Noll looked at him and remembered the lad's mother. Eh, Peter was just like her. Soft but stubborn sometimes too. 'What's got into you? Why have you changed your mind?'

'Because she's a nice girl and it'd be a dreadful thing to do to her. A gentleman just wouldn't!'

Noll looked at him, muttered something and did the unthinkable—pushed his food aside and left without a second helping or another of his many daily cups of tea.

When the house was quiet Peter went up to his bedroom and stared bleakly out of the window. He might be trapped here, as his mother had been, but no one could make him kidnap Georgie Seaton, not even his father. As for ravishing her, even the thought of that sickened him.

Why had he been born to such a man? He thanked heaven for his mother's blood, for the morals she had gently taught him.

And he tried yet again to think of a way out of this dreadful situation.

–

After a midday meal during which the two men hardly said a word to one another, Peter went up to his bedroom again, feeling rather sleepy. He had nothing to do and it was cold outside, with snow threatening, to judge from the heavy clouds which had been building up all morning. As his father didn't approve of fires upstairs, the room was too cold for comfort so he lay down on the bed and pulled the covers over himself.

Half an hour later his father opened the door and walked across to stare down at the sleeping figure on the bed. He shook Peter just to be sure that the laudanum had worked and when his son didn't stir, went up to the attics and got out a travelling bag. Back in Peter's bedroom he stuffed it full of a selection of clothes, not wishing to entrust this to the servants, then slung a warm cloak across the foot of the bed in readiness.

Won't do it, indeed! he thought. You'll do as I tell you, my lad. You're too weak to hold out against me.

Downstairs he went out through the back door and hurried across to the mill, stopping in the doorway to look up at the sky. Damned weather! Why did it have to threaten snow today of all days? But it hadn't started snowing yet and would surely hold off long enough to serve his purpose.

In his office he rang his little handbell briskly and when Gerry appeared, said only, 'Tell them it's on for an hour's time. I've packed him a bag and they're to take his warm cloak.'

'What about the Seaton girl? What's she to wear?'

Noll grinned. 'I told Jack to get her some nightgowns and wrappers, no outdoor clothes. We don't want her running away, do we?'

'No. Of course not.' Gerry went to do his master's bidding, but to his mind, this was a bad business and nothing would persuade him otherwise. He felt sorry for that poor lass, he did indeed.

He sent a lad to his home with the message and waited for the three men to turn up with the carriage, as promised. They arrived in an elderly posting chariot whose paintwork was faded, pulled by two sturdy horses. He went to fetch Noll, who came out to gesture to them to drive round to the rear of the house. Gerry hesitated, then trailed behind them.

Jack got out of the carriage followed by another man, a huge fellow with a broken nose. The driver stayed where he was, huddled in a heavy coachman's cloak, with extra capes over the shoulders. His hat was pulled over his ears and a muffler wound round his neck.

'Nice day for a kidnapping,' Jack commented.

Noll put one finger to his lips. 'Shh, you fool! Don't shout it out for all the world to hear. Just wait there till I get rid of the maids, then I'll show you where Peter's room is. You'll have to carry him down to the carriage.'

'Hasn't he got feet of his own?'

'He's a bit reluctant to upset the young lady—comes of being brought up a gentleman—so I gave him a little dose of sleeping juice. When you get there, you're to lock him in the bedroom with her and take her clothes away. She can only have the nightdresses and shawls. Even if he never lays a finger on her, she'll need to wed him if they've spent three or four days and nights together.'

His eyes narrowed and he looked at the two men. 'But think on! I'd be very angry indeed if either of you touched her. Remember that.'

'We'll remember. But we'd better get a piece of rope and tie him up before we leave. We don't want him waking too soon and causing trouble on the way there, do we?'

'Good idea. Go and fetch some rope, Gerry. Plenty of it. Now, you lot wait there a minute.'

Noll went into the kitchen, where he looked at the cook and said simply, 'You've had your orders.'

She nodded, wiped her hands on a cloth, used it to pull a pan off the hot part of the hob then took the maid up to the attics, where they'd been instructed to stay for the next half-hour and not look out of the windows. Both of them were too glad of a rest to disobey.

Noll waited until the sound of their footsteps had died away, then went to the back door and beckoned. Jack and Hobb hurried across, followed by Gerry with a coil of rope. Noll led the way upstairs to Peter, who was still sleeping soundly. 'Don't know when he'll wake. Hard to judge the dose.'

'Doesn't matter now.' Hobb tied Peter's hands and feet, wrapped him in the cloak then slung him over his shoulder.

When Noll pointed to the bag of clothing, Gerry picked it up, then they all went downstairs again as quietly as they'd gone up.

Within minutes the carriage was driving away.

–

Georgie walked home, as usual, along the lane behind the church, deliberately not keeping up with Hepzibah, who turned to her half-way along to say, 'What's the matter with you today, girl? Going too fast for you, am I?'

'Yes.'

Rolling her eyes at the heavens, Hepzibah noticed the first of the snow fluttering down, tiny flakes but coming from a sky which seemed to hang down almost to the church spire with the weight of further falls. 'Drat it! I knew it was going to snow. It's been snowing already on the tops.'

Georgie looked up and sighed. 'When we lived out in the country I used to love snow. It was all white and beautiful there, but in a town it soon turns dirty and there's no pleasure in walking through brown slush.' She looked ahead and frowned. 'What's that carriage doing there? There's hardly room to get past it. I don't recognise it, do you?'

'No.' Even as she spoke, the door of the carriage opened and a man jumped out, coming towards them with a smile. 'I wonder if you could direct me to Mr Berringham's house, ma'am?'

'There's no one of that name in Tapton,' Hepzibah began, 'and—'

A second man had followed the first and suddenly she felt uneasy, however polite her questioner had been. She didn't have time to say or do anything, however, because the larger man suddenly grabbed her, putting his hand across her mouth to prevent her from screaming, and the one who'd spoken did the same to Georgie.

Being more agile, Georgie managed to break the man's hold for long enough to scream for help, but there was no one nearby and it took him only a minute to squeeze her throat in a certain place that rendered her unconscious. He pushed her limp body into the carriage then turned to help Hobb tie the wildly struggling Hepzibah up, stuffing a handkerchief in her mouth before putting her into the carriage as well.

The driver immediately told the horses to 'Walk on' and they clopped gently round the church towards the main square.

Terrified, Hepzibah tried to struggle, but the big man only laughed at her and held her still as the carriage rumbled out of the town. The other man tied up Miss Georgie, joking about her pretty ankles to his companion.

It was dim inside the carriage with the blinds down, but not too dim for her to see a man's body lying on the seat opposite, covered in a cloak and seeming totally unconscious—or dead? Then she noticed that his ankles were bound together, so he must be a prisoner too. Dear heavens, what did these villains want? Were they going to kill them all? Why? She managed to turn her head enough to see that Georgie was stirring.

She could feel the carriage climbing now, so guessed they'd left the town behind, but heading in which direction she couldn't tell. Some time later the vehicle drew to a halt and the man who seemed to be the leader opened the carriage door and dragged Hepzibah out. She tried to struggle, thinking he was going to kill her.

He spoke in a strange hoarse voice. 'Be still, you silly bitch and you'll not get hurt. Now listen to me.' He gave her a shake to make sure she was paying attention. 'Tell your master not to come looking for her. She'll not be hurt but she'll be well hid. We'll let him know when she's ready to come home.'

He reached behind her and loosened the bonds a little, then pushed her over so that she fell into the snow, which was quite deep up here.

By the time she'd freed herself the carriage had disappeared. She stood up and tried to brush her clothes down, looking round and recognising where she was. Despair filled her. The place had been well chosen. It was quite a way out of town on foot. What's more, there was a crossroads just over the brow of the hill, so the carriage could go in any direction, and there were no farms up here on the tops. With a sob she turned towards the town. It would be a long walk back in weather like this, and she was only wearing her normal shoes, not her heavy winter boots.

Wind whistled round her and she shivered as she tried to pull the cloak round her more warmly. Tears tracked down her cheeks as she walked. What did they want with Miss Georgie? Why hadn't she taken better care of the lass? She should have guessed that a strange carriage standing behind the church meant no good.

Darkness was falling fast and she tried to hurry, but the snow made the going difficult and when she fell heavily, she stopped trying to hurry and concentrated only on getting back to Mr Ben in one piece. He'd know what to do, if anyone would.

But how would he find Miss Georgie? It was dark now and she still had some distance to go. Her limbs felt heavy and she was so cold it was an effort to keep moving. When she saw the lights of a farm and found a track leading in that direction, she sobbed in relief and began to stumble towards the lights.

Hammering on the door she called for help. Someone opened it and a voice said, 'Nay, it's a woman, our Hettie.'

The man put an arm round her and led her inside. She was shivering violently and couldn't stop weeping.

–

When Nan came across to the mill and burst into his office without knocking, Ben guessed something was wrong before she even spoke and was round the desk to her side. 'What is it?'

'Hepzibah and Miss Georgie haven't come back, sir. And they won't have gone to the shops, not in weather like this. Look how hard it's snowing now.'

He frowned out at the whirling snow. 'I'll go and see if they're still at school. You go back to the house.' Throwing on the old cloak he used for crossing the mill yard and cramming his hat on his head, he ran out into the whiteness and within minutes was at the villa, where the glow from the lamp inside the hall shone out softly on the falling snow through the panes of coloured glass. He hammered on the door and as Meg opened it, asked at once, 'Is Georgie still here?'

'No, sir. Everyone went home early today because of the snow.'

Martha appeared in the doorway of the parlour. 'Do come in and close the door. What's wrong?'

As he followed her into the cosy warmth, he announced, 'Georgie and Hepzibah haven't come home.' He saw the surprise on both sisters' faces. 'I wanted to know if they were here, but Meg said they'd left early.'

'They did,' Penelope confirmed.

'I'll go and ask around town then. Perhaps they went to the shops.'

Martha shook her head. 'I shouldn't think so. You know how Georgie hates the cold. She was complaining about having to walk home in the snow.'

'I'll still have to check whether anyone's seen them. Please excuse me.'

When he'd gone, Martha paced up and down the parlour a few times, then declared, 'I'm putting on my boots and cloak and going after him. If something's wrong, he may need a woman's help with Georgie.'

Penelope didn't attempt to argue. 'Should I come with you?'

'No. It'll be best if you wait here.' She paused at the door. 'She can't have run away, surely?'

'On a day like this? And with Hepzibah? Definitely not.'

Martha left as soon as she was warmly clad, not even thinking that the lane was dark and no one around. She'd have run if the ground underfoot hadn't been slippery with snow. The mill was lit up brightly but the house beside it showed only a lamp outside the front door and a dim light inside the front parlour.

As she raised her hand to knock, footsteps hurried up and Ben joined her. 'I thought you might need a woman's help if—' she hesitated, then said it, '—in case anything has happened to them.'

'That was kind of you.' He threw open the door and waved her inside.

'Is there any news of them at all?' she asked before he had even closed the door.

'No. They definitely didn't go into town after they left your house.'

In the hall, which was lit by an oil lamp on the wall, she raised her eyes to his face, hating to see how ravaged by anxiety he looked. 'Is there trouble with Brindley's workers again? Could they have attacked them?'

'I very much doubt it. It's been very quiet lately in town. And on a day like this… well, I'm at a loss to think what can have happened to them.' He saw her shiver and realised they were still standing in the hall. 'Come into the parlour. There'll be a fire there.' While he busied himself making it blaze, she turned up the lamps.

He stood holding his hands out to the warmth of the fire and gesturing to her to join him. 'Where can she be? And Hepzibah's missing too. Georgie might do something foolish, but Hepzibah definitely wouldn't. All I can think of is that someone else must be involved.' After a pause, he added, 'It was kind of you to come. I'm going to close the mill early and set some of the workers from the mill to searching for Georgie.'

'I could stay here in case she returns and needs a woman's help, if you like.'

His gaze was warm. 'Would you?'

'Of course.'

'It's particularly kind after I was so rude to you the other day. I do apologise for that, Martha. Sometimes I'm a bit too sharp, I know.'

'That's all right.'

Their glances locked for a moment or two, then he said, 'Let me show you through to the kitchen. There's only Nan here today, as Cook's mother's ill, but I'm sure if you need anything, Nan will be able to get it for you. She's very willing, but not good at thinking for herself, so I'll be doubly glad to have you here.'

When he'd gone, Martha left Nan and went back to the parlour. After pacing up and down, she picked up a novel which she herself had lent to Georgie but soon put it down again. Again and again she was drawn to the window, looking out and praying to see them returning. But there was only the snow and an occasional passer-by hurrying to get out of the cold.

The siren shrieked its message early and soon the operatives were pouring through the gates, some talking earnestly, others with their heads down, their only thought to get home.

A short time later a group of men, Ben and Daniel Porter among them, came out of the mill yard and headed off in different directions.

The search had begun.

Time seemed to pass very slowly and after a while, she went to the kitchen and asked Nan for a pot of tea. The maid had tears on her cheeks and was so upset she nearly scalded herself when she tried to fill the teapot from the big kettle. Martha jumped forward to take the cloth from her and push the kettle back on to the hob.

'Oh, Miss! Miss, I'm that sorry.' Nan began weeping again. 'Where can they be?'

'I don't know, but getting hysterical isn't going to do anyone any good,' she said firmly as the sobbing continued. 'Pull yourself together, Nan, and we'll both have a cup of tea. After that we should make sure there's plenty of hot water, yes and food too. Ben's sent out some of his men to hunt for signs of Georgie and Hepzibah and they'll be cold and famished when they return. Some hot soup might be good too, perhaps? Are you anything of a cook or shall I see what I can find and make it.'

'Oh, Miss—' Nan's face crumpled again.

Martha spoke with deliberate sharpness. 'No more tears! We're going to need your help. What about the soup?'

'There's a leg of lamb and the gravy from yesterday. I can make some broth quite quickly. Cook's been teaching me for a while now.' She took a deep breath and gave Martha a wavery smile.

'Good.'

For a time they worked together, Martha peeling potatoes and chopping onions and Nan cutting up the meat.

When there was nothing left to do but let the soup simmer in the big pan, Martha suddenly wondered where they were to feed the searchers, because there wasn't enough room in the kitchen. She fetched her cloak and went out to find the watchman, persuading him to light a fire in the old mill and herself lit the lamps there. Even that short outing had her shivering by the time she returned to the house and she was covered in snowflakes. It was a dreadful night, the worst of the winter so far.

What if Georgie and Hepzibah were outside in such a storm?

Next she and Nan carried the big pan out to the schoolroom and set it on the closed stove there, which was now radiating a welcome warmth. The work of fetching bowls and cups across helped keep them warm, but each time they went outside they were assaulted by an icy wind as well as thickly falling snow.

Ben was the first to return, for he knew someone needed to direct operations. He paused in the doorway of the schoolroom for a moment to watch Martha and Nan. In just this way had his mother worked with their servants, not directing them from a distance, but sharing the tasks.

Martha felt the draught from the half-open door and swung round. When she caught sight of him she hurried across to close the door and help him off with his cloak. 'You're soaked!'

'Never mind me!'

'It'll not help anyone if you catch your death of cold. Nan, will you go and fetch your master another coat, please?'

As the maid snatched up her cloak and hurried across the yard, Martha took Ben's arm and pulled him across to the fire, then began tugging at his coat. 'You've got to get this off.'

Bemused, he let her help him and even chafe his frozen hands, because of course he hadn't thought of gloves and you couldn't keep your hands crammed in your pockets all the time.

As they stood there by the closed stove, they both stilled and stared at one another.

'You're a wonderful woman, Martha Merridene,' he said suddenly. 'My mother would have been behaving in just the same way today.'

'I like to think I'm practical.'

He reached out to tuck back a strand of hair that had escaped. 'More than that, Martha. Much more than that. You're—'

The moment was lost and he cut off his next words sharply as Nan erupted into the room, shaking the snow

253

from her shawl and hurrying across to him with a coat held out. 'I brought you a muffler, too, sir, because there's nothing like a muffler for making you feel warmer, I allus think.'

'Would you like a bowl of soup, Ben?' Martha asked. 'We have some ready for the men who've been searching.'

She frowned as she thought she heard him say, 'Dear, practical Martha,' in a low voice. But she must have been mistaken because he sat down at the nearest table and began spooning the hot soup Nan had brought him into his mouth, sighing with pleasure as its warmth slid down his throat.

One by one the men came back to the mill, to be directed by the watchman at the gate to the schoolroom, where they fell enthusiastically upon the meaty soup and bread, washed down intermittently with strong tea, as they reported their findings.

No one had seen Georgie or Hepzibah, but Daniel and another man had been told about a strange carriage.

'It was an old one, rather shabby,' Daniel said. 'It turned into the square earlier and went round behind the church. Mr Perston, the chemist, noticed it and wondered where it was going, but he had some customers and didn't see it leave. He thought it might be coming here.'

'We've seen no carriages,' Ben said, his voice harsh and his face deeply lined with worry. 'And how can a strange carriage be connected with Georgie?'

'It's all we have to go by, the only strangers seen in town.'

'Yes.'

'Brindley's will be stopping work soon,' Daniel offered when Ben said nothing more. 'If you like, sir, I could go and ask one or two of my old friends there if they've seen anything unusual? The mill's nearer the edge of town than you are. Maybe someone was looking out of the window and saw the carriage leaving? No one saw it on the other side of town, so it can't have gone that way.'

Ben nodded, fumbling in his pocket and coming up with some coins. 'Take them for a drink if you think it'll loosen their tongues. But finish your soup first. It'll do no good for you men to get chilled and catch your death of cold.'

Daniel nodded, spooned up the soup quickly and was soon off.

Ben looked at the other men. 'Will you wait here for a while, in case we need you? You'll be fed and I'll pay you extra for your help.'

Ross Turner spoke automatically for the others. 'Nay, sir, we need no payment to help with this. It's the lass's safety that counts. I don't like to think of her and my cousin Hepzibah out in a blizzard like this, 'deed I don't.'

There was a chorus of agreement and heads nodded vigorously.

'Thank you. I'm grateful.' Ben stood frowning in thought for a while, then asked Ross to go and tell Jonas Wright what had happened. He left the men sitting round the tables and beckoned to Martha. 'I think they'll be more comfortable on their own. And there's nothing we can do at the moment, *nothing.*'

His voice was so bitter, she put her hand on his arm and somehow found herself holding his hand as they chased across the yard with snow driving against their faces in fat wet flakes that were piling up on all the ledges and windowsills now.

When they got inside the kitchen, he let go of her hand and brushed the snow from her hair and face. 'I'm glad you're here.'

'So am I. You shouldn't be facing this alone.'

'But I'm glad it's *you*, Martha. I don't think anyone else could help me as much.'

She stared at him in shock. What did he mean by that?

He looked down at her. 'This isn't the time to talk of what's between us. But we shall do once Georgie is back.'

To hide her confusion, Martha went to hold her hands out towards the fire, which gave her the opportunity to turn her back to him. He couldn't mean... surely not... ? She was well past that sort of thing, at almost twenty-nine.

Wasn't she?

He watched her with a wry smile on his face. He knew she felt something for him, you couldn't mistake a mutual attraction. But she had seemed shocked at what he said. Well, she'd just have to get used to the idea. Her behaviour tonight had set the final seal on the feelings he too had been denying. She was a woman in a million. Hepzibah was right.

Then his mind turned back to Georgie and anxiety took over once more.

When there was a knock on the front door Martha was greatly relieved because she hadn't dared look at Ben in case she'd mistaken his meaning.

And in case he saw how confused she was about her own feelings.

–

Penelope waited in the kitchen with Sally and Meg, worried when they heard nothing from Martha.

'What can be going on?' she burst out after several hours had passed.

'I don't know.' Sally looked at the window. Not only was snow falling still, but it was piling up everywhere. 'It's a dreadful night to be out.'

'I'm going to Mr Seaton's house to see what's happening,' Penelope said a few minutes later. 'Anything's better than sitting around waiting like this, knowing nothing.'

'Not on your own, you're not,' Sally said at once. 'Someone must have kidnapped Miss Georgie and you're not risking yourself. I'll come with you.'

'Can I come too?' Meg asked. 'I'd be feared to be left on my own here after the break-in.'

So all three of them dressed as warmly as they could, linking arms and walking the long way round via the square, because as Sally said, there was no need to make it easy for anyone to attack you in the dark lane behind the church.

The last of the shops was shutting down, but all of them had left lamps burning outside tonight. The proprietor of the grocery store waved to them and shouted to ask if there were any news of Miss Georgie.

'We haven't heard anything,' Penelope shouted back. 'We're going to see if we can help.'

It seemed to take a much longer time than usual to make their way to the mill house, because the going was treacherous.

–

Georgie was terrified when they stopped on the moors and she saw the man called Jack pull Hepzibah out of the carriage. As he climbed back in alone, she strained against the gag in her mouth, making gurgling noises, desperate to know what he had done to her companion.

He laughed at her efforts. 'You might as well save yourself the trouble. I'm not taking that out until we arrive where we're going, and I shan't be answering any questions, neither.' As they set off again, she carried on making noises and struggling against her bonds, so he said suddenly, 'I didn't hurt her, just set her free.'

Relief surged through her and she stopped wriggling, watching her captors by the light of the small carriage lamp flickering as it swung to and fro on its hook. They were travelling very slowly and once the man called Jack muttered something about 'Damned weather.'

The man hidden by the cloak didn't move and she was worried that he might be dead… that they meant to kill her too… or ravish her, something the heroines in novels always feared more than death itself, something they were prepared to kill themselves to avoid. She wasn't quite sure what ravishing involved, but it must be a truly dreadful fate.

Eventually the carriage slowed down almost to a halt and made a turn to the left, the horses hooves sounding muffled on the snow.

'Here at last!' the big man said. 'I'm frozen.'

Georgie was chilled through as well, but the terror that surged around inside her was worse than anything else. Where were they? What did these men intend to do to her?

Chapter 14

Noll beat a path to and from the window in his office. 'I can't believe it! Of all the sodding nights for there to be a blizzard!'

Gerry stood near the fire, still brooding on the events of the day. In the end he could hold back no longer. 'You shouldn't have done it, Noll. It wasn't right.'

'Who cares about what's right or wrong?' his companion snapped. 'If I only did what was right I'd still be poor like you.'

A minute later, he said in a gentler tone of voice, 'I'm sorry I said that, lad. You've been a good friend to me an' I shouldn't be taking my worries out on you.'

Gerry shrugged. 'You allus do.'

'Do I?'

'Aye.' With a rusty spurt of laughter, he added, 'Even when we were lads together you did.'

'We were a right pair of young hellions, weren't we?'

Gerry nodded.

Silence hung over the mill office and even the noises that usually penetrated its walls weren't there. Outside both sight and sound were muffled by the clinging, drifting curtain of white. The wind had dropped a little, but snow was still falling, thick and heavy, relentlessly taking over the town.

'Let's go across to the house. I've a bottle of finest Geneva there.'

For once Gerry didn't meekly agree. 'I'd rather go home if you don't mind. The wife will be worriting that I'm not back an' it's not going to be easy walkin'. That snow's getting' worse by the minute.'

Noll pursed his lips. 'All reet, lad. You get off home.' He sat there a few minutes longer, alone and wishing he wasn't. Stupid fool! he told himself and stood up abruptly, going to push the coal aside so that the fire would die down. He let out another rusty laugh as he looked at the poker. He could afford to keep fires burning all night in every room if he wanted, and yet he still broke up a fire to save the last bits of coal.

He was amazed at how deep the snow was in the mill yard and by the time he got across it, his feet and lower legs were soaked and he was covered in huge white flakes. 'Jack'll not be able to send me word in this weather,' he muttered as he went inside the back door. He'd just have to assume everything had gone as planned.

Wincing as his bad hip throbbed out a protest, he climbed the stairs and put on some dry clothes. 'Who'd a thought it?' he muttered again. 'Couldn't have chose a worse night for it, not if we'd tried.'

Then he grinned. 'Them two young 'uns will have to huddle up close to keep warm, so it isn't all bad.' He went down in his slippers and dressing gown, with an old shawl of his wife's round his shoulders, to stir up a blaze in the parlour and ring for his dinner.

–

As the carriage turned off the road, the huddled figure opposite Georgie stirred. Jack leaned across and flipped

260

the cloak off his other prisoner. 'About time you came out of it, young fellow.'

She strained her eyes in the dim light. Surely that was… it couldn't be… but it was Peter Brindley! And like her he was trussed up securely. This was like a nightmare, with neither rhyme nor reason to anything that was happening.

The carriage was now jolting along slowly over very rough ground and the passengers were bumping about like sacks of oats. Georgie couldn't help moaning as she slid towards the edge of the seat but the large man opposite grabbed her before she could fall. While he was holding her, he made free of her breasts in a way that terrified her. She jerked away from him, her instinctive scream choked off by the gag. The other man intervened.

'Let her go. If you do that again I'll cut your hand off,' Jack rasped.

Even though he was much bigger, the fellow cringed back. 'I only touched her.'

'Don't. She's not your meat.'

Georgie sagged back in relief and as the carriage drew to a halt soon after, she managed to stay on the seat without anyone's help. By now Peter Brindley had his eyes wide open and looked as shocked as she felt. It was a further source of relief to her that he wasn't involved in this kidnapping, for that's what it must be.

But who was? And why had they done it?

'Carry her inside first,' Jack ordered, fumbling for the door latch. 'And no touching. Then come back for him.'

Hobb grunted and picked Georgie up roughly. Jack followed them across the snow to the front door of a long, low dwelling, leaving the coach door open and Peter lying there helpless with the snow blowing in on him.

By the time Hobb returned, Peter had pulled his wits together and worked out that his father must have engineered this. He said nothing, however, as he was carried inside, pretending to be half-stupefied still.

He was thrown on to a bed beside Georgie, who was lying there with her hands bound, looking terrified. Damn his father! How could he treat a nice girl like her in this way?

Jack, who had been lounging near the door, now came over with a knife. 'Stay there, Hobb. We don't want them escaping, do we?' He made much play of testing the blade of the knife, enjoying the sight of his two captives cringing away from it. However, a desire for some strong drink and warmth cut the game short and putting the knife away, he untied the ropes round Peter's ankles and then Georgie's wrists.

She cried out in pain as circulation began to return to her numbed arms.

Jack laughed. 'It'll soon pass, then you can untie him.' He turned back to Peter. 'We'll bring you some food later—as long as you behave yourselves. Try to escape and you get nothing to eat or drink for a day.' With a laugh he left the room, leaving them with one candle flickering in the many drafts and a low fire burning in the rough fireplace, not nearly enough to warm the room properly.

As soon as she could control her arms, Georgie pulled the gag out of her mouth and turned to do the same for Peter.

'Are you all right?' he asked. 'They haven't hurt you?'

'No. They pushed me into the carriage and tied me up, but didn't hurt me. What can they want?' She didn't wait for an answer, assuming he didn't know, either. It took her a while to undo the ropes, then she watched in sympathy as he too suffered the pain of returning circulation.

'Do you know who those men are?' she whispered glancing towards the door as if she expected them to be eavesdropping.

He looked at her and decided abruptly to be honest. If she understood that he meant her no harm, they could perhaps work together to escape. 'They've been hired by my father.'

For a minute shock kept her silent, then she gasped, 'But why would he do that?'

'Because he wants me to marry you and this is his way of making sure you have to. I think he means to keep us here together for some time, compromising us.'

She stared at him in consternation.

'I'm sorry. I'm so very sorry. Believe me, I didn't agree to it. That's why he had me kidnapped too.' He closed his eyes, feeling utterly humiliated by the whole situation. 'Please don't hate me.'

Her voice was gentle. 'I believe you. It's not your fault, Peter.'

He opened his eyes again and took her hand. 'You're very generous.' He saw her shiver and wrapped the blanket round her.

'What can we do?' she asked in a low voice.

'I don't know. We can't escape in weather like this—and I don't think Jack's the careless sort, anyway. We'll just have to see what happens.' He saw the gleam of tears on her cheeks and pulled her to him. 'Ah, Georgie, don't cry. We'll get out of this somehow.'

Neither of them heard the door open, but Jack's jeering laughter made them jerk their heads round.

'Right old pair of lovebirds already, aren't you?' he mocked. He threw a small bundle of clothes on the bed. 'You're to get your clothes off, young lady, and put these on.'

She gasped as she looked at them. 'But that's a nightgown!'

'Aye.'

'I won't do it!'

He grinned. 'You can do it yourself or I'll bring Hobb in to do it for you. He'll enjoy that.'

Peter stood up and Jack immediately drew a knife out. 'Careful! Don't you come any closer or I may get careless.'

'Surely this isn't necessary?' Peter pleaded. 'It's too cold in here. She'll freeze to death if she's only got nightclothes.'

'Orders from my employer.'

'My father, you mean?'

Jack shrugged. 'You were stupid to tell her, but what's done is done. Now, are you going to get those clothes off yourself, Miss, or must we do it for you?'

She gulped and looked at Peter.

'I think you'd better do as he says.' In a whisper he added, 'I give you my word it'll make no difference to how I treat you.' He looked across at Jack. 'She'll not do it while you're standing there.'

Jack held up his hand, fingers spread out. 'Five minutes. And put the things she's wearing on the floor near the door.'

When he'd gone, Georgie began to sob.

'I'm sorry, but he means what he says and there isn't time to cry. I'll turn my back and you change quickly.' He got up off the bed and went across to stare out of the window as she changed near the fire.

Feeling utterly vulnerable, she scrambled out of her clothes and into the nightdress, relieved that there was a shawl with it. 'I'm changed now,' she said in a small, frightened voice.

Peter turned round and his heart went out to her. She looked so young and afraid. 'Wrap the blanket round yourself as well or you'll catch cold.'

The door opened again without warning and Jack picked up the bundle of clothing.

'We need more blankets,' Peter said angrily. 'And more coal, too.'

Jack considered this and nodded. 'I reckon you're right. No one expected a night like this. We're all snowed in together. Jolly, isn't it?' He raised his voice, 'Hobb! Bring us some more coal and another blanket or two, and look smart about it.'

When they were alone again, Georgie began to cry. She was filled with embarrassment to be wearing only a nightgown, she was hungry and tired, but most of all she was terrified of what was going to happen to her.

Peter went across and took her in his arms, cuddling her close and shushing her as she wept against him. Anger seethed in him at the thought of what his father had done and his own helplessness galled him.

-

Hepzibah sat in front of the fire, clad in one of her hostess's nightgowns, with a shawl round her shoulders and on top of it a blanket. She hadn't been able to speak, only shiver when she fell through the door but now she was beginning to thaw out and needed to get their help to start the hunt for Georgie.

'Ready to tell us what happened now, are you, love?' the farmer asked.

'Yes. But you won't believe me...'

When she'd finished they both sat gaping at her.

Hepzibah looked at her host. 'Can you lend me some dry clothes and take me into Tapton, please? I know it's late and the weather's bad, but I've got to tell Ben what happened.' She hated the thought of going out into the cold again, but it had to be done.

Her host exchanged glances with his wife and shook his head. 'Eh, I can't take you anywhere tonight, love. We'd both be dead afore we'd gone half a mile. It's as bad a snowstorm as I've ever seen.'

She sat there in dismay. 'But they've got Georgie!'

'Aye, and that's bad, I agree, but killing ourselves won't help the lass, will it?'

–

Ben opened the door to find Penelope Merridene and her two maids standing there. He urged them quickly inside, but snowflakes still whirled in with them.

'We couldn't wait any longer, not knowing what was happening,' Penelope said apologetically. 'Is there any news?'

He shook his head.

'There must be some way we can help.'

'Your sister's been organising Nan to feed the men helping me search, but at the moment everyone's waiting for Daniel to come back. He's gone to see some of his old friends from Brindley's and will try to find out if they saw anything today.' He eased his shoulders and neck as if they were hurting him. 'We don't even know where to look, only I'm sure Georgie wouldn't have planned to go for a walk on such a bleak day, let alone a sensible woman like Hepzibah going with her. I can only conclude that someone must have kidnapped them.'

'Can we stay? We might be able to help.'

For a moment or two a smile replaced the anxiety on his face and he said, 'Of course. Your family is very kind.'

'Me and Meg will go to the kitchen,' Sally said firmly. 'No need to show us the way, Mr Seaton.'

Ben hung up Penelope's cloak and ushered her into the parlour.

Martha joined them shortly afterwards. 'I've been turned out of the kitchen. Sally's taken charge there and Nan seems relieved to have her. They've decided to make a big batch of scones in case more food is needed. I hope that's all right, Ben.'

Penelope noted the use of his first name but didn't comment.

Someone else knocked on the front door and he went to open it, returning with Daniel who, since he was soaked to the skin and covered in melting snow, was protesting that he wasn't fit to enter the parlour.

His teeth were chattering and his face was so white with cold that Penelope moved to his side instantly, pulling him closer to the fire before Ben could say anything else.

'S-sorry,' Daniel managed. 'So cold out there.'

'Get that wet coat off before you do anything else,' Penelope ordered. 'Mr Seaton, have you something dry that Daniel can wear? Martha, will you go and fetch him a hot drink?'

When they'd gone, she helped him remove his sodden outer garments, and when he tried to protest against baring his chest, she brushed that aside and pulled his sodden undervest from him. 'I have no shame when it comes to looking after people I care about,' she teased softly.

'Eh, lass, I never know what you're going to say or do next.'

Ben returned with a woollen dressing gown and an assortment of clothing. 'They'll be too big for you, but they'll keep you warm at least.'

'I'll leave you for a moment,' Penelope said hastily.

While she was out, Ben watched Daniel pull on the dry clothes, then asked, 'Are you warm enough to talk now?'

Daniel nodded and as Martha came in with a big tin pint pot of tea and put it into his hands, he began sipping it as he started telling them what he'd found.

'One of the lads from Brindley's had sneaked out to the privy. He saw a carriage drive into the mill yard and go round to the back of the house. He stayed hidden till everyone had gone inside because they fine 'em at Brindley's for going to the privy except at lunch time, you see.'

'There couldn't be two strange carriages in town on a day like this.' Ben let out a growl of anger. 'That *must* mean Noll's involved.'

'Who else could it be anyway?' Daniel said. 'I was certain of that afore I even went asking.'

Martha joined in. 'It might be his son. Peter Brindley seemed rather interested in Georgie.'

There was a pregnant silence then Daniel cleared his throat and offered his other news. 'There's more. One of the women at Brindley's was taken ill a little later and had to go home, so I went to see her, which is why I was away so long. She saw the carriage come out of the mill and turn towards the town as she was walking home. That'd be about three o'clock.'

'Just before Georgie left school,' Penelope said thoughtfully.

'We'll have to get up a search party and find out where they went when they left town,' Ben said.

Daniel shook his head. 'You can't.'

'What do you mean?'

'I've never seen it snow so thickly. There'll be no search parties going out across the moors tonight and I doubt if anyone will be able to get up there tomorrow, either. The snow's settling and it's hard enough to walk round the town. It'll be impossible to move across the moors in safety.'

Ben stared at him as if transfixed, then let out a long, shuddering sigh. He turned instinctively to Martha as he asked, 'What am I to do? I can't leave things like this. There's Hepzibah as well as Georgie, and I—' He swung round and went to stand by the window, too upset to continue.

Martha went to stand beside him, her hand on his shoulder. 'I doubt you have much choice, Ben. No one can do the impossible and it'd not help your sister to get yourself killed.'

For a moment they stood there looking out, then he said, 'You're right. I'd better send the men home.'

'Let's send them with something in their bellies, at least. I'll go and tell Sally.'

He nodded, looking upset and not seeming his usual confident self. He followed Martha out of the room, putting on his greatcoat and taking Hepzibah's old shawl from the hook near the back door to wrap round his head. As he opened the door, wind screamed into the room and he paused to yell, 'I'll bring the men over here if they want a bite before they set off. And I'll send the watchman home, too. He'll freeze to death out there on a night like this and we can lock the gates. I doubt anyone will be breaking in.'

Martha helped Sally get food ready and the men stumbled inside, crowding into the kitchen covered in snow, which melted rapidly. She didn't comment on the mess they made, but offered them tea and buttered scones. They didn't waste time, eating these rapidly, drinking the hot tea and then going out again into the wind and snow with a chorus of thanks.

When she turned round, Ben was standing by the back door, still clad in his outdoor things. He looked so agonised she went across to him. 'Let me help you out of these wet things now. You won't be going out again, I'm sure.'

He let her do as she would then stood there staring at her, misery in every line of his face. 'I've failed to look after her.'

'This wasn't your fault. No one can keep another person totally safe, not even if they make them stay inside a house. Ah, Ben, don't blame yourself like this!' And she was in his arms, hugging him close and letting him hug her.

'The minute it's clear enough, I'll be out searching for them,' he said in a muffled voice, his head close to hers.

'Of course you will.'

He moved back a little, then bent his head and took her lips in the gentlest of kisses, his own lips still feeling chill against the warmth of hers. She was so surprised she didn't protest and then so caught up by the wonder of the kiss that she found herself kissing him back. When he pulled away again, she felt flustered, not knowing how to face him, and said quickly, 'Er—we must get you warm again.'

He didn't protest, had already guessed that she wasn't used to being kissed or courted. He didn't even know whether she was unmarried simply because she'd had no choice or whether she had chosen spinsterhood, as some women did. He wasn't a ladies' man, never had been, couldn't frame fancy speeches.

But for all its gentleness, the kiss still burned on his lips like a promise. And if it hadn't been for the worry about his sister, he'd have been proposing to Miss Martha Merridene, spinster of the parish, this very night.

–

When they were alone together, Penelope went to sit beside Daniel. She saw him shivering and moved closer to him, taking his hands in hers. 'You feel cold still?'

'Aye. It's a white hell out there. Never seen the like of it. I nearly got lost, fell over a few times…' He sighed and let his head rest on her shoulder.

'Your mother?'

'I sent her word I was helping Mr Seaton and that our Meg was staying here with me.'

For a few minutes they sat there then he turned and looked right into her eyes. Her expression was so filled with love that his heart melted within him and he couldn't resist kissing her. She fitted into his arms as if made for him, giving her lips happily, her own arms going up around his neck.

'Don't tell me we shouldn't love one another,' she begged when the kiss ended.

'I've given over telling you that.'

He smiled, such a fond smile that she felt warmth curl through her, and as his hand tightened on hers, she raised it to her lips and pressed a kiss against it.

'Will you marry me, Penelope love?'

The question was asked so simply, she answered in the same way. 'Yes, of course I will.'

'I don't know how we'll manage it, we may have to wait, but one day...'

'One day it'll be possible.'

They sat smiling at one another then moved closer for another kiss, this time one with passion and hunger in it.

'What on earth do you think you're doing?'

Martha's voice made them both jump in shock and pull apart, then Daniel stood up and Penelope joined him.

'I'm kissing the man I love,' she said calmly.

Ben moved into the room, ranging himself beside Martha, a grim expression on his face. 'Porter! A word with you outside.'

Penelope grabbed Daniel's hand and held tight. 'No. I apologise for forgetting where we were, but Daniel wasn't forcing himself on me.' She stared them both steadily in the eyes as she added, 'And our love won't go away just because you think it isn't *suitable*.'

'I can speak for myself, love,' Daniel said mildly, looking dignified for all the odd collection of garments he was wearing. 'Miss Merridene, I've fallen in love with your sister and if I can, I mean to marry her. I know I'm not good enough for her, but she doesn't seem to mind about that, so I intend to work my hardest and prove myself worthy.'

Penelope gave them a rueful smile. 'We didn't mean to announce our feelings yet, especially at a time like this, but they can't be ignored and I don't really care what other people think. I'm lucky to have found love for a second time and I'm not going to give him up.'

Martha hesitated, then stepped forward to hug her sister before turning to Daniel. 'I've no intention of being estranged from my only sister, so I'd better welcome you into the family. But I do hope you'll wait until you're in a position to support a wife properly.'

Ben watched them in astonishment. 'Are you just going to—to accept it?' he asked Martha.

'Yes, I am. Penelope's old enough to know her own mind.' She was both glad for her sister and envious. Why did Pen find it so easy to fall in love, not just fall, but admit it and do something about it? If Martha had ever had a real chance of such happiness she knew she'd have agonised about it, worried—and probably thrown it away. She'd always felt so responsible for her sister and father. And now, suddenly, she wasn't responsible for anyone but herself. That felt so strange.

And she had her own future to worry about. She shouldn't have let Ben kiss her like that, she really shouldn't. It was for comfort, that was all it could be.

Ben looked at the couple standing hand in hand smiling at one another. How easy they made it all seem! He watched Penelope persuade Daniel to sit down again by the fire and suddenly, envy for his Assistant Engineer shot through him. He was quite sure his own path wouldn't be nearly as smooth. Martha had kissed him, but afterwards she'd seemed flustered and embarrassed, withdrawing from him and finding an excuse to seek her sister's company.

And now she was avoiding his eyes, speaking briskly, keeping her attention on her sister.

Something told him marrying Martha wasn't going to be easy.

Chapter 15

The door opened and Hobb came into the room carrying two dishes of stew with hunks of bread sitting on top of them.

Jack followed, his wicked-looking knife much in evidence. He watched Peter carefully as Hobb deposited the plates on a scarred chest of drawers to one side then they both backed out of the room.

Georgie was sitting on a rickety wooden chair in front of the fire, wrapped in a blanket but still embarrassed by her state of undress. When Peter brought her a dish across, she shook her head. 'I'm not hungry.'

'You need to eat something or you'll not keep warm.' He held out the plate again. 'Please try.'

She took it from him and began to pick listlessly at the food with the spoon which was the only eating implement offered.

Feeling hungry he went to sit on the bed and was surprised to discover that the food was good. 'I wonder who's doing the cooking? I'm sure Hobb and Jack didn't make this.'

'I expect they have a woman looking after this place for them.'

He looked at her thoughtfully. 'I wonder if we could appeal to her for help? If she'd take pity on you and help us escape, we could promise her money.'

Georgie took another cautious spoonful, trying not to let the blanket slip and reveal her nightdress. 'I shouldn't think she'd dare do anything to upset them.' She shuddered at the thought of that knife, so shiny and sharp-edged.

'You never know. Money can make a big difference.' He flushed. 'I don't have any or I'd give it all to see you freed, but surely your brother would pay well for your safety?'

She nodded. 'He doesn't know where I am, though.'

'I don't know where we are, either,' he confessed.

Half an hour later the two men came back. Hobb picked up the dishes, leaving their two half-empty glasses of water behind.

Jack stood in the doorway looking at the captives. 'Can I just have a word with you in private, Mr Brindley?'

Peter was sure that if he left the room it would make Georgie less trusting. 'You can say what you have to in front of Miss Seaton. I presume it's another directive from my father?'

'It is indeed. He's going to keep you two here, alone together, until Seaton agrees to you getting wed.'

Georgie began sobbing and Peter went over to her, laying one hand gently on her shoulder.

'Don't touch me, you monster!' she cried, jerking away from him.

'I'm not a monster. Why do you think they had to kidnap me too?'

'It was probably all a trick to make me trust you.' She looked round wildly. 'I'll kill myself if you touch me!'

He squatted down so that he was on a level with her, picking up her hands and holding them in his. 'Georgie, it wasn't a trick. I did refuse to be part of this kidnapping.

But unfortunately, once we've been here for a few days you'll be compromised.'

She shuddered and pushed him away, flailing out with her hands.

He pulled her to her feet, though she resisted.

'What are you doing?'

'I can't speak to you properly like this. Come and sit on the bed beside me.'

'No, no!' She began to scream and struggle wildly.

–

When Martha woke up, she couldn't think where she was for a moment. She jerked upright and stared round. The room was filled with dim grey light and her sister was sleeping peacefully beside her. Pen always could sleep anywhere, she thought resentfully. Getting up, she found her cloak more by chance than by remembering where she'd laid it, and swung it round herself, shivering in the icy air.

In the grate some embers were still alight so she poked a stick of kindling carefully into the centre, trying not to disturb the small glowing patch. To her relief the kindling caught and she began to build up a fire with small pieces of wood and coal.

While she was waiting for it to take hold she moved across to the window, her bare feet silent on the thick carpet. Outside she could see no sign of life, nothing except shadowed whiteness. What time was it? Surely at this hour there should be people at the mill getting the machinery ready for the workers to arrive? But there was no sign of footprints in the pristine snow in the yard below her. Was the whole world still asleep?

At that moment a man came out of the back door, which was just below this bedroom. He stood for a moment on the kitchen steps, huddled in a cloak. Ben. She recognised him at once. Only as he began to move did she realise that the snow was at least two feet deep. He went across to the big gates and opened the little doorway in one of them. Some people were waiting outside and after a few words with their employer, they went away again, all except a boy and three men, one of whom was Daniel, she realised.

The men tramped through the snow to the mill, following Ben in single file and using his tracks, then vanishing inside.

Though she felt cold, she stayed there staring out, her thoughts churning round in circles. She'd been so tired she'd fallen asleep straight away last night, even though this was a strange bed and she was wearing one of poor Georgie's nightgowns, which was far too short for her. She'd meant to think about things before sleeping. No, she corrected mentally, to think about the way Ben had kissed her.

It had just been a kiss of friendship, surely? Only how was she to judge, she who'd never been kissed on the lips before? It had been very gentle and not at all alarming, in fact, very pleasant. She touched her lips, remembering.

He hadn't meant anything by it—had he?

She clutched the cloak around her, trying to understand her own feelings, and all she could think of was the way people had laughed and sneered back in Woodbourne when a spinster of many years' standing eventually got married. She'd hate people to talk like that about her. Of course 28 wasn't 48, but still… she had learned many years ago that gentlemen weren't interested in her in that way and therefore she mustn't get her hopes up. Or let herself be made a fool of.

She saw movement at the mill door and a man and boy came out with shovels and started digging a proper path through the snow. Of Ben and Daniel there was no sign.

'Are you going to stand by that window all morning?' a sleepy voice asked behind her.

She summoned up a smile and turned round. 'I didn't know you were awake.'

Penelope yawned and stretched with little murmuring sounds of satisfaction. 'I slept very soundly.'

Martha tried to divert her sister's thoughts from herself. 'Daniel arrived a few minutes ago. He and Ben went into the mill.'

'You call him Ben now, do you?'

'When something like this happens, it makes you feel closer to your friends.' She changed the subject hurriedly. 'I wonder how Georgie and Hepzibah are—and where they are.'

'For a minute I'd forgotten. Oh, Martha, I do hope they're both safe! Let's get dressed at once and see if there's anything we can do to help find them.'

'I doubt there will be. The snow seems to be about two feet deep, so they won't be able to send out search parties until it thaws.'

'Well, we can try to keep up Ben's spirits, at least.' She looked down at herself and grimaced. 'Though I think perhaps we'd better go home and get some clean clothes. If we're going to stay here, we should bring our own night things too.'

'We may not be able to get home so easily.'

'Oh, I think they'll dig paths round the town centre. If we wait till later, we'll get through without trouble.'

When they went down after a quick wash in icy water, they found Sally in the kitchen with Nan and Meg, preparing breakfast.

'You should have rung for some hot water,' Sally scolded.

'We managed,' Martha said. 'We got the fire burning again so weren't too cold.'

The kitchen was wonderfully warm, though, and Penelope went to stretch her hands out to the glowing stove.

'I'll have some tea ready in a few minutes and Meg's lit the fire in the parlour if you ladies would like to wait there,' Sally said pointedly. 'I don't want you under my feet. Nan and I have to get breakfast for Mr Seaton and yourselves, and then who knows what? I've already got some bread proving.'

'Whatever time did you get up?' Martha asked in surprise.

'I couldn't sleep. No use lying here, I thought, so up I got.' She looked at them and her gaze softened. 'I'll keep praying for that lass and Hepzibah, but my place is here, helping look after those people as can *do* something to rescue them. At my age I couldn't go tramping across the moors, even if it hadn't snowed. Now then, off with you!'

Penelope rolled her eyes at Martha behind their stern handmaiden's back and followed her to the front of the house and the parlour, which wasn't nearly as cosy as the kitchen.

Martha wished she were as certain of her role as Sally was. How could she best help Ben? She knew her presence here helped keep his spirits up, but what would happen when he went out looking for Georgie and Hepzibah? As she thought the situation through, she realised that if

Georgie had been interfered with—everyone's unvoiced fear—the poor girl wouldn't want a group of men rescuing her. She'd need a woman's help.

And if Hepzibah was hurt, she wouldn't want men tending her, either. *That's what I can do!* Martha thought as she went across to look out of the window. *I can go out with the searchers and be ready to help Georgie and Hepzibah. I'm a good walker, as strong as most men. I'm sure I won't hold them back.*

She watched people struggling through the snow to get to the mill entrance and then returning with joyful faces. The word 'holiday' rang out more than once as those who'd arrived early turned back the others. Since the parlour looked out to the front, she could see that the nearby snow was well trodden down on the footpath, though still lying deeply on the street, with no signs of wheel marks.

She looked up at the sky. It didn't look as heavy today, surely it didn't? Would it snow again or not? How soon would they be able to leave the town to search for Georgie? And would she be able to persuade the men to let her go too?

Her lips tightened. She'd find a way. She had to. She was quite sure that she would be needed.

—

Ben returned to the house soon afterwards, trying to keep at bay his desperate anxiety about his sister and Hepzibah's safety. The steam engine was idling and keeping the mill from freezing, but he couldn't in all conscience let his operatives spend the day in wet clothes, then go out again into the bitter cold. Nor could he settle to anything himself until he knew what had happened to Georgie.

A few people were staying at the mill to keep an eye on things and he'd make sure hot food and drink were sent out to them. They would have the old mill house to retreat to, with a fire to keep them warm. And maybe after this was all over, he'd build a covered walkway from the gate to the mill and also across to the house, or a room where the workers could get warm and dry their outer clothes.

Spoiling them, Brindley would call it. Well, Owd Noll was heading for real trouble the way he ran his mill. There had been plenty of accidents there, though not fatal ones, thank goodness. That was a miracle in itself. Daniel had left rather than take the guards off the machinery, but the new engineer was a dull fellow, barely capable of doing his job and was certain to do anything his employer asked of him without question.

Well, that wasn't Ben's business. He had enough on his own plate. But he and Jonas had discussed the situation quite a few times, worrying about those poor, thin children and stunted, hollow-eyed adults. And if they ever worked out a way to help them, they would take action.

Before he went inside he looked up at the sky, wondering if it was his imagination that it seemed lighter, looking as if it'd lost some of its grey heaviness by dumping its load of snow. Yesterday had been the worst snowfall he could ever remember, a real blizzard, and there would be deep drifts out on the moors for days. Even if it didn't snow again, he knew they'd not be able to get far out of town for a day or two—and by that time, who knew what would have happened to Georgie and Hepzibah? He stood still for a moment, oblivious to the icy wind as anguish about where his sister could be washed through him yet again.

He had failed her!

The minute he got inside the back door, Sally greeted him with a pair of slippers and an order to get out of his wet shoes before he tramped snow all over the house. 'And you'd better change your trousers, too, sir. Those are soaked.'

'But I'm going out again as soon as I've eaten.'

'Then you can change back into the wet ones before you do that, can't you? But if you sit around in them, you'll catch your death of cold and that will help no one.'

She sounded so like Hepzibah he didn't protest further.

And it was comforting to be gently scolded like that. Almost as comforting as holding Martha's hand had been.

–

Noll watched his operatives arrive for work, chilled and soaking. They should get sacks for weather like this and put them round their shoulders, he thought, forgetting that he'd refused to give them the old sacks from the mill, because he could get money for them from a rags dealer he knew.

When he went out to make his first round of the mill, he found himself beyond his knees in snow and yelled at Gerry to get a path to the house cleared at once. Ignoring his soaking trousers, he marched round, yelling at one group of workers who had let the fluff pile up under the machines. 'Get that lot cleaned up.'

'We'll do it as soon as they turn the machinery off for the night,' Gerry said soothingly. 'And they'll not get paid extra for staying behind, neither.'

'They'll get it done straight away. I don't want dirty fluff blowing up on to my clean yarn.'

'Them kids are stiff with cold. They'll not be as nimble today,' Gerry said placatingly. 'Best leave it till later.'

'They'd better be nimble. If they're not, they can find work elsewhere. I want it done now.'

Behind him he heard someone muttering a protest and swung round, yelling, 'Quiet!' If he'd known who it was, he'd have sacked them on the spot.

As he left the mill to go back for his breakfast and change his trousers, he turned back to Gerry. 'Don't forget to get the fluff cleaned out.'

Shaking his head, Gerry went back inside.

Noll went to change his trousers, then stuffed himself full of good food and toasted his feet in front of the fire.

His pleasure was rudely interrupted when someone hammered on the front door and refused to be told by the maid that the master wasn't available. Noll stood up and shoved his feet into his slippers, intending to go and tell whoever it was to clear off.

But before he could get to it, the door of his cosy parlour was flung open and Ben Seaton burst in.

'I want a word with you, Brindley!'

'I'm busy.' Noll saw such determination in the other man's face that he yelled, 'Fetch Gerry!' to the maid.

Ben turned and shut the door in her goggling face, then moved across to the older man. 'I want to know what's happened to my sister?' He watched Noll stare at him as though in puzzlement and yet felt quite sure the fellow was involved. Well, as Daniel had said, who else could it be in a small place like Tapton?

'How should I know what's happened to her? Have you lost her?'

'She's been taken away—in a carriage that stopped for a while in your mill yard.'

Noll was so shocked that Seaton knew about this, after all the care he'd taken, that he stammered, 'How did you—' before he realised he'd given himself away. He snapped his mouth shut on further careless words.

'How did I what?' Ben moved forward till he was standing toe to toe with Brindley. 'How did I find out?'

'I was only wondering how you came to that conclusion,' Noll said, forcing himself to speak mildly. Seaton seemed bigger than he'd remembered. How had he found out about the carriage, dammit? They'd had the operatives shut inside the mill while the vehicle was there, so who could have betrayed him? Whoever it was would lose their job and be booted out of town as well. He decided not to say anything about Georgie marrying Peter, not yet. He'd send round a note in a day or two, make Seaton sweat until then.

Ben guessed what Noll was thinking and said quickly, 'I was told by several people who saw the carriage going into your yard and coming out again yesterday afternoon.'

'Nothing to do with me. I was inside the mill all afternoon. Had a bit of trouble with one of the machines.'

There was a knock on the door and Gerry came in without waiting for an answer.

'Ah, there you are. I was just telling Seaton here I was in the mill with you all afternoon yesterday. He says a carriage came to the house then.'

'You were with me all afternoon,' Gerry agreed at once.

'The carriage must have been summat to do with our Peter,' Noll added.

Ben looked at them both, eyes narrowed, certain they were lying. 'Where *is* your son? I want to speak to him as well.'

'Went off to stay with friends,' Noll said promptly.

'In all that snow? I don't believe you. And besides, he doesn't have any friends round here.'

Ben's expression was so dark and threatening that Noll said quickly, 'Better go and fetch help from the mill, Gerry lad. Seaton's gone mad.'

His deputy turned towards the door, as obedient as a puppet. Ben was reaching out to stop him when there was a noise from the back of the house, voices shouting and a woman screaming.

'What the hell's that?' Noll asked. 'Go and find out, Gerry.'

But before the other man could make a move, the door of the parlour burst open for a second time that day. This time a group of the mill workers pushed inside, led by a huge man whose face was so ravaged by pain and grief that it upset Ben even to see it. That was how he'd feel if anything happened to Georgie.

'Get him!' the man yelled and they all surged forward.

For once Ben found himself outnumbered and could do nothing to prevent them dragging Noll Brindley outside. When he tried to follow, he found the door barred by two men who'd stayed behind, two large men with grim expressions.

'We've no quarrel with you, Mr Seaton,' one of them said. 'So you'll kindly stay here while we deal with him.'

'What do you mean, deal with him?'

'Do to him what he did to them two childer this morning.'

'Explain yourselves.'

'He insisted on the little lasses cleaning the machinery while it was still running.' Great tears were pouring from the man's eyes as he spoke and his voice stumbled and

286

faltered as he tried not to sob. 'The machinery's not been running well since Daniel Porter left an' today it suddenly—well, it threw out a gear an' they were under— oh, dear lord, their hair was caught up and they were killed. Two little lasses. *Two!* I can still hear the way their screams cut off.'

Ben's eyes filled with tears of sympathy, but he knew if there was trouble as a result of this, the men would suffer the full penalty of the law for it, not Brindley, who would claim it was just an accident. 'You still can't take matters into your own hands.'

'We can and we shall,' the other man said in a tight, bitter voice. 'Someone should have stopped that sod years ago. You don't know what a hell it is in this mill, Mr Seaton. It's not like your place, where you treat folk fairly. But even *he* doesn't usually send the childer under them back machines while they're still working. I'll give Cox that, he does keep the worst from happening when he can and…' He broke off to shake his head and knuckle away a tear, but he didn't move from the doorway.

'What are they doing to him?' Ben asked.

'Sending him to clean his own machinery—while it's still working.'

Ben tried to push forward but they barred the way. 'Don't do it. Go and tell them to let him go.'

'Nay. He deserves it. One of them lasses was nobbut eight, for all they pretended she were ten. The poor creature only started work here last month.'

Ben walked over to the fire. 'You might as well warm yourselves up while we wait.' As the men, both of whose clothing was still wet from their walk to work, moved instinctively towards the warmth, he pushed one aside so forcefully that he fell over and was out of the room before the other could stop him.

He ran through the kitchen, praying he'd be in time, but even as he started across the yard, he heard a chorus of wild shrieks and yells, with some cheers, and knew something had happened. He passed two still bodies lying on the snow, covered by a piece of canvas, but the snow was stained red under their heads. He didn't stop, having to force himself through the crowd now.

When they saw who it was they fell silent and parted to let him through.

Gerry stepped forward to bar the way. 'You're too late, Mr Seaton. He's killed hisself.'

Ben looked at him in shock, moved him aside and saw a bloody body lying in a tangled heap beneath the machinery.

'You couldn't never tell Mr Brindley anything,' Gerry went on. 'He allus had to know best. I told him not to get under the machinery, but he would do it, said it was easy, said the childer must have been careless an' he'd show 'em what was what.' He looked the other mill-owner in the eyes and dared him to say different.

Ben hesitated. He knew perfectly well that the operatives would have forced Noll under the machinery, knowing it would likely kill him, and that the man would never have crawled under there willingly. But when he looked round at the thin people, stunted in growth, hollow-faced from lack of good food, their clothing little better than rags, he suddenly knew he couldn't bring down the wrath of the law on them, for all these bystanders would likely be arrested too. Whether it was right or wrong, he simply couldn't do that to them.

He took a long, slow breath and then nodded. 'Foolish of him, but as you say, he always thought he knew best.'

A sigh ran round the crowd.

'Well, you'd better send for the magistrate, Cox. Don't move him. Leave everything as it is. Tell him what you told me.'

Gerry closed his eyes for a minute, swaying visibly, though whether from relief or delayed shock, Ben couldn't tell. 'Go and sit down, man,' he said more gently. 'There's nothing anyone can do till the magistrate arrives. It's been a dreadful—um, accident.' He looked across at the big man whose daughter had been one of the two killed. 'I'll pay for a proper funeral for those poor lasses. We can give them that, at least.'

The man nodded, but like Gerry he too seemed only half aware of what was going on around him now that the moment of mindless fury had passed. He seemed near to collapse and two others came to lead him away, giving Ben nods as they passed, as if to approve of what he'd said.

As he turned to walk out, somewhere not too far away he heard a woman weeping, on and on, a hopeless dirge of grief that followed him all the way out of the mill.

He prayed that he wouldn't lose Georgie, prayed with all his might. What had young Brindley done with her— and why?

-

Peter pulled Georgie over to the bed and plonked her down on it. It had suddenly occurred to him that her screaming and shouting would sound good to those no doubt listening outside. On that thought he went and jammed the chair back under the door handle. He didn't

289

want any of their captors wandering in while he was in the middle of this.

When he went back to Georgie, she shrank away from him, so he sat down on the bed a little distance away from her and waited.

'What are you going to do?' she asked in the end, her breath still catching on sobs and her face full of fear.

He kept his voice low. 'I'm not going to do anything to you, but we must come to an agreement, work together against them if we're to have any hope of escaping.'

'Do you really think we can?'

'I think we must try.' He reached out and took her hand, looking at her very solemnly as he made his promise. 'I won't touch you or hurt you in any way while we're here, Georgie. I can promise you that, at least.'

She looked down at his hand and then gave him a wobbly smile. 'I know. I'm not afraid of you, Peter.'

When she didn't pull her hand away, he felt better somehow. He might be helpless in some ways, but not in others.

Chapter 16

Nothing could be done to start a search for Georgie and Hepzibah that day, because the snow had gathered in drifts on the moors outside the town. Ben stubbornly insisted on going out to see how far he could get and came back soaked and shivering. Patches of snow on his clothing turned to water as he stood in the kitchen and Sally scolded him softly as she got him a cup of tea and helped him out of his clothes.

'You know,' he said with a wry smile. 'You and Hepzibah are so alike, you could almost be sisters.'

'I take that as a compliment, sir. And I'm praying hard that they'll come back safely.'

'Thank you. Are Martha and Penelope here still?' At her nod, relief surged through him. The last thing he wanted at the moment was to be alone to face the horrors his imagination kept dredging up.

'They're staying here again tonight in case they're needed. Meg's mother and Daniel are going to stay in our house to keep the fires burning and be on hand. Martha's arranged all that.'

She would, he thought, but didn't comment on her efficiency, just finished the cup of tea and went upstairs to change.

When he joined his guests in the parlour, he had to explain for a second time how deep the snow had been in parts and how impossible it was to get out of town. 'I'll try again tomorrow morning, see how far I can get.' He cast a resentful look out of the window. 'If it'd just start thawing, we'd be able to get through, I'm sure. As soon as there's even half a chance, I'll get a search party together.'

'When you do, I'm coming with you,' Martha said, chin up, ready to do battle.

He stared at her in surprise. 'It's a kind thought, but I'm afraid you'd hold us up.'

'I don't think so. I'm used to taking long walks in all sorts of weather and,' she hesitated and finished in a rush, 'Georgie may need me if—well, if the worst has happened.'

'The answer is still no. I'm not putting your life at risk.'

'If you don't take me, I'll follow you. You can hardly tie me up, can you?'

He looked across at Penelope. 'Will you please try to talk a little sense into your sister?'

'I'm afraid I agree with her. Georgie may indeed need a woman to look after her and Martha *is* a strong walker.'

'But her skirts will hamper both her and us. What's more, they'll get soaked and she'll be chilled through before we've gone very far.'

So Martha said what she had been thinking. 'I'm not going to wear skirts. I'm going to borrow some trousers and wear those. If you can find me an old pair of yours today, I'll alter them.'

He opened his mouth to refuse, then thought of Georgie and changed his mind. 'Some of my clothes from when I was a lad are stored in the attic. You'll probably find something that fits you better than my present things. But if you slow us down at all, I'll send you straight back, I warn you.'

Her eyes met his in a challenge. 'You won't need to. If I find I'm slowing you down, I'll go back of my own accord.'

'I still don't like it.'

She stiffened and for a moment tension crackled in the air, then she said quietly, 'I'll go and look for those clothes.'

They were in the second trunk she opened, so she and Penelope set to, adapting two pairs of his trousers, to be worn one on top of the other for warmth. They also found an old jacket, flannel underwear and shirts. When she was clad in several layers, Martha stared at herself in the mirror. He might have found her worth kissing before but he wouldn't now. She looked and felt strange, but was nonetheless determined to carry this through.

It seemed that fate was on their side because a thaw set in during the early afternoon. The sound of dripping water alerted Penelope, who ran to the window and called out to her sister to join her.

'Thank goodness,' said Martha. 'Now he can't stop me going with them.'

–

Just before dusk a man walked slowly into Tapton supporting a woman, both of them covered in snow and looking exhausted. One of the shopkeepers sent a lad running to fetch Mr Seaton and he came in time to see Hepzibah, white with cold and exhaustion, staggering along the street on a stranger's arm.

'Georgie?' he asked at once, going to help her.

She stopped and clutched him, her face crumpling as tears filled her eyes. 'I don't know where she is, Mr Ben. They threw me out of the carriage on the moors and if

I hadn't found a farm—this is Mr Hough whose farm it was—I'd be dead.'

'Come on. We need to get you warm—both of you.' One on either side of her, the two men helped her along the street.

Inside the house Ben guided his housekeeper into the kitchen, which was always the warmest room. He sat her and her rescuer in front of the fire and didn't question them while Sally bustled about getting a bowl of hot soup for them both then sending Nan up to warm Hepzibah's bed.

By the time they'd finished eating, darkness was falling fast and Mr Hough was looking out of the window anxiously. 'I'll not get back tonight.'

'We'll find you a bed here,' Ben said at once. 'We're very grateful to you for your help.'

'Thank you, Mr Seaton. But there wasn't much I could do, not nearly as much as I'd have liked.'

Ben turned to look at his housekeeper. 'Have you recovered enough to tell me exactly what happened, Hepzibah?'

She explained in detail and they all listened, not interrupting until she'd finished.

'Have you no idea who the man hidden by the cloak was?' Martha asked.

'None. But I could see that his ankles were tied up and he was wearing a gentleman's boots. Who *are* these villains and what do they want with Miss Georgie? I'm to blame. I should have looked after her better.' She began sobbing, utterly worn out by her worries and her gruelling walk through the snow.

Penelope went to put an arm round her. 'I think you've done everything you could, Hepzibah, including walking to Tapton on a day when most people would have stayed indoors.'

'I had to let Mr Ben know.'

'And he's grateful, but you're exhausted and the best place for you now is bed. Let me help you upstairs.'

Ben watched them go, sighing. 'I'd hoped she could give us some hint of where to look.'

Mr Hough cleared his throat. 'Begging your pardon, sir, but I think I can make some suggestions. You see, there aren't many dwellings up beyond us, it's mostly moors, and I know all the places with buildings. The other farmers wouldn't harbour villains, I'd stake my life on it, but there are a couple of houses it might be worth checking. There's nobody living in one of them, but it's a sound enough building still. The other belongs to a widow who scratches a living any way she can since her husband died. My wife won't have anything to do with her, which will tell you the sort she is. People say she has a brother in Manchester who sends her money, or she'd have gone under by now.'

After a pause for thought, he added, 'If your sister isn't at either of those two places, then they'll have taken her further afield and I can't help you—though I don't see how they could have got much further in that blizzard. It's still pretty bad on the tops, you know. We nearly turned back once or twice, only your housekeeper was desperate to get to you and the going got a bit easier as we came lower down, so we pressed on.'

'You must give me all the details you can. We'll start searching tomorrow.'

'I'll do better nor that, sir. Me and my son will guide you out to the places I mentioned.'

The two men shook hands.

Penelope went to bed early, claiming exhaustion, and Martha, after a moment's hesitation, settled down opposite Ben in front of the parlour fire. She knew she'd never sleep if she went to bed now. They sat in silence for a while, then she said thoughtfully, 'I don't understand why they had another prisoner. Who can he be?'

'I don't know. Peter Brindley is missing, but if he's part of the plot, why would they have to tie him up? It doesn't make sense.' He clicked his tongue in exasperation. 'If only Brindley hadn't died! I'm sure he's behind this and I'd have forced him to tell us where she is.'

'The magistrate recorded a verdict of accidental death, didn't he?'

'Yes.'

'Was it?'

He was shaken out of his somnolence. 'What made you ask that?'

'Something Daniel said.'

'I wasn't there. The workers say it was. I took their word for it, because I didn't want to see them get into trouble. The magistrate has asked me and Jonas to keep an eye on the mill until young Brindley can be found, so I've set Gerry Cox in charge and warned him to treat the operatives better. If it was up to me, I'd be raising their wages and improving conditions there, but I don't have the authority to do that.'

She couldn't find it in herself to regret Noll Brindley's death, however it'd happened. He'd been a nasty little man, and from what she'd seen and heard, his workers had been treated appallingly. 'Are we going out to hunt for Georgie tomorrow?'

'Yes. Well, we are unless it snows again, but I don't think it will. It feels much milder outside. We'll leave as soon as it's light.' He looked at her and added, 'I wish you'd think again about coming with us. I don't want to expose you to danger.'

'I shan't change my mind.'

'You're a stubborn woman!' he said angrily. 'How am I to protect you out there? It'll be as much as I can do to lead the others.'

She was just as angry. 'You won't *need* to protect me. I keep telling you that. Why will you not believe me?'

'Because you're a woman and women simply aren't as strong as men.'

She hated it when people said that to her. Since she was fourteen she'd had to be strong in so many ways, both physical and mental. It might make her seem unfeminine, stop men from being attracted to her, but it had been necessary—still was. 'I'll prove you wrong on that tomorrow.' She stood up, not tired but sure they'd only quarrel if she stayed. 'And I'll bid you good night now.'

He didn't call after her or wish her good night, and as she lay in bed she scolded herself for caring about that. She was thinking some very foolish thoughts lately.

–

Georgie woke up with a start, to find herself nestled in Peter's arms. He opened his eyes and for a moment looked equally surprised.

'Are you all right?' he asked gently.

'Yes.'

There was a knock on the door and it was flung open without more ado. Jack and Hobb stood in the opening, grinning.

Peter got up, snatched his cloak off the top of the bedcovers and flung it round himself, then fetched Georgie's from the chair.

'Your father will be very pleased at how cosy you're getting,' Jack said.

'Hang my father. We need some more coal.'

'Hobb will bring you some.'

'Surely you're not going to keep us here much longer?' Peter asked. 'After all, we've spent the night together. That was what my father wanted, wasn't it?'

'We'll be here a day or two yet.'

'I don't understand the need. Take us back to town now. I'll make it all right with my father.'

Jack's grin broadened. 'Can't take anyone anywhere. We're snowed in. Looks like we'll all be here for several days.'

Georgie uttered a cry of distress, and when Hobb had brought the coal and left, locking the door behind him, she looked at Peter. 'What are we going to do?'

'There's nothing we can do about the weather. He's right there.' He felt her shiver. 'If you sit down, I'll put some more coal on the fire. It's grown cold in here.'

But she didn't sit down. Instead she pulled the cloak round herself and wandered across to the window, staring out over an expanse of dazzling white. That horrid man was right. They were trapped here. No one would be able to rescue her even if they knew where she was. Tears trickled down her cheeks and she kept her back to the room, trying to control her emotions. She had never felt so helpless in her whole life.

Peter came across and put his arms round her from behind, staring out with her. After a while he turned her round gently, set his hands on her shoulders and looked at her very solemnly. 'When we get back—well, I don't know what your brother will say. He'll be furious and rightly so, but if he feels it that we should marry because your good name is compromised, then I can think of nothing I'd like better.'

'That's just what your father wants.'

He sighed. She was right and there was no changing that. 'I know. I'm so sorry, Georgie. I hate my father. He made my mother's life a misery and has done the same to mine. I'm trapped with him because I have no money of my own and wasn't brought up to earn any.'

'What about the mill? That'll be yours one day.'

'Have you seen it? It must be the most miserable place on earth and he treats his operatives abominably. It sickens me to see the poor creatures. You must have seen them, too. They're half-starved, utterly worn down by life. As for the children… they're all shrunken and worn. That's the worst thing of all, to see the children.'

'When the mill's yours, you can change all that, surely?'

He gave a mocking laugh. 'What do I know about running a mill? Anyway, my father will probably live till he's ninety and I'll die first.'

'Why is he so eager for you to marry me? Is it for my money?'

'Not really. He wants grandchildren whom he can train in his own ways. He thinks I'm too much of a fool to bother with.'

'I don't think you a fool.'

'I'm glad of that, at least.'

She continued to look out of the window and lean against him, feeling comforted by his closeness. It suddenly occurred to her that he had just proposed to her and she gave a wry smile. Not how she'd expected her first proposal to be made. And yet… he was gentle and kind and she felt at ease with him, even now. 'You know, I think I'd like to marry you, Peter.'

He kissed her cheek. 'You must be the only woman in the world who would.'

'Don't be silly.'

He laughed and kissed her nose, then they went back to the fire, she sitting on the only chair and he sitting on a folded blanket at her feet. After a while he leaned against her knees with a weary sigh and she dared to stroke his hair. They passed the day chatting, never short of something to talk about, sharing memories of their childhoods, sharing too their hopes for the future.

'You don't see me as a child, do you?' she asked at one stage.

'No. I see you as a woman—and a very desirable one, too.'

She smiled, a secret, satisfied smile. With him she felt like a woman and was glad it was just the two of them and that those horrible men were elsewhere.

If she married Peter, she'd have someone all her own—and a life of her own, too. As long as old Mr Brindley didn't interfere.

But would Ben let her? Would he allow her the money she'd inherited so that she and Peter could make a new life for themselves?

And what did old Mr Brindley intend to do with them when they got back? She was sure he'd have made plans to take over their lives and force them to do as he wished. He was that sort of man.

Whatever his plans, she'd be ruined unless she married Peter. She was well aware of that.

But she wasn't having Owd Noll bringing up her children, not under any circumstances. She'd have to persuade Ben to intervene and help Peter. Surely he would?

–

They planned to set out at first light, Ben and seven of his men, Mr Hough and Martha. He left Ross Turner in charge of the mill and instructions with Sally and Hepzibah to provide warm drinks and soup for the operatives at midday, if they could, for it was still bitterly cold. He sent the same instructions to Gerry Cox, telling him to get Brindley's housekeeper to do the necessary cooking.

The messenger said Cox had looked dumbstruck when he heard this.

Ben made sure each of the men going with him was warmly clad, delaying the start to raid the attics again for extra garments for those whom he knew to be short of money and therefore of warm underclothes.

Then they set out, tramping through the slush in town then making their way up into a white landscape, where shadows looked blue in the distance, black close at hand. The going was hard, but the thaw had got rid of some of the snow, and as long as they kept to the roads which were clearly marked by the dry-stone walls running on either side of them, they managed.

As they got right out on the moors, however, the going became more difficult and their pace was inevitably slowed.

Martha was well aware that Ben was watching her surreptitiously. Well, let him watch! She was doing no worse than the other men and it was a relief to be out of the house, in spite of the cold wind chafing her face.

She was secretly delighted by the trousers, finding them so much easier to walk in than long skirts and petticoats.

At one point Daniel came to walk beside her. 'Penelope was right.'

'About what?'

'You're a good walker.'

She smiled at him. 'I think she's right about you, too. You'll make her a kind, loving husband.'

His beaming smile lit up his whole face. 'I still can't believe it.'

She couldn't help being a little jealous of the joy he and Penelope showed at the mere mention of each other's names. No wonder her sister had seized this chance for happiness, even though the world might call it a mismatch.

When Ben came to walk beside her a little later, he greeted her with a scowl so she scowled right back.

'How are you going, Martha?'

'As you can see, I'm fine.'

'Hmm.' He trudged along beside her without speaking.

Of course it would have to be just then that she slipped and nearly fell. And he would have to catch her! 'Thank you.' She let go of him and started moving again.

'Please go back, Martha!'

'Just because I nearly fell? Certainly not. Several of the men have fallen. It's unavoidable in conditions like these.' She heard him mutter something under his breath which sounded like, 'Stubborn fool of a woman', but didn't challenge him. She needed her breath for walking. They all did.

Soon after that they reached Mr Hough's farm, where his wife burst into tears of relief at seeing him come home safely, then started laughing at herself within the minute for being so foolish. She insisted on everyone crowding into her kitchen, regardless of the moisture they carried in with them even after kicking their snowy feet and legs against the outer wall.

She made them a hot drink and a jam butty each— which Martha found to be a slice of newly-baked bread, with butter and jam spread thickly over it. She ate her butty with relish and by the time Mr Hough's son Ted had got ready to lead one group, she was quite ready to set off again. When Ben looked at her and frowned, she put up her chin defiantly, upon which he shook his head and gave her a wry smile.

After about a mile, the two groups split up, Ted leading their group to the farm occupied by the widow, Mr Hough taking the others in the direction of the deserted building. By that time Martha was definitely feeling the strain of walking in such conditions, but nothing would have made her admit it, let alone go back. Besides, some of the men were clearly in the same state as she was because the snow was laying more thickly up here and made trudging along difficult.

But oh, she liked these moors, the vast spaces and rolling uplands! They seemed to call to her and she promised herself to go for long tramps across them when the weather improved, even if she had to hire a guide to do it.

Ben watched her covertly, admiring her rosy cheeks and sparkling eyes. She was a woman in a million and had kept up without any more difficulty than most of his men. But he couldn't help worrying about her, all the same, just because she was a woman. If they did meet these villains, he'd make sure she was kept out of the way, by force if necessary.

Then, when this was over and his sister safe, he meant to speak to Martha, ask her if he had any chance with her. He gave a wry smile. If they could stop quarrelling for long enough. He couldn't understand why tension sometimes sizzled between them, while at other times they got on so well together. He knew she was attracted to him, knew it as well as he knew his own feelings for her. But what did a plain man like him know about wooing and marriage? All he knew was that he loved Martha and wanted to be with her.

He thought, hoped, prayed that she loved him too. If she didn't—he couldn't bear to think about that...

Pulling himself together, he began to talk to Ted about this farm they were heading for, asking what it was like, how exactly it was situated.

-

Georgie woke that morning feeling even more down-hearted than usual. Their imprisonment felt to be going on and on, and it seemed as if the walls were closing in on her and the room getting smaller each time she woke. If it hadn't been for Peter she would have gone mad, she was sure, but he was there, speaking to her gently, protecting her from Jack and Hobb's innuendoes as much as he could, and sleeping with her in his arms every night, though he'd not touched her in any other way.

Although it hadn't snowed since the blizzard, the moors were still blanketed in white and that made escape impossible. Besides, she didn't have any proper clothes. You couldn't trek across the snow in a nightdress and shawl. And their captors were always extremely careful when they brought food and drink or took away the slops, so neither she nor Peter could work out a way to get past them. Even the window was nailed shut and the door was solidly built, always locked.

'I'm useless to you,' he said suddenly from beside her.

'Why do you say that?'

'Because I can't find a way to rescue you.' He let out one of his bitter, unhappy laughs. 'I'm useless at everything I try. You should pray that no one makes you marry me.'

Her heart went out to him. They'd exchanged many confidences over the past few days and she'd grown fond of him. How could she not? Behind the bravado was a very unhappy man, one with little confidence in himself or his abilities—but who'd protected her in the only way within his power. She'd grown to love him, but he wouldn't believe her when she said so. 'I keep telling you that I *want* to marry you, Peter, and I mean it. I think Ben will try to prevent it, but I shan't let him stop us.' After a moment's thought, she added slowly, 'Maybe we should give him reason? Sleep together as your father hoped for.'

He stared at her in shock then a sad expression settled on his face. 'No. I won't do it, hard as it is to resist you. In that at least I shall have something to be proud of.'

'Don't you *want* to love me?'

'More than anything, my darling girl. And if I were a better man, if I had anything—anything at all!—to offer you, I'd ask your brother's permission to marry the minute we get back. But I've nothing, Georgie.'

'Couldn't you learn to do something, even work in the mill with your father? Perhaps if you showed yourself capable, he'd let you make some changes there.'

'I doubt it. He's a cruel, ruthless man, interested only in making money.'

'Then we'll have to find you something else to do,' she said firmly. 'If you really do want to marry me, that is.'

His face was so full of love she could have no doubt he meant what he said. When he drew her towards him and kissed her, she went willingly. If he loved her like this, with her hair a mess, only a torn nightgown to cover herself with, then it was truly love. Something inside her eased at that thought and she raised one hand to caress his cheek and hair. 'We'll work something out,' she said confidently. 'I'm not giving you up.'

'You almost make me believe it's possible.'

They went to stand at their favourite spot by the window, arms round each other's waists, staring out as they often did at the moor, watching the patterns of light play across them as cloud shadow was followed by sunlight and then by shadows again.

Only today they saw something moving across the snow.

'What's that?' she asked, pointing.

'It looks like—it is!—men's heads. Someone's coming up the slope towards the farm.'

'Could it be rescuers?'

'I don't know. I hope so.' And he didn't know whether to be glad or sorry at the thought of rescue. His time with her had been sweet, so very sweet.

Chapter 17

The farm was a small place, one storey high, built of whitewashed, plastered stone with a grey slate roof and set in a shallow depression below the road. The white-wash was patchy with mould and looked grey against the dazzling white of the snow. In a few parts the plaster had broken off, exposing the stonework beneath.

As they got closer, Ben let out an exclamation. 'Look! There's a coach outside the back.'

'This must be the place, then,' Daniel said.

Snowdrifts in a hollow forced them to tramp further round the walls so that they approached the farm from the front again.

'They must have seen us by now,' Ted muttered.

'Well, according to Hepzibah, we outnumber them, so—'

A shot rang out, ploughing into the snow in front of Ben.

'Take cover!' he yelled, pulling Martha down behind him. When he'd checked that the other men had sought shelter in the lee of a nearby wall, he turned to gaze at her and say grimly, 'If you don't promise to stay here and leave this to the men, I'll tie you up myself.'

'I'll come no further, I promise you,' she said quietly. 'It's afterwards you'll need me. And Ben—'

'Yes.'

'—be careful yourself.'

A moment longer he stared at her, then, satisfied she meant what she said, he nodded and moved on.

–

Peter and Georgie heard Hobb call out from somewhere in the house and the outside door banged open.

'They've seen them too,' she said. 'What if they send them away again, pretend they haven't seen us? They'll come in here and keep us quiet, I'm sure.'

Peter stepped away from her and went to get the chair, setting it under the door, their only form of privacy and that a dubious one. 'I don't know how long that'll keep them out for, but we have to try.'

'Let's put the bed behind it as well, and the chest of drawers. Then let's break the window and scream for help.'

'You're indomitable.'

She laughed aloud. 'Come on. Let's do it!'

–

In the kitchen of the farm Jack was cursing under his breath. 'How the hell did they find us?'

Hobb and Dirk said nothing, waiting for his instructions.

Suddenly they heard the sound of furniture being moved about inside the bedroom. 'What the hell are those two doing?' Jack snarled, then glanced back at the group of men approaching the farm. 'I'll slow those sods down. You go and fetch the girl, Hobb. She'll make a useful hostage. Leave *him* locked in the bedroom. Knock him on the head if he objects.' He picked up the pistols which were lying ready loaded on the table, sticking one in his belt and holding the other ready to use.

When Hobb tried to open the bedroom door, it wouldn't budge. 'They've set summat behind t'door!' he yelled. From inside he heard the splintering of glass and then two voices began calling for help.

'Kick the bedroom door down an' shut them two up, Hobb,' Jack ordered. 'I'll deal with those sods outside.'

His henchman began to kick the door and it gave a little. He turned to Dirk. 'Come and help, you!'

With two men throwing themselves against it, the door jerked open little by little until Hobb could push his way inside. He almost burst out laughing at the sight of the two occupants, clutching one another with scared expressions on their faces. 'Come here, Miss Georgie! You're wanted.'

'No.'

Peter set her behind him, which made Dirk chuckle. He left it to Hobb to deal with him while he grabbed the lass and pulled her towards the door. It wouldn't take two of them to deal with that runt.

–

Martha watched her companions creeping forward towards the house inch by careful inch, taking advantage of every bit of cover. She looked round, wondering what she could do to help. There must be something, surely? Then her eyes lit on what seemed to be a shovel handle, leaning against a wall, its lower end hidden by snow. She wriggled sideways towards it. She had only promised to go no closer to the house, after all, not to sit still. Protected by a curve in the wall, she pulled the wooden handle out of the snow and found that it was indeed attached to a shovel, a rusty old thing, but it seemed stout enough. It'd make a weapon of sorts, if nothing else. She began to edge along the wall towards the curve, wanting to get a better vantage point.

As she stared at the farm, she saw that the man with the pistol was still standing by the door. He yelled a threat to shoot anyone who came close and Ben held up one hand to prevent his men from moving forward into the line of fire.

The armed man then turned his head for a moment to yell something through the doorway behind him and from where she was standing, she saw another man came out of the house and vanish into a tumble-down outbuilding at the rear. He emerged leading two horses, which he proceeded to harness to the carriage. She suspected that this activity was hidden from Ben and the rescuers by the house.

The kidnappers were trying to escape! What could she do to prevent them? Should she go round to the other side of the building and warn Ben? She looked down again at the shovel, remembering how narrow the entrance to the farm had been. Was there time to block it with snow and prevent the carriage leaving, or at least slow it down? Coming on foot, they'd found the snow untouched near the gate, which showed that no one had left the farm since the blizzard. Perhaps she could pile it higher?

Bending low to stay hidden, she hurried back the way they had come. At the entrance to the farm she saw a broken gate leaning against the perimeter wall. It had come off its hinges and goodness only knew where the other gate was, but perhaps she could use it. If she could move it.

Throwing down the shovel, she started to drag the gate across to the entrance. At first it resisted her efforts, but as she struggled it moved a little, then a little more, then fell across the gateway, with a couple of slats falling off it. She had to jump out of the way but laughed exultantly at this. Panting, she dragged the gate a little further then began to shovel snow around it, able to tilt one end into the snow, so that the gate stood half-upright in the middle of the entrance, a clear sign to both horses and driver that they couldn't pass.

It was surprising how quickly the pile of snow grew, because it was soft enough to let her shovel it freely. She kept looking over her shoulder to make sure no one surprised her and when she paused for rests, she listened hard. Her hands were hurting and she looked down, surprised to discover blisters. But there was no one else to continue the work so she carried on shovelling the soft white snow into a pile that grew higher by the minute in the middle of the entrance.

It wouldn't hold them for long, but maybe it'd hold them for long enough.

–

Hobb disposed of Peter with a massive blow to the chin, laughing to see him fall so easily. Dirk had already begun pulling Georgie out of the bedroom, though the little hellcat fought and struggled against him.

'Bring a blanket, you fool, or she'll freeze to death,' Hobb said, then raised his voice to yell, 'Peg, come here and help!'

Jack's sister was in a foul mood. 'I never agreed to this. Our Jack's gone crazy, shooting at folk, kidnapping lasses. They hang you for this sort of thing, you know.'

'Only if they catch you,' Hobb snapped, sick of her whining. 'You keep Madam here in the kitchen till Jack calls for her.' He forced Georgie down in a chair and she pulled the blanket round her, jerking as far away from him as she could.

'He wants you two to harness the horses,' Peg said. 'Didn't you hear him yelling?'

'Too busy getting the girl and shutting Brindley up.'

As the two men went outside Peg picked up the poker. 'Give me any trouble, young woman, and I'll knock you senseless. I'd really like to hit you, because you've been more trouble to me than you're worth.'

Georgie glared at her but sat still.

When the carriage was ready Jack yelled, 'Bring the girl out.'

Peg dropped the poker and grabbed Georgie's arm, twisting it behind her to make sure she didn't try to escape and then dragging her to the door.

Jack edged towards the corner of the building, from where he could still keep an eye on the intruders but also watch his companions. 'Good girl, Peg. Bring her here to me.'

'I'll give you "good girl"!' she muttered. 'This'll cost me my farm.'

'You know you hate living out here and I'll make it up to you. Just get into the carriage and keep a tight hold of the lass when I tell you. She's the key to our success.'

'Don't worry. I will.'

He turned to yell at the attackers, 'We've got the girl and if you try to stop us leaving she'll be the one to suffer.' He dragged Georgie forward to where they could see her, then pulled her back and shoved her towards Peg. 'Into the carriage.'

Ben had been edging forward a little every time he thought the villain's attention was distracted and was now able to see the rear of the farm. He could only crouch there, heartsore, watching as his sister was led out, wrapped in a blanket that was half falling off, since one arm was twisted behind her. Beneath it she was only wearing what looked to be a nightdress. What had they done to her? Where were her clothes? She'd freeze to death in that meagre garment.

He didn't own a gun, didn't want to, but now wished he had borrowed one before he set out. He'd have happily shot anyone who hurt Georgie. After they'd threatened to harm her if he tried to prevent them leaving, he shouted, 'If you harm her in any way I'll find you and kill you myself.'

'What would we harm her for when you'll pay us good money to get her back safe?' Jack mocked, suddenly deciding to hell with Noll Brindley and his plans—he'd make as much as he could for himself out of this now that they'd been rumbled, then run away somewhere no one would ever find him.

As the carriage began to move slowly out of the farm-yard, Ben saw another man rush out of the house with a knife and try to cut the harness.

The largest of the villains jumped down and thumped the fellow before he could damage the harness. He fell like a stone, nearly under the horses' hooves and his attacker kicked him out of the way before getting inside the carriage again.

'That man's young Brindley,' said Daniel suddenly.

'It can't be! Why would he be trying to stop them?'

'I don't know, but he's definitely not on their side.'

As they watched, the big man thrust Georgie forward into the gap left by the open door of the carriage. He held a knife in front of her while the one with the pistol climbed up to sit next to the driver.

Ben cursed under his breath, feeling frustrated beyond measure. 'As soon as they start up the track towards the road, follow them but keep your distance,' he ordered and there were murmurs of agreement from his men.

—

As the carriage rumbled slowly up the gentle slope, Dirk glanced behind and said, 'They're following us.'

'They're only on foot. We'll soon leave 'em behind once we get on the road,' Jack gloated, pleased with the success of their escape. He raised his voice to call, 'Whip the horses up a bit, lad.'

'They can't go any faster. It isn't safe in all this snow.'

'Do as I tell you!'

Dirk yelled at his horses, who moved a little more quickly only under the persuasion of the whip cracking above their heads. As they turned the final bend he yelled in shock at the sight of the makeshift barrier and reined in the animals, which were trying to turn aside to avoid the piled snow and gate.

Jack dropped his pistol and clung for dear life as the carriage rocked wildly.

Georgie, still standing in the doorway of the carriage, felt Hobb's arm slacken and seized the opportunity to throw herself out and roll away across the snow. She stumbled to her feet as Hobb jumped after her, knowing she hadn't a chance against a huge man like him, but still not willing to give in without a fight.

Then a figure she recognised as her teacher ran forward to stand in front of her holding a shovel poised in mid-air like a weapon.

Hobb stopped dead. 'Come and help me with these two, Dirk.'

'Can't. Got to calm these bloody horses. You'll have to clear that mess away.'

Jack picked up his pistol again and roared, 'Come back over here, you stupid bitch, or I'll shoot you.'

'Shoot me, then!' Georgie yelled back before Martha could stop her. 'I'd rather die than go anywhere with you.'

Martha saw he really did mean to shoot and pulled her foolhardy young companion down to lie on the ground just as he pulled the trigger.

Cursing loudly as the shot meant to hit Georgie in the arm went wide, he cast that pistol aside now that both its chambers had been fired and began to fumble in his belt for the other one. But the horses were still upset and the loud noise had made them start rearing and whinnying again. One of them was trying desperately to free itself from the tangled harness and the carriage was rocking about even more wildly than before. It took all Jack's strength not to fall out. 'Get her back here, Hobb!' he roared.

Just as Hobb reached Georgie, Ben came up from behind the carriage. The relief in her face alerted her pursuer and he swung round as Ben lunged for him. Both men struggled to move through the snow and went down in a welter of fists and feet.

Jack managed to pull the second pistol out and tried to aim it at Ben, but the men were rolling to and fro and he couldn't get a good shot in. Then a big snowball took him in the face and by the time he had spat out the snow and wiped it from the eyes with the back of one hand, Daniel was dragging him out of the carriage and fending off his attempts to turn the pistol on him.

One of the other men came to Daniel's assistance and they stopped the fight quite simply by pushing Jack's face down into the snow.

While this was going on, Peg got out of the carriage on the other side and started back towards the farmhouse, stopping short when a man moved in front of her.

'They made me do it,' she whined, cringing as if expecting a blow.

'Tell that to the magistrate!' He grasped her arm.

Martha could feel Georgie shaking with cold. Sure that the other men wouldn't let Ben be defeated by Hobb, she hauled her companion to her feet and wrapped the cloak more tightly round her. 'I need to get her back to the kitchen fire,' she called out to Daniel and began urging Georgie to return to the farmhouse. She looked at the woman. 'You'd better come with us.'

'Hadn't I better keep hold of her?' the man asked. 'Who knows what she'll do?'

'I don't think there's anywhere she can escape to and if she tries anything, I'll be happy to thump her myself,' Martha said grimly. 'I'm a good deal bigger than she is.'

The woman muttered something beneath her breath but fell in behind Martha and Georgie.

Dirk was still busy calming the horses and had signified that he didn't intend to resist any more, so the only ones left still struggling were Ben and Hobb. Daniel took his muffler and bound Jack's hands behind his back, then went cautiously up to the struggling pair. They were evenly matched, but he didn't see why Hobb should have the opportunity to land any more punches on Ben's already bruised face, so waited until he saw his way clear, then dived into the fight to pull Hobb's head back by the hair and hold it for long enough for Ben to land a massive punch on the man's temple that knocked the light of battle from his eyes and made him sag back.

'I could have finished him off on my own,' Ben growled.

'If you want Martha to be attracted to you, you'll do better with your face in one piece.' As Ben gaped at this frank speaking, Daniel kept a wary eye on Hobb. 'We'd better tie him up before he comes to or we'll have it all to do again.'

Ted had stepped in to help Dirk with the horses and at last the two animals were standing still, quivering in reaction to the near accident. 'One of 'em's scratched hissen,' Ted called, 'but I think the poor creatures will be all right.' He looked at Dirk. 'You aren't going to give us any trouble, are you? Good. Then help me get this thing turned round and back to the farm.'

Seeing that everything was under control, Ben looked round for Martha and his sister.

'They've gone into the house,' Daniel said. 'Georgie was only wearing a nightgown under that cloak.'

Ben's face lost its look of triumph and took on a grimness that boded ill for her kidnappers.

'You go back to her,' Daniel said softly. 'I'll sort this lot out.'

'Thanks.' Ben set off as quickly as he could manage, but had to slow down as he slipped and slid on the trampled snow.

–

Outside the back door of the farmhouse the three women found Peter Brindley standing unsteadily, clutching the door frame for support, looking dazed and chalk-white.

Georgie forgot her own troubles and flew across to him, putting her arm round his waist in a gesture so familiar it was obvious to Martha she'd done this before. 'Are you all right, Peter? I saw them hit you again.'

He clung to her. 'Feel dizzy.'

'Come inside.' She forgot the others as she guided him through the back door.

Martha jabbed her forefinger into the woman's back and Peg went forward at a run. Shutting the door behind them, Martha looked round the kitchen, nose wrinkling at the grubby state of the room. 'Build the fire up,' she ordered and the woman hurried to obey her, recognising the voice of authority.

Georgie had sat Peter down on a high-backed wooden settle and was examining his head, making soothing noises and seeming quite unconscious of the fact that she was scantily clad in a nightgown.

Martha blinked in surprise at the pair of them, then moved forward to say, 'Don't you have some clothes, Georgie?'

The girl turned. 'What? Oh, they took them away.'

'I know where they are,' the woman volunteered, adding, 'They made me do this. I didn't want to.'

'Never mind that, go and get her clothes right away.'

When the woman returned, Martha had to tap Georgie on the shoulder to get her attention. 'You'd better go and put your clothes on. I'm sure the men will be back in a minute.'

'You won't—hurt Peter?'

'On the contrary, I want to look at his injuries.'

Georgie returned to the room very shortly, hair in a tangle still but respectably clad, at least. 'It wasn't Peter's fault,' she said at once. 'They kidnapped him, too, you know.' She went across to stand by him, holding his hand.

Martha looked from one to the other, recognising the same sort of invisible connection she had seen between Daniel and Penelope. How had this happened so quickly? She'd have sworn the two of them barely knew one another before this incident.

Just then the door banged open and Ben almost erupted into the room. 'Georgie, are you all right?'

'Yes, thanks to Peter.'

Ben looked from her to the man on the settle. 'Is there somewhere else we can go to discuss this matter, Brindley?' he asked, his tone frigid.

'There's a bedroom,' Georgie said acidly, 'but since Peter and I have spent the last few days in there, I don't feel like going back, thank you.'

If Ben had been frigid before, his tone was positively icy now. 'I'm not including you in the invitation, Georgie. We'll step aside for a few minutes, if you please, Brindley.'

Georgie set her hands on her hips. 'No, you won't! Can't you see he's injured?'

Martha didn't know what had been going on, but clearly Georgie had not only survived it, but found love in the process.

'I need—to speak—to him,' Ben said, articulating each word as if it was an effort to hold back his anger.

'Well, you'll have to wait. We're tending his injuries first.'

'He needs to explain himself to me, as your brother.'

Georgie rolled her eyes. 'You're really good at ordering people around, Ben Seaton, but you're not going to spoil

319

my life and you're not going to shout at my Peter while he's in no state to stand up for himself.'

Ben gaped at her. *'My Peter?'*

Peter hauled himself to his feet. 'He's right, love. He and I do need to talk.'

'Don't you dare call my sister "love"!'

'Oh, stop shouting at people, Ben. I'm perfectly all right—and didn't you hear me say that that is thanks to Peter, so stop treating him like—like a pariah.'

Martha put her hand on Georgie's shoulder. 'Your brother's been out of his mind with worry about you.'

'I can speak for myself, thank you, Martha.'

He didn't even look at her as he spoke and suddenly she began to grow angry. Was she so unimportant?

Into the heavy silence, Georgie announced, 'You may as well know that I love Peter. He saved me from them and we're going to be married and—'

'Over my dead body!'

'We've been living together ever since they kidnapped us and—'

'If he's bedded you, I'll kill him,' Ben said flatly.

'Well, he hasn't!' she flung back at him. 'He hasn't touched me at all in that way. But I wish he had, then you'd *want* me to marry him.'

Ben stood there, opening and shutting his mouth, clearly at a loss at this unexpected attack.

'I think we can postpone these discussions until we get back to town, don't you?' Martha said coldly. 'Georgie needs a bath and a change of clothes and Mr Brindley really does need his injuries tending properly.'

'The matter is only postponed,' Ben snapped. 'I'll go and see if the carriage is ready.'

'What's made him so bad-tempered?' Georgie demanded as soon as he was out of the room.

It was Peter who answered. 'Worry about you. I don't blame him in the least.'

'Well, I do. And for once, he's not telling me what to do.'

Peter grinned. 'You're turning into a fearsome woman, Georgie Seaton.'

Her anger faded and she returned his smile. 'Sometimes you have to fight for what you want.'

'You're sure?'

'Very sure,' she said quietly.

Martha didn't comment on that exchange.

—

Outside Ben found that his men had tied up the prisoners and discovered a cart and sorry-looking horse in the ramshackle stables, so he left them to escort the prisoners to the magistrate in that and joined the women, Daniel and Peter in the carriage, with Ted driving.

The journey back into town was slow, because of the bad roads, and passed mostly in silence. All of them were tired and cold, longing to get back to the comforts of dry clothes and a fire.

It wasn't until they were nearly there that Ben remembered something. 'I forgot to inform you, Brindley. There was an accident in the mill and your father was killed.'

Peter stared at him as if he couldn't believe his ears.

'Did you hear what I said?'

'Yes. He's dead? Really and truly dead?'

There was such relief in his voice that Martha's heart went out to him.

Georgie beamed at Peter. 'There. Now we can improve conditions in the mill, just as you wanted.'

Ben looked at Martha and said in a low voice, 'I'm getting more and more bewildered by these two.'

'Then I suggest you postpone further discussions.'

Her voice was so curt that he realised she was angry about something. He forgot his sister and opened his mouth to ask what was wrong, but just then the horses came to a halt.

Daniel, who'd been watching them all but saying nothing, hid a smile. Ben Seaton seemed to have no idea how to treat a woman and in the heat of the moment had barked out orders to her as if she were his servant.

He heard Georgie whisper to Martha, 'Don't leave me alone with Ben!' as he helped the two women out of the carriage and his grin broadened.

The front door of Seaton's house was flung open and Hepzibah burst through it, followed closely by Penelope. After that it was impossible to hold a conversation as explanations were demanded, half-started, interrupted and begun again. Ben strode into the house, forgetting Brindley, so Daniel helped Peter inside.

'I should go home and change my clothes.'

'You should come inside and stay with Georgie if you want to marry her.'

'I do. But will he let me?'

Daniel shrugged. 'I think she's probably as stubborn as he is, and he's a bit distracted now by Martha.'

Peter eyed him in puzzlement. 'Martha?'

'Mmm. He seems interested in her, but he's making a hash of dealing with it.' He guided Peter into the front parlour and when the other man collapsed on the sofa with a sigh of relief, went to put more coal on the fire and wait for the womenfolk to come downstairs again.

Ben strode in to join them. 'I can't get any sense out of them and they won't let me talk to Georgie.'

'She needs to put some clean clothes on,' Daniel said mildly.

'And Martha's angry with me about something.'

'You've been barking orders at her again.'

Ben stilled and frowned at him. 'Have I?'

'Yes. It's something you do from time to time.'

Ben caught sight of his face in the mirror. 'Oh, hell! I didn't realise I looked so bad. No wonder Hepzibah wanted me to go and bathe my face.' He saw Peter behind him, sitting slumped on the sofa, his face chalk white except where it was bruised by the blows he'd received. 'You'd better come too and let her minister to you. Your face is in a mess.'

Peter nodded and then as he stood up, swayed. 'Sorry. Don't feel well.'

'You took a nasty blow on the head,' Ben allowed.

They supported Peter into the kitchen where Hepzibah had a bowl of steaming water ready and insisted on tending their injuries. 'Miss Penelope's dealing with Georgie and I said I'd look after you. Meg, pass me that cloth.'

She sat the two battered men down by the table and washed their cuts, applying a soothing salve to them, then ordering them to go and sit down in the parlour while she got some hot food ready.

Drawn together by this nursery treatment, Ben and Peter went back to the parlour and Daniel stayed behind in the kitchen. 'They need to talk,' he said by way of explanation to Hepzibah.

'So Georgie told me. He hasn't hurt her, then?'

'She says not, says he protected her.'

She whisked out a handkerchief and blew her nose, then squared her shoulders and got on with her work, muttering, 'I don't know what the world's coming to, I really don't.'

In the front parlour the two men sat down and stared warily at one another.

'I haven't touched her in that way,' Peter said suddenly. 'I wouldn't do that, though my father hoped it'd happen.'

Ben nodded, suddenly feeling too tired to be aggressive.

'I can't believe he's dead. An accident, you say?'

Ben nodded again.

'Are you sure it was an accident?'

Another long silence, then, 'No. I'm not sure. But I let the magistrate believe it was. I still can't decide whether I was right or wrong about that. Your father insisted on the children cleaning the machinery while it was running and two little girls were killed. I think the operatives forced him under the machinery as he had the children, and he too was mangled. But afterwards they said your father went under willingly to show them it wasn't dangerous.'

'He'd never do something that put himself at risk.' After a short pause, Peter added, 'I hope you don't expect me to say I'm sorry he'd dead. I loathed him.'

'No, I don't expect that.'

'I've watched him use his operatives shamefully and hated to see it.' He paused, then said in tones of shock, 'I suppose that means I own the mill?'

'I should think so.'

324

'I don't know the first thing about running a mill. I only know I don't want people treated so badly from now on.'

For the first time Ben's gaze was approving.

After chewing his forefinger for a few seconds, Peter said in a rush, 'I know you don't want me to marry Georgie, but I love her and she loves me, heaven knows why. If I sell the mill, surely it'd bring enough for us to live on?'

'It's not sellable as it is. Everything's run down. Your father took money out but put nothing back in.'

Georgie came into the room just then, clad in fresh clothes and looking surprisingly untouched by her adventures. She went to sit beside Peter and said quietly to Ben, 'We *are* going to get married.'

'Not yet you aren't.'

'What do you mean by that?'

'I mean if Peter can learn to run that mill, bring it up to scratch again and earn enough to support you in comfort, then maybe I'll let you marry him.' As she opened her mouth to protest, he said firmly, 'You're too young, Georgie, and so is he. You both need to grow up.'

After a few minutes' thought, she said slowly, 'Then we'll get engaged. I do insist on that, Ben, because I know my own mind. And in the meantime, I'm going to help Peter with the mill, just as your mother helped our father.'

'Maybe.'

'Definitely.' She looked sideways and the love in her face made Peter raise her hand suddenly to his lips.

'I don't deserve you, Georgie, but I think you'll be the making of me.'

She kept hold of his hand for a moment or two, her eyes searching his face, then nodded. 'That's settled then.'

Ben could only look at them and smile wryly. Even his little sister found it easier to declare her love than he did. On that thought he stood up. 'You'd better get home and change your clothes, then, Brindley. I'll come round tomorrow morning and we'll go through your mill together. I'll be happy to share my knowledge with you and help you in any way I can. You may find Cox useful once you've made it clear how you want him to work.'

Peter stood up. 'Thank you.'

'I'll see you to the door,' Georgie said.

'Where's Martha?' Ben asked as she passed him.

'In the kitchen. We didn't like to disturb you.' She looked at him speculatively. 'Isn't it about time you asked her to marry you?' She slipped out, leaving him scowling after her.

The scowl was still on his face as he marched along to the kitchen, to find Martha and Penelope taking a cup of tea with Hepzibah. 'May I have a word with you, please, Miss Merridene?' he asked formally.

Martha looked at his tense expression and wondered if he was going to complain about something else. 'We were just about to go home, weren't we, Penelope?' When there was no answer, she looked sideways. 'Penelope?'

'No, we weren't. At least we were, but I think you should go and see what Mr Seaton wants first.'

But Martha felt suddenly panicky and couldn't move.

Ben went round the table and took her hand, pulling her with him and shutting the kitchen door behind them with a bang.

After dragging back at first, she suddenly gave in and went with him.

The two women left behind exchanged glances.

'I hope he doesn't make a mess of it,' Hepzibah said.

'Asking her to marry him?'

'Yes.'

Penelope smiled. 'He probably will. He's not good at flowery speeches, is he?'

'No. Never has been. But he's a loving lad underneath and I think they'll suit one another.'

'So do I.'

–

In the parlour Ben let go of Martha's wrist. 'Will you sit down, please?'

She rubbed it, though he hadn't really hurt her. 'There was no need to manhandle me.'

'I had to speak to you.' He took a step forward and she backed away. 'Will you stand still!'

'Don't shout at me, Ben Seaton!'

He opened his mouth, then shut it again, looking at her in despair. Then the words came out in a rush. 'I'm no good at fancy speeches, never have been, but surely you must realise how I feel about you?' When she didn't say anything, just stared at him wide-eyed, he said, 'Oh, Martha,' then grabbed hold of her and pulled her towards him, 'Martha, you will marry me, won't you?'

She couldn't say a word, could only look at him, her eyes huge, her mouth slightly open at the abruptness of his proposal.

It was the mouth that did it. So soft and inviting that he had to kiss her. With an inarticulate growl, he pulled her closer and bent his head.

The kiss began slowly and gently, and she couldn't seem to stop him. When it deepened, she was so lost to good sense that she kissed him right back and even flung her arms round his neck. When he stopped kissing her, she would have fallen if he hadn't been holding her so tightly.

'Well?' he asked.

'Well what?' She couldn't think straight, let alone remember his question.

'Are you going to marry me?' Then he saw fear replace the soft warmth of her gaze. 'What is it? Surely you're not afraid of me?'

It came out as a whisper. 'Yes. I am.'

'But Martha, darling Martha, you must know I'd never hurt you.'

'I'm afraid of how you make me feel,' she explained. 'I'd never realised—never felt anything like...' Her voice trailed away.

'Come and sit down.'

She found his shoulder just the right height to lean against. 'I'm twenty-eight,' she said suddenly.

'I'm thirty.'

'What will people say about a spinster like me getting married?'

He saw that her hands were shaking and forgot his own worries in the need to reassure her. Clasping them in his own, he said gently, 'I think people will be happy for you. Your sister, for one. And Georgie. She said it was about time I asked you to marry me.'

'She did?'

'Yes. She likes you. Then there's Hepzibah. She told me to marry you a while back and I wouldn't want to be in your place if you told her you'd turned me down. She'd scold me for making a mess of it. I'm shaking in my shoes at the thought.'

She was betrayed into a gurgle of laughter. 'You're not afraid of anything or anyone, Ben Seaton.'

'I was afraid of asking you to marry me, I promise you, terrified in fact. Because I'm not good with words and if you turn me down, I don't know what I'll do. You're not going to do that, are you, my darling?'

'No.' When she raised her eyes, she saw joy spread across his face like sunshine and could feel a warm tide of happiness flowing through her. 'No, I'm going to accept your kind offer.' And suddenly she had no doubts. She could feel herself blushing as she said it for the first time, 'I love you, Ben.'

'I love you, too.'

They sat for a long time, murmuring endearments, making plans, or just sitting quietly enjoying one another's company.

Neither of them heard the tapping on the door, not the first time and not the second.

When Georgie pushed it open a little, she could see them sitting on the sofa together, so pushed it fully open and marched into the room, setting her hands on her hips as she confronted them. 'Ben Seaton, you've been in here for over an hour and we're all *dying* of curiosity.'

The two lovers were startled and turned to face Georgie, Hepzibah and Penelope, all standing just inside the doorway.

'Well?' Georgie demanded when her brother still didn't speak. 'Are you going to marry Martha or not?'

He rose to his feet, pulling his beloved with him. 'Of course I am, and—' The rest of his words were lost as Georgie squealed loudly flung herself at him to give him a hug, then turned to do the same to Martha. 'I couldn't have borne it if you'd not agreed to put up with him,' she said. 'I need a sister-in-law much more than I need a teacher.' She clapped one hand to her mouth. 'Oh dear, the school. Whatever's going to happen to it now?'

'Who cares?' Penelope asked. 'This is much more important.'

'We'll ask Jenny Barston to take over the school, of course,' Martha said at once, with something of her old crispness of tone. 'She'll be delighted to get away from her relatives.'

Ben put his arm round her shoulders and beamed at the three women. 'Never mind that.' He turned to Martha. 'How soon can we be married?'

'Oh. Well. I don't know. There's a lot to do, plans to make and—'

'As soon as you like,' Penelope said firmly. 'Daniel and I will have to wait until he's established, but there's no reason whatsoever for you two to wait.' She grinned at her future brother-in-law. 'I'll make sure she doesn't delay things, Ben.'

'We'll have the first banns called on Sunday, then,' he decided. 'Because I'm marrying you as soon as I can, Martha Merridene.'

And Martha found she couldn't protest, because becoming Ben's wife was the thing she wanted most in the whole world. Blushing and laughing, she accepted everyone's congratulations, but her eyes kept going back to him and her smile was soft with joy.